ALSO BY BRENDA L. THOMAS

The Velvet Rope
Threesome: Where Seduction, Power & Basketball Collide
Fourplay . . . the Dance of Sensuality
Kiss the Year Goodbye
(with Crystal Lacey Winslow, Tu-Shonda L. Whitaker
& Daaimah S. Poole)
Four Degrees of Heat
(with Crystal Lacey Winslow, Rochelle Alers
& ReShonda Tate Billingsley)

Published by Pocket Books

every woman's got a secret

BRENDA L. THOMAS

Pocket Books

New York   London   Toronto   Sydney

POCKET BOOKS, a division of Simon & Schuster, Inc.
1230 Avenue of the Americas, New York, NY 10020

ISBN-13: 978-0-7434-9706-0
ISBN-10:   0-7434-9706-6

This Pocket Books trade paperback edition January 2007

10 9 8 7 6 5 4 3 2 1

POCKET and colophon are registered trademarks of Simon & Schuster, Inc.

Manufactured in the United States of America

For information regarding special discounts for bulk purchases, please contact Simon & Schuster Special Sales at 1-800-465-6798 or business@simonandschuster.com

To my beautiful and precious granddaughters,
Jazzyln, Briana, and Jada,
who give me all the love I'll ever really need.

acknowledgments

Dear God, I couldn't have done it without you!

This is often the most difficult page to write because there are so many people to thank: family, friends, faithful readers, book clubs, bookstores, reviewers, fellow authors, and those people who simply decide to take a chance on reading someone different. But then there are the ones who rough it out with me over and over again for the sake of my literary passion.

My closest friends who never complain as they listen and support me through many drafts, second guesses, and often give up their own personal stories to make it flow. Carmen Carrion, Kim Gerald, Aisha Jordan-Moore, Leigh Karsch (webmaster), Denise Robinson, Renee Washington, and Sharon Woodridge.

Many thanks and much love goes to my friends Pamela Artis and Christopher Payne, who asked way too many questions as they plied through numerous emails and versions of the manuscript. Of course there were those to whom I became a welcome nuisance as I shouted out questions in the office, my Jeff Crew (Erica DelGrippo, Kari Kulp, Cyndi Lavorgna, and Michael Pocceschi).

If you wonder where some of the crazy stuff comes from, a big shout out goes to my nephew Terrell Thomas for keeping me current, and my outlaw Kim Rawlinson for the fight scenes. And no way can I forget Mr. Grant, an avid reader who proved how steam could rise from the love scenes.

To the authors who've become my friends and to whom I often turn, Steve Perry (*Man Up!*) and Nikki Turner (*Riding Dirty on I-95*). Nakea Murray, thanks for keeping me in touch with everything books.

There are always those who never leave your side probably because they can't (they're waiting on the big one) and that's my brothers, Joe, Gregory, and Jeffery. However, my son and daughter, Kelisha and Kelvin Rawlinson, don't care if it ever comes as long as I keep on trying.

Saving the best for last, the #1 man in my life, my Dad, Thurmond Thomas, who will forever be the anchor that keeps me grounded.

every woman's got a secret

PROLOGUE

August 2006
Caroline Y. Isaacs

I opened my eyes and took in my bedroom to be sure I was awake this time. Glancing around, I was relieved to see everything looked familiar. Once again I wondered how many bad dreams I'd have to awaken from only to realize that I wasn't dreaming at all. I brought my hands up to my face and squeezed them together in hopes of ceasing their trembling. I turned them over for yet another inspection. My poor nails, chewed down to the cuticles, leaving the skin ragged and tender.

I turned over and lay on my stomach, my face hidden in the pillow, allowing myself to revisit that night with my eyes closed, just barely awake. I saw her lying there, her eyes bulging out of their sockets, gagging for another breath that I wouldn't allow her to take.

I'd been back home in Beverly Hills for damn near two months and still the only communication I'd allowed myself had been with the pizza and Chinese food delivery people. In the last three weeks I hadn't even bothered to lift a finger to shower, wash my grimy hair, or clean my dust-covered condo. After all those court appearances and doctor's appointments to prove that I wasn't crazy, I just didn't have energy for anything.

I rolled over and kicked back the covers. Maybe today would be the day I got my ass up and at least made it to the shower. Maybe that would help me drown out the memories of her.

Good girl. You're up, I encouraged myself. Fifteen steps into the bathroom, and onto the only other place I'd been spending time, the toilet. And that's when I saw it again, the black orchid tattooed to my ankle. With my index finger I tapped at the skin and it still trickled with blood. I'd scraped at it so bad the other night with a nail file, trying to erase the memory. Like girlfriends we'd gotten the tattoos together, before I had a clue to who she was, before she began to whittle away at my life. How could I not have known, after spending an entire summer with her, that she could be so vindictive? With an unexpected teardrop splattering onto my thigh, I was content to accept that today was not the day. I climbed back in bed.

There had to be somewhere else for me to live, some way to forget, or at least, some way to learn to live with it. If only I'd caught on to her earlier, I could've held on to what had been mine. I could've held on to Julius.

But I couldn't change the past. It was over. Marí Colonado was dead and I'd killed her with my bare hands!

Marí Colonado

'm not leaving the world like this, on the grounds of the Isaacs' estate. I have planned too long to redeem my family to lose this fight. With my eyes I plead for mercy, but my thoughts are cut short because she's strangling the words from my throat. No! I refuse. I've come too far to give up. This bitch doesn't deserve her life—doesn't appreciate how easy it came to her and at the expense of someone else.

I'd only been a teenager when every day I had to hear my father rave about pretty little Caroline Isaacs. It was always about what a good athlete she was, what a good student she was, and what a shame her parents had no time for her. Because she'd captured my father's attention, I had to compete with her every way I knew how. But no matter how much I tried, how many awards I received, good grades I made, it was always about Caroline. I may have been able to deal with that, but then she'd taken away my mother. For that I intended to exact revenge.

I'd done everything according to plan. I'd taken away the simple things she'd treasured: her health, her hair, her family—who I turned against her—and best of all, I'd taken her man. How funny when the tables are turned.

The cement pebbles of the patio dig into my back. Reaching up, I slap at her face and am even able to land a few punches. Faintly, I hear Maurice screaming at her to let me go. I knew he'd choose me over his sister; he loves me because I'd proved to him and to everyone else that I'm better than Caroline Isaacs.

Caroline's nails gouge deep into my neck, breaking the skin. I gaze at her face, covered with sweat, her eyes so wide that the lashes touch her eyebrows.

I feel myself fading. It would be easy to let go now, into that peacefulness called death. As her grip tightens, my body stops squirming, and that's when I know that death won't be so bad after all. No more scheming, plotting, or risk of being discovered.

Straining, I open my eyes for the last time and pray that somehow they reveal to her that despite everything, I'd actually grown to love her. With that I give up the fight, satisfied that she'll never forget me.

1
CITY OF ANGELS

May 2006
Caroline Y. Issacs

Backing out the driveway of my sweetie Julius's Malibu
bungalow, I was already reminiscing about what a hot
night we'd had. Had I not had a full day ahead of me, I'd
have gone back inside for more. I pushed the button to
slide back my convertible roof and I pulled out of the gates
of Tara West. The condos and the beautiful landscaping
were surrounded by palm trees and bordered by the Pacific
Ocean. Now safe on the street, I dialed my parents, who'd
been on vacation in Thailand. I'd had minimum contact
with them while they were gone, so I was eager to know
they'd made it home safely.

"Hello?" My mother's sleepy voice answered the ringing
phone.

"Mom, hey, you're home. When did you get in?" I asked, turning the corner onto Greenwater Lane.

"Late last night. We're still in bed. Where are you, honey?" my mother asked in between yawns.

"On my way to the studio."

"Why don't I call you later when we're both up? I have lots to tell you. We brought you back some beautiful things."

Just then Mary J. started belting from my speakers. I reduced the volume and said, "All right, Mom. I love you."

"I love you too, sweetheart. See you soon."

It had been six months since I'd seen my parents, so I was about due. I usually went to visit them in Philly, and at other times my brother Maurice and I would join them wherever they were vacationing, but Thailand was a little more than I could handle. All those bugs and the rain—I'm too spoiled for that kind of adventure. No sooner had I hung up the phone than it rang again.

"Kia, hey, what's up? Are we still doing lunch?" I asked my best friend.

"Yeah, but I can't be too long. I have a photo shoot at two-thirty and you know how your ass likes to stop and talk to everybody you know."

Kia may have been unmanageable as hell when it came to money, but she had me beat when it came to time management on any day.

"Are you saying I can't stick to a two-hour lunch?"

"Please . . . you always need longer than that to finish a meal. I'll meet you at the Ivy at one o'clock."

"Cool. I'll see you there."

Kia and I had been friends since I moved out to LA five years ago, when we'd both been living at the Four Seasons.

Both of us had been far away from home, me loving it and Kia in tears every night, as she'd never been too far from her family in West Virginia. The furthest she'd been was New York, where she'd begun modeling, but since acting was her goal she'd moved out to LA and was now bicoastal. So here we were both caught up in the glamorous world of Hollywood, Kia as a high-fashion model and me as a veejay for VMT. But it was no wonder how we'd remained friends. We'd both learned early on that the only way female friendships survived in Hollywood was by maintaining a no compete clause. My goal was to have my own talk show—and yes, my idol was Oprah. For Kia, well, her goal was to one day slip into Halle Berry's shoes.

Driving along the scenic Pacific Coast Highway, I was glad my days started late because I'd never been one for early mornings. I usually tried to get into work by 10:00 A.M. and out of there when my show ended at 7:00 P.M. I switched the CD from Mary and opted for the radio, my ears craving some variety, but it was more of the same. All the deejays did was play the same tunes and talk the same trash everyday, making me glad my short career path had led me to TV instead of radio. At least being a music television veejay gave me the opportunity to not only be seen but to be up close and personal with my audience.

Forty-five minutes later I was pulling up to the circular five-story Lowery Building, where I hosted *Top of Da Charts*, an urban music video show.

"What's up, Linney?" the parking attendant said, greeting me as I drove over the speed bump past his booth.

"Freddie, what's it look like today?"

He stepped out of the booth to light his cigarette. "Gonna be a big one."

I backed into my reserved spot but not before noticing the growing line for the studio audience that Freddie was referring to. Crazy how these folks lined up for a show that wasn't scheduled to begin for over five hours, but that's what made us number one.

The studio was on the first floor and we shared a floor of conference rooms on the third with our sister radio station, which was housed on the fourth floor.

I took the elevator to the second floor, where our offices were located, and pushed through the heavy wooden doors.

"Morning, Caroline."

"Good morning, Ms. Gwen," I replied to our receptionist, who was about fifty years old and well versed in everything hip-hop. She didn't take any crap from visitors or staff.

Without looking up she nodded her head toward a cup of hot water and lemon she had ready for me everyday when I arrived. It all started a few months ago when I'd suffered with laryngitis, so regardless of what time I arrived, she'd have it waiting.

I stepped around the UPS boxes that were stacked in the lobby and began making my way down the winding hallway, past walls lined with platinum records and autographed artist's photos.

Before I could reach my office, my assistant, Erica, approached me at a light trot from around the corner.

Erica was twenty-nine and had been at VMT when I arrived from Philly. Initially we'd rubbed each other the wrong way, which was probably my fault because I'd felt so out of place when I arrived. I think she'd thought that at the age of twenty-one I'd be too immature for the job, and I had to admit a few times I made quite a fool of myself. But now I was twenty-four and a lot less insecure. I simply referred to her as E.

"Linney, good morning. First thing you should know is that your guest has been changed today from Diamond Studz to Raw Dawg. He's arriving around five-thirty, so there won't be time for a preshow interview."

"Morning, E. I'm not surprised," I said, jangling my key ring for the right one.

"Here," Erica said, stepping in front of me to unlock my office door.

"E, Raw has been on the show three times in the last two years and he's never arrived early enough. Just because he has a new album coming out we're supposed to drop everything for his ass. Next you'll tell me that he's not going to perform either," I said, while stashing my backpack into my bottom desk drawer and kicking it closed.

"Nope. He's going to show his new video and spend time talking with you and the audience. You know he likes to give you exclusives."

I switched on the computer and said with a smirk, "That ain't all he'd like to give me."

Erica picked up the remote and turned on the television that was suspended from the ceiling. "You might wanna see this. Ree-Ree was on Leno last night and she mentioned how you inspired her."

"Smart girl," I said, watching the fourteen-year-old song-stress from the suburbs in Philly, not far from where I'd grown up. "So what else is up?"

"We'll also be running three other artists' videos from Dawg's label and you'll have one open slot and the closing video." Erica propped herself on the corner of my desk and opened her leather folio.

"Here's your script for the interview," Erica said, handing me the predetermined questions sent over from Raw Dawg's publicist.

"Thanks a lot," I grumbled. "I thought this was *my* show. Looks like today is gonna belong to Raw Dawg and his label. Is that it?"

"The studio is going to be packed. Guess you saw that coming in. The audience probably heard he was coming."

"I don't have to guess how that happened," I added, certain the leak came directly from his label.

"Here, let's go over your schedule for the day," she said once she'd pulled it up on Outlook.

Erica began reciting from the timetable we both leaned over to see.

"Production meeting is starting later today, like around eleven-thirty, so you can go to wardrobe first, but I'll come get you when they're ready. Then you'll have a two-hour window for lunch or whatever. Three-thirty I've got you set up for phone interviews and some calls. Five-thirty you're back to wardrobe and then . . ."

"Six o'clock you're on," we both said together.

"Oh yeah, and over there" Erica pointed to the small conference table—"I've set up a stack of new videos that came in yesterday for you to take a look at." She then dashed out the door to a meeting with the station's publicist

If one more thing landed in my small and overcrowded office, I'd have to literally sit on my desk. I reviewed the list of calls Erica had pulled from my voice mail, returned a few, and then headed over to wardrobe to see my stylist. Raphael, who'd come highly recommended, had been with me for the last year. He was a thirty-year-old white queen who handled my makeup, hair, and clothes for the show. And if I needed him for special events, he was always on call. Raphael was tall and thin, with bleached blond hair and a year-round perfect tan. He was one of the few people I knew who was a native of LA. His favorite pastimes were gossiping and surfing, but he also loved beautiful men and beautiful clothes, in which order I'm not sure.

I tapped on his open door and Raphael waved me in.

"Linney, git in here, girl. I have some funky pieces for you. Here, sit down," he said, pushing a high stool to the middle of the floor.

"Well, let me see what you got," I said, and then kissed him on the cheek. Raphael always wore the best cologne and smelled so good that I'd usually go out and purchase whatever he was wearing for Julius once I got a whiff.

Looking in the three-way mirror in front of me, Raphael pushed his fingers through my hair, trying to decide how he'd style it for today's show.

"Mmmm, what am I going to do with this today?" he said, now brushing my hair. "So, tell me, girlie, what color, designer, fabric, whatever you want, to put on that cute bottom of yours. I've got everything fresh."

"Why don't you just pick?" I said to him, because I knew that's what he wanted to hear.

He removed two dresses, a pair of shorts, a tank top, and three different pairs of jeans from one of the racks, spreading them out on the dressing table. I stood up to take a look.

"Here's what I'm thinking. . . . A few have been altered already, and the others I can touch up. This one is from Dolce," he said, holding up a beautiful printed halter. "The jeans and tank are Baby Phat, and wait a minute, this is from . . ." —he looked in the collar for the label—"Missoni. Is that what you're feeling?"

I disregarded what he'd laid out when I glimpsed a sexy turquoise Gucci jumpsuit with a low-riding waist still hanging on the rack.

"You keeping that for yourself?" I asked, pointing to the piece.

He covered his mouth to hide a girlish giggle. "What makes you think I don't already have one?" he asked, pulling down the jumpsuit and adding a funky belt from Christian Dior.

"I know you're waiting to tell me where you hung out last night—go on," I said as I slipped my foot into a pair of three-inch Samanta heels he slid in front of me. That was all Raphael needed to get him going on celebrity gossip.

"You are not going to believe who I met last night. Oh, girl, you ain't gonna believe it."

"Probably not but go ahead."

Clasping his hands to his cheeks, he said, "Boateng! Linney, that man is so exceptionally fine."

"Who?" I asked while taking a stroll around the room in the high-stepping shoes.

"You know, the men's designer from London, the brother. Are they too high?" he asked, pointing to my feet.

I had no idea who he was talking about, especially someone who only designed for men. It didn't matter to Raphael because he would tell me everything regardless of if I wanted or didn't want to know.

"We were at the Blue Pelican and he and his wife walked in and oh, girl. I could've eaten him right up. Oh yes, a scrumptious thing he was."

You couldn't help but laugh when Raphael talked about men; he was just like having a girlfriend. As Raphael continued to talk about last night, who he'd seen and who he'd like to do, thirty minutes passed and I'd tried on two outfits.

In the midst of him telling me who he thought needed to come out of the closet and what celebs simply didn't know how to dress, Erica came through the door.

"You ready, Linney?"

"And hello to you too, Ms. Erica," Raphael said.

"What's up, Raphael?"

"Without a doubt, let's go," I said, leaving him with the decision of how to put my outfit together.

"Hey, we're not finished here yet," he said, posing in the doorway.

"Be back with her at four-thirty," Erica promised him.

Erica pushed the button for the elevator to take us upstairs to the executive conference room. "Linney, I wanted to remind you that I have a stack of résumés for you to look over."

"Résumés for what?"

"Uh, your summer interns, remember?"

"Sure I do," I lied.

Inside the cluttered third floor conference room I found Sharon, the show's producer, Brad, the director, and three production assistants.

"Good morning, Caroline," said Sharon.

Sharon Stone Face Washington, was how we referred to her. Sharon's demeanor was strictly business. Always in a skirt suit, as if she didn't know the phrase chill out was in the dictionary. I would be uptight too if I had as much at stake as she did. The word around the studio was that she'd taken a cash-out from a major network after a highly publicized sexual harassment case, which explained why she was determined to prove her professionalism.

"Looks like we have a full house. What's the hot topic?" I asked, spinning around one of the swivel chairs to sit on.

"Summer ratings," Brad gestured, swishing the spreadsheet in the air.

On the other hand the show's director, Brad Cohen, had been nicknamed the "Grease Man" by Raphael. He was good at what he did, he could cut up a tape to perfection, but his only topic of conversation was food. Brad claimed to have been to every restaurant in California and maybe across the country, however all we ever saw him eat were tuna sandwiches, which he washed down with coffee. None of this helped his breath especially.

"We were just going over some of the feedback on your blog. I think you'll find it interesting," Sharon said.

Caroline Tells All was a Web blog I started one night while I was trying to respond to the show's many e-mails. Once we announced it on the air, the Webmaster had to create additional space on our site just to keep up with the entries. It was a way to give the audience a look into my life and a supposedly candid view of what happened behind the scenes and in the streets, and the audience in turn was able to add comments.

My fans weren't the only ones interested in Caroline Tells All. Celebrities and their publicists were wearing out my phones with requests to leak gossip on them, especially around album release time. In just a few months it had gotten so controlled by the industry that I secretly vowed to one day add some of the real underground stuff that nobody wanted put in print. But I had to be careful because I didn't want myself or our show to be caught in the middle of a record label war.

The thing nobody knew was that my brother, Maurice, sometimes would have his friends put comments on my blog to add fuel to the fire about things I couldn't personally put out there.

I reached over to gaze through the printouts. "I hope there are no crazed stalkers in the pile."

"No stalkers, but your fans love you and the females think you should start having some of your favorite designers on as guests. What do you think?" Sharon asked, twiddling her pen.

"This is a music video show," Brad added, before refilling his coffee cup.

"I think it's something we should at least consider. Everyone knows these artists are trendsetters when it comes to fashion," Sharon piped in.

I winked at Erica, who wore a size six same as I did, and always welcomed whatever I passed off to her. "So long as they fill up our closets. But for real, isn't it enough they get credit at the end of the show?" I asked.

"It's what the audience is asking for," Sharon said, ever the diplomat.

"If you think it'll help the ratings, maybe we could try one or two along with the actual artist wearing the clothes to see what the response is," Brad suggested. "Can't hurt."

For my ears only Erica mumbled, "Next we'll be doing makeovers."

"Caroline, the audience is also asking when you're going to bring some athletes on," Sharon added.

"Sharon, they gotta start making some rap songs that aren't bullshit," I said impatiently. "Now can I see the ratings, since you saved that for last?"

"It's about the same, which isn't good, since the competition plans to go head to head with us on a reality show in thirty days."

"So what's the plan?" I asked, glancing down at the multicolored spreadsheet.

Brad took a bite from his tuna sandwich like it was a delicacy.

Sharon opened her notepad. "Don't know. That's why we're all here for a good ol' brainstorming session. We need to come up with some fresh ideas for a summer show if we don't want to air reruns all summer."

"All right, everyone, let's see what we've got," I said.

For the next two hours we went from one stupid idea to another, none of which sounded impressive to me or anyone else. Since it was my show, the situation was left in my hands. I didn't have much time either, because the summer was about to kick off in one month. All some kids did with their summer vacation was sit in front of the TV and watch videos the entire day, and those kids were our worst critics.

After our meeting I went back to my office to get my purse, then walked down Robertson Boulevard to meet Kia at the Ivy, but not before stopping at Lisa Kline to pick up two items they'd been holding for me.

I saw Kia waving at me from where she stood beside the restaurant's white picket fence. She was a country clean white girl and to hear her tell it, she'd gone from trailer trash to the cover of *Vogue*. Kia stood exactly six feet tall in her bare feet and weighed 125 pounds with no signs of anorexia. Her biggest complaint was still having to be shoved into skimpy and tight clothes, so when she was off camera she chose to wear free-flowing sundresses like the Free People number she had on today.

I knew her waving was all for show, to make sure the paparazzi's lenses that were always focused on the Ivy could get a good shot of not only her face but of the beautiful six-month-old cleavage she was sporting.

Seeing my shopping bag, Kia teased, "Linney, I know you ain't been shopping. It's impossible for you to get anywhere on time if there's a store within a hundred miles."

"I'm not late, so shut up."

Kia and I hugged, then followed the hostess inside. Before we could get to our seats my cell phone rang. I saw that it was Julius so I picked up.

"Hey, Jules baby," I said into the phone. "Did you finally get your butt out of bed?"

"How's a man supposed to get up for work when you knocked me out like that last night?"

Julius was a budding sports agent who'd left the law firm he'd been with to start his own agency. So far he had three clients, two football players and one hockey player. I'd met him about two months after I'd moved to LA, when he was still an uptight lawyer. He was four years older than me, certainly mature, which was just what I needed to keep me grounded. Julius and I didn't live together, but most of my nights were spent at his house in Malibu when he wasn't out of town schmoozing prospective clients.

During the time we'd been together, a solid two years, marriage had come up more than once, but he wanted to wait until he had a more solid financial situation. Mine was as solid as it would ever get, since I'd already been deemed a trust fund baby. Julius wanted to make sure that he could give me whatever I needed so I'd never have to touch that money. At the rate he was going it wouldn't be long, so when he told me to keep his spot warm, I was sure we were both on the same page.

The waiter pulled out my chair, seating us outside on the shaded patio. I didn't bother to look at the menu because I'd be having my usual.

"Don't act like you didn't enjoy that little show I put on for you," I told Julius.

"What was that, anyway? My private welcome home party?" he asked, referring to the well-rehearsed strip show I'd performed when he'd gotten home after being in Dallas for three days.

"That sounds about right. But don't go taking your ass out of town any time soon. Where are you now?"

"On my way to meet a client. You coming back over to-night? Because I want to know if my spot is gonna be warm."

"You think you can handle some more of me?"

"Bring it on home to big Papa, baby!"

I could feel the smile spreading on my face when I hung up.

Kia didn't miss it. "You two are sickening."

I sipped my water. "Don't hate me just because the men you're seeing can't bring it like mine."

"At least I have options when one of mine is out of town. I'm telling you, you're going to get bored one day having just one man to turn to," Kia chided, referring to the three men she was currently dating.

"Never! I love that man to death," I boasted.

Kia threw up her hand and flagged me. "Anyway, new subject. What's going on? Who's on the show today?"

"Raw Dawg bombarded his way on, promoting that new album of his."

"That boy is really feeling you, Caroline. You might wanna check him out, is all I'm saying."

"I am not interested—no way, no how. You know my rule; I never, ever date rappers, singers . . ."

". . . Actors, actresses, nobody, absolutely nobody, in show business," Kia finished. She knew me well.

"So have you heard anything yet?" Kia asked.

"About what?"

"Come on, *People* magazine . . . You know what I'm talking about. You have to make it again this year," Kia cried, visibly more excited that I was.

"I don't know. I mean, if I make the list this year, it'll be the fourth time in a row. Isn't that asking a bit much?" I pondered, yet still glad that my name was in the running. "But how about you making *Maxim*'s Hot One Hundred?"

"Yeah, and you know what I had to do to get on it too. But for real, Linney, how could being named one of the fifty most beautiful people ever be a bit much?"

She was right. I did want to make the list, but I also didn't want it to get old. Would fans stay interested year after year?

"It's no biggie; it's only because I'm in people's living rooms everyday," I stated, realizing that in Hollywood everything was about making lists—even the negative lists. As long as you made one you were still visible.

"You're telling me that being beautiful has nothing to do with it. Stop downplaying yourself."

"Well, looks definitely help," I consented, wondering if being beautiful would be enough for me to reach my career goals.

The waiter appeared at our table.

"What are we eating?" Kia questioned, as if she expected us to get something different than our norm.

"Caesar salad, mescalun salad, or arugula salad?" the familiar waiter asked, well aware of our eating habits.

"We're so stuck in our ways. Why don't we just order fat ass burgers with fried onions and mushrooms, and some cheese fries with salt, pepper, and ketchup?" Kia urged, nudging me with her foot under the table.

"Yeah, right, and then neither one of us will have a job." I looked up at the waiter and simply stated, "Caesar salad for me and arugula salad for my friend. That way we can share."

While we picked at our lunch I signed a few autographs and posed for a few pictures with passersby. I usually didn't like to be bothered while I was eating, but in all honesty I really did want to make that list again. So if that meant signing autographs and answering a few questions, then so be it.

"Have you made any vacation plans for the summer yet?" I asked Kia, who was signing a picture of herself on the cover of *Vogue*.

"No, I'm going to be working. I'm leaving in a few weeks for Brazil, a *Town & Country* shoot, then I have a private show for La Perla's new line. What about you?"

"Nothing yet. Julius wants us to do something, and I'll probably fly out to see my parents."

I made my way back to the studio and was in with Raphael by three o'clock for hair and makeup that would take at least an hour and a half. Styling my hair always took the longest amount of time. I'd always had shoulder-length hair and some might even describe it as "good hair," but there was nothing thick about this limp stuff. Even though I preferred less infusions and hair spray, I knew I needed it to hold my look in place. I kept threatening to cut it but every time I mentioned it, Sharon jokingly threatened me with my job. Since she didn't have much of a sense of humor, I didn't take any chances.

While Raphael worked me over, I met with the show's publicist in reference to three charity appearances she wanted me to attend. Then I returned a call from my agent about a possible perfume endorsement. Erica also sat with us for a few to read through some of the fan mail that came in by the bin from the post office. For me it was another day at the office that was only halfway through.

By five-fifty I was waiting behind the thick blue velvet drapes for my music to be cued up to go on stage. I noticed Raw Dawg slip into the studio and up behind me.

"Hi, Raw. I didn't think you were making appearances yet for the new CD."

I could overhear his publicist telling Brad that he would be performing and what he needed for his setup.

"You can get me whenever you want, Linney," he said all up on my butt.

I responded with a kiss on his check. "Is that so?" I asked, swaying my hips to the beat of the music.

"I'll bust some rhymes if you chill wit' me tonight."

There wasn't time to answer his invitation because I was bouncing out from behind the curtain and onto the stage to begin my monologue.

"Linney here, y'all, with *Top of Da Charts*! What's happening? I've got a hot, hot show today that's gonna turn you on your heels, so I hope you came prepared with your Nikes, your Adidas, whatever it is you call your dancing shoes, 'cause Linney promises that today's guest is gonna turn it out!"

"RAW! RAW! RAW!" the audience chanted practically making the stage vibrate.

I yelled to my deejay, "Cue it up, Wakeel," and he brought up the first video of Raw Dawg's duet with the Marley brothers.

We showed two videos and three commercials, then were back, and I officially announced our guest for the day. Raw Dawg lumbered his way around the corner to the stage and threw up the V sign for his label before pouncing down onto my couch. As usual he sat closer to me than any of my other male guests, and it wasn't just because he had two of his artists with him.

After the audience's response I began like clockwork with my round of questions. I read sporadically from the teleprompter and he casually answered me as if he had no idea what I would ask. While Raphael touched up my hair and lip shine during a commercial, Raw started in on me with his rap game.

"You ready for me yet? I'm telling you, Linney we could do some things."

"Why do you ask me that every time you see me when you already know what the answer is? I'll tell you again, Raw,

I'm in a relationship with one person and you're in a relationship with what . . . several?"

He put his hand, three fingers of which were filled with bling, on my knee and squeezed it. It wasn't that Raw wasn't attractive. Oh yeah, he was built better than most athletes, even had begun a line of workout clothes for men and women and had already opened his first gym in Cincinnati. He was an entertainer and I didn't do those.

"Don't believe the hype, Linney. All this could be yours."

I'm assuming he was referring to the rumor that he was so well endowed that his profession prior to rapping was servicing women in exchange for money.

"Just not mine alone," I added.

With that he nodded to one of the many guys in his crew who   just as we went back on air—rolled out an eight-piece Louis Vuitton luggage set filled with apparel from his sports line. He'd timed it perfectly so I had no choice but to show my gratitude in front of my audience by giving him a hug and thanking him for my gift.

All of this gave him ample opportunity to try to kiss me, and if I hadn't turned my head quick enough, it would have been on my lips instead of my cheek.

After two more videos Raw asked the audience whether or not they wanted him to perform. They responded with a screaming yes. He took the stage to my right where his deejay was set up, and I went to stand with the audience. As always his performance was outstanding and, unbeknownst to the audience, well rehearsed. Not much was spontaneous when he was releasing a new album.

When the show ended I changed out of my stage clothes, Raphael broke down my makeup, and I guzzled a quart of water. Being under all those lights and talking for an hour straight sometimes took all my energy, especially when I hadn't gotten enough rest like last night, when I stayed up late playing around with Julius.

Finally I made it to my office, where I spent another two hours returning some calls and taking a telephone interview from a writer with *Blender* magazine.

There was also an e-mail I needed to respond to from *Vibe* magazine requesting my opinion on Raw Dawg's new release. While answering their questions, I simultaneously popped in one of the music videos to be aired next week. After that I began reviewing the list of top ten videos that would be played on Friday's countdown show.

Breaking my concentration, Sharon appeared in the doorway of my office and said, "Great show, Caroline."

"Thanks."

"I need you to come in early tomorrow for our meeting."

"Anything in particular happening?"

"Besides needing a summer theme, I want you to settle the intern thing."

By 8:30 P.M. I was starved and ready to make my way back to Julius's house. When I phoned him his cell went straight to voice mail, which meant he'd be home late, so I decided that for dinner I'd pick up sushi at Mama Foo's. My Julius was not a sushi man.

When I got to the reception desk I heard Erica calling after me. I couldn't believe she was still in the office.

"Hey, wait up!" she yelled down the hall just before I was out the door.

I turned around to see what the big rush was. "What is it? I'm outta here."

"I know, I know, but you need to be here in the morning by nine for the interviews."

"Interviews?" That quickly I'd forgotten about Sharon's reminder.

"Yeah. Here's the folder of résumés I put on your desk while you were at lunch. Remember you have to select a summer intern. Did you forget?"

"You know I forgot," I said, retrieving the folder from her hands. "I'll look over them tonight."

When I arrived at Julius's he still wasn't home, so I let myself in with the keys he'd given me. Placing the bag of takeout on the dining room table, I noticed that Julius had left me a note letting me know he'd had to make a quick trip to San Diego and would be back around midnight.

I was actually kind of glad he wasn't there so I could veg out in front of the television, maybe do my own brainstorming of sorts, but I needed to shower first.

Julius called just as I finished moisturizing myself.

"Hey, you get my note?"

"Yes, baby. How'd things go?" I asked, walking into the kitchen. "Football player, right? Tight-end."

"Very good, Caroline."

"How was your day?"

"Not bad," I answered, undoing the container of mango tango and salmon skin rolls.

"I saw you had Raw Dawg on. You didn't let him make no moves on you backstage, did you?"

"Yeah, right. You know I belong to one man. Speaking of which, what time are you flying back?"

"It'll be late, but keep my spot warm. Matter of fact, I need it to be hot tonight."

Julius Worthington's spot would always be warm with me because I had no interest in any other man. With that I sat cross-legged on the couch to chow down. Later I opted to enter my thoughts into Caroline Tells All.

> All right y'all, tomorrow I'm interviewing for my summer intern. I'm hoping that person is ready to get their grind on and have some fun. Know anybody who wants to fill those shoes?
>
> Anyway, tomorrow's the day. So y'all intern wannabes better be somebody hot and fresh off the block, 'cause Linney don't do no knock offs.

2
THE INTERN

When I turned over in the morning, it wasn't the alarm clock that woke me but the smell of bacon frying. I hadn't heard Julius come in during the night but could tell that he'd made it to bed because, as always, the sheets had come loose from his side.

I'd promised Sharon that I'd be in early and was already regretting it. I made my way into the bathroom and stood for a moment in front of the mirror. If only *People* magazine could see me now. Eyes crusted with sleep, hair all over my head, and skin with marks from the pillow—far from beautiful. I took Julius's robe down from the door just as he stepped through the doorway with a breakfast tray.

"Where you going? Get your butt back in bed so I can serve you breakfast."

"Whatever you say, but I'm supposed to be in early," I said, eagerly climbing back under the covers.

"How was San Diego?" I asked as he sat the tray in front of me.

He picked up the fork and began to feed me eggs. "It went well. I think my guy might get slotted on their roster."

"Chargers, right?" I asked, never having been a sports buff. Hell, I had a hard enough time keeping up with the entertainment industry. Rappers wanting to act, actors wanting to rap—there was way too much crossover for people who couldn't do both.

"Here," Julius said, handing me a hot buttered grand biscuit.

"You know I can't eat all this food," I stated as I washed the biscuit down with a sip of green tea.

"I don't think a little scrambled eggs and bacon are going to put any weight on you."

"If I gain an inch Sharon will notice. And you know Raphael's butt notices every change in me."

Julius moved closer. "Let's see if they notice this." He planted a wet kiss on my neck and then gently sank his teeth in, sending a chill through my body.

I wiggled away. "Come on, don't start. I have to be in early." I glanced over at the clock radio. It was 9:30 A.M.

"Girl, you know I didn't fix you breakfast for nothing. I even put syrup over your bacon like you like it."

I'd noticed the dripping sticky stuff on my bacon, which I couldn't resist. I picked up a piece and held it in my mouth for him to bite the other end. We both chewed until our lips met.

"You love me?" I asked.

Julius didn't answer, just devoured my lips and what was left of my bacon. He caught the tray just as it was about to topple over.

"Let's get this shit out of the way. Breakfast is over." He sat the tray on the floor next to the bed and pulled the comforter down from me, but not before I had a chance to dip my fingers in the syrup.

I rubbed my sticky fingers across his lips to taste and he in turn took them in his mouth.

"That's the sweetest thing you got?" he asked, then positioned his body on top of mine. Julius was already hard but I knew he wasn't in a rush. He never was. Julius never wanted a quickie. He had to have long engaging sex, which didn't always work for me because I had a schedule that I had to stick to, but this morning would have to be an exception.

He began with my nipples, tickling them with the very tip of his tongue. He was always so gentle with me, as if I would break, and though I enjoyed his fragile treatment, sometimes I wished he'd just tug on them a little bit harder, maybe rough me up a bit in the sack. But I'd never tell him that. Julius was too much of a man to be told how to make love to his woman.

As his tongue moved down my belly and around the curves of my hips I knew where he was headed. He stopped, glanced up at me, and said, "You don't think I fixed breakfast for nothing, do you?"

I backed up further against the headboard, bracing myself for what was to come. Gripping his shoulders, I held on, trying not to scream out when his tongue made its way inside me. I was so sensitive down there that half the time I couldn't stand for him to give me oral sex, but I also loved it so much that I couldn't stand for him not to.

As I attempted to squirm away from him he held me tight by my hips while he covered me with his mouth.

"Juuuuules, oh, Juuuules . . ." I screamed out in pleasure, one small orgasm already behind me.

I put my arms under his and tried to pull him up to me, but he shook his head no.

"Stay right here, baby," he mumbled, never bothering to take his lips away.

This was way too much for the morning. I tried harder this time to pull him up, and this time he let me—he was ready.

With Julius now up on his knees, his face glazed with my juices, I pushed him over on his back. I knew what I wanted and so did he; it was my turn to perform. I climbed my small frame on top of his sexy lean body, easing down on him, because even though I was wet, his dick was morning hard. With him inside me I hesitated, allowing myself to adjust to its width and length. He grabbed my hips and gestured for me to get up and ride him, and I knew that as soon as I did, one, maybe two strokes, I would come. And I did. It poured out of me as if a dam had broke loose.

Julius bent my head towards him for a kiss. "Come again for me," he said, smiling and holding firmly onto my shoulders so I couldn't move.

I wasn't smiling now because coming for me was serious, and what was more serious was making him come, and that too I'd mastered. I did as he asked and I rode him from the front and from the back until my juices splashed against his chest. Exhausted, I put my hands around his neck and rolled over for him to get on top, and as soon as he sunk into me he told me what I wanted to hear.

"I'm coming, baby. Hold on, I'm coming."

It was almost eleven o'clock when I rushed past Ms. Gwen, who handed me a cup of hot water and lemon. Erica was also standing watch in the reception area waiting for me. I was sure the heads who watched me whiz by were the summer intern candidates waiting to be interviewed. Erica was quickly on my heels.

"What happened to your early morning, Linney? You only have an hour left for interviews, then a production meeting," Erica said, her leather folio held tightly under her arm.

"I know, I know," I replied, dancing into my office to the music that played over the intercom.

She whipped some papers from the folio and stated, "Here's the stuff I posted on your blog this morning about your off-camera interview with Raw."

"When did that happen?" I asked, aware that I hadn't interviewed him off camera, but realizing this was the thing that kept viewers interested.

Erica opened the blinds and turned on my computer. "It didn't, but I took care of it this morning. His publicist already called and thanked me."

"I tell you, E, what would *Top of Da Charts* do without you?"

"I don't know, but you'd better hurry up and hire one of these interns so I can get some help. You want your messages?" Erica asked as she opened Outlook to my calendar.

I sipped on the lemon tea. "Naw. Let's just get rolling on the interviews."

"Here, I knew you'd forget your folder," she said, passing me the stack of résumés that I'd never bothered to look at last night.

"Okay, who's first?" I asked, then sat down behind my desk.

Chris, the first candidate, a nineteen-year-old Asian boy, was attending UCLA seeking a degree in filmmaking. His goal was to be a director and he was a little bit too glamorous for me. He might've been better off working for Raphael. His clothes were impeccable, screamed designer, and he had eyebrows arched so perfectly that I had to ask him where he'd gotten them done. Hell, he'd probably be ready to slide onto my studio couch the first time I called in sick.

But from talking with him it was evident he was more interested in Hollywood than music videos. I knew he needed to be interning at Miramax instead of on a music video show and told him that much, even offering to have Erica make a call to some of our contacts over there. No need to lead him on.

Next up was a sexy sister, Tamara, whose Korean hair weave was as perfect as my $1,200 infusions. She wore a little too much makeup and showed too much skin, but she was up on her music video trivia. She could answer any question I had about videos, directors, and especially about rappers.

Her knowledge might've gotten her the position until she slipped up and told me that she'd recently starred in a video where she'd been clad in a G-string. It seemed her goal was to open an agency called Video Chicks.

Next.

If I hadn't met Kelly Osbourne before her makeover, I would've thought the punked-out rocker candidate slouched in front of me was her twin. In talking with Angel I could tell she was an intelligent girl, having graduated summa cum laude from Yale. But I just couldn't get past the piercing, one in her bottom lip and another through her nose, or the tangled web of blond dreadlocks hanging down her back. She had no clue about how to conduct herself in an interview and needed to acquaint herself with some grooming techniques.

After I closed the door behind her I buzzed the receptionist. "Ms. Gwen, how many more of these clowns are out there?"

"One more, Linney."

"Give me a sec to get something to drink."

I took a bathroom break and asked Erica to bring me a bottle of water. What I really wanted was some food because I'd never really gotten the chance to eat the breakfast Julius had prepared, except for the piece of bacon he'd wrapped around his dick for me to chew on.

Just when I was about to call in the next ridiculous candidate, I heard laughter out in the hallway.

I peeked out the door. "Is there a party without me?"

"Caroline, here's your next candidate, Marí Colonado," Erica said, moving to her right so I could see the girl.

Marí stood about five and a half feet tall, had dark brown eyes, high cheekbones, and skin that was a ruddy shade of brown. But what she had that every Hollywood actress paid mucho dollars to get were beautiful thick lips.

"I apologize," the pretty little Puerto Rican girl said as she reached out to shake my hand. "I was making a lot of noise. I was telling your staff about my run in with Nikki V. yesterday."

Nikki V. was the diva of East Coast radio. We weren't exactly friends because she was always riding me on the air about how my show was boring and how I flirted with all my male guests.

Another issue was that she felt I'd gotten hired based on my looks. Also she felt I'd been too young to have landed such a hot job. There was no doubt I'd been fortunate to get this position. During my junior year of high school back in Philadelphia the station's reality show came to the school and did a piece on wealthy suburban teens. Lucky for me, I was picked to host the show because they said I'd been so camera friendly, but I knew it was because of my looks. And so I became their high school correspondent, which continued after graduation and landed me in my current job.

Nikki V., on the other hand, was thirty-five and had worked the ropes by having been an intern and possibly sleeping her way to the slot of a nationally syndicated radio show, where she provided lots of gossip.

"And what did ol' Nikki V. have to say?" I asked, my back against the doorjamb as I checked the little chick out.

She shrugged her shoulders.

"I doubt if it'll be anything I haven't heard," I remarked.

She lowered her eyes, embarrassed, I was sure, at being put on the spot. Then she did a good job of mimicking Nikki V.'s New York accent. "She ain't nothing but a lil' trust fund brat riding on her daddy's money. She gotta let somebody who needs a job do hers," she said. "You know, the usual thing she says on the air."

The girl was right. I'd heard it all before, countless times, about me riding on the fact that my father was a world-renowned plastic surgeon. Was I not supposed to enjoy the financial benefits of that? Some people, I'd learned, were just pure haters.

Raphael was laughing so hard I thought he was going to pee himself. Erica stood there shaking her head.

"Where did you see that diva to get that big dose of crap?" I asked, looking from Erica to Raphael. I thought to myself, how bold of the candidate to tell me something like that, and I was curious as to how she'd responded to the queen of the airwaves.

"I interviewed with her last week," the girl replied.

"Really . . . So how did you respond to her bashing me?"

"I simply told her that trust fund or not, I preferred to work for the young and beautiful, and I kindly walked out of her office, after she'd offered me the intern position."

"Ohhh, I am liking you already. Come on in and tell me all about yourself," I said as we sat in the chairs opposite my desk. I glanced down at her résumé to make sure I had her name right. "Marí."

"Sure. I just turned twenty-one; I received my under-graduate degree from Loyola, where I'm also taking some additional courses in business management."

"What brings you to *Top of Da Charts*? Interning here ain't easy."

"Working hard is all I know, especially if I want to reach my goal in life."

"And what would your goal be?" I inquired, noticing that Marí's tight ponytail was off center.

"Oh, maybe Oprah's job, or I could take over *The View*."

She surely hadn't said that to win me over, because I hadn't told anyone of my goal but those close to me, so another brownie point for the Puerto Rican.

"I like your spunk, Marí, but how well do you know this business?" I asked, again glancing down at her résumé and noticing she'd worked at Loyola's campus radio station.

"I absorb everything radio and television and I know celebrities. I read the dailies, the monthlies, and your blog. Before I came here this morning."

"And what did you think of my off camera interview with Raw Dawg?"

"Sounded kinda shady to me, maybe a bit contrived," she said, more as a question. I'm sure she was worrying that she was being too honest.

I chuckled because Erica wouldn't think that was so funny. But I was feeling Marí and her spunky attitude. I needed a dose of that and so did the show, which made me come up with a question I hadn't asked the other candidates.

"Marí, here's a question for you. If you had to suggest a summer show idea for *Top of Da Charts*, what would it be?"

I could tell I had her stumped as she lightly drummed her fingers on the arm of the chair.

"Take your time and think about it."

There was a tap on the door; it was one of the PAs telling me that I had ten minutes before our production meeting.

"I don't know . . . I have an idea," Marí said hesitantly. "It might be stupid or you might've already thought about it."

"Marí, come on, don't wimp out on me now."

"Okay, but you're gonna think it's stupid. How's this? Why not think about taking the show out of the studio and on the road."

"On the road? Now why would we do that?" I asked, amused by her idea.

Little Ms. Marí sprung to life and I could hear her Hispanic accent very clearly. "It's like this. You're always stuck in the studio, with the same audience, mostly kids from out here who live in La La Land. So why not be adventurous, take your show on the road, you know, hitting different clubs, interviewing the folks who are partying, and you know, it would—"

"It would create a following and with the right amount of hype, people would be waiting when I arrived," I interjected.

"And your ratings would run off the charts," she added nodding.

I stood up to let the idea run loose a bit. "And every celebrity would want to be on my show. They'd be begging."

"Exactly. So what do you think?" Marí asked, her eyes following me as I walked the room.

"I think I love it! You're hired and you can start tomorrow." I said, elated by Marí's creative thinking.

Her big brown eyes stretched open with surprise. "Just like that? But wouldn't you like to go over my résumé? What about my college GPA and the references that I've got for you?"

I put my hand over hers on the arm of the chair. "Marí, so long as you're not a spy for Nikki V., then we're on. Plus, let me share something with you. I sat in a two-hour production meeting yesterday and nobody, including myself, had an idea even half as good as yours."

She jumped up from her seat, then took my hand in both of hers, shaking it until I pulled away.

"Caroline, thank you so much! I'm so excited. This is going to be great. I can't wait to start, tomorrow, *really*."

"You bet. I'll see you at eight-thirty. Well, you should be here by then, but I'll see you around eleven," I said, as we both made our way out of my office.

"I promise you, Caroline, I'm going to be the best intern you ever had."

"I can see."

"And can I say one more thing?"

"Sure, go ahead."

"I can't believe you're really this beautiful in person."

I felt my eyebrows rise in question.

"No, I mean sometimes you can't believe everything you see on TV."

"Gotcha. Thanks, Marí."

I watched Marí as she practically skipped down the hall, and it excited me that some fresh air would be coming to the studio. Not only did I have a new intern but I also had a new idea for the summer show to take to my production meeting.

I took the elevator up to the conference room, where the rest of the staff had already gathered and were chowing down on lunch.

"Did you have time for your interviews, Caroline?" Sharon asked, already aware that I hadn't made it in early.

I scooped up a banana and a bottle of water from the spread on the credenza. "Interviews were a bore until the last one and she, what do they say, hit the bat out the box?"

"Not quite. More like hit the ball out the park, I think," Brad offered.

"Yeah, well, she came up with the best idea, so there's no time to be eating," I said, looking over at Brad. "I have an idea to pitch that you're going to love."

Now I had their attention.

"We're all ears, Ms. Linney," Brad said while he picked an onion from his tuna to eat.

"We're going on the road!"

"What are you talking about and who is this intern?" Sharon asked.

"Like I said, we're taking *Top of Da Charts* on the road. We'll do our shows from different cities. I don't know what cities or how we'll do it, but I guess that's your job to figure out. But for right now I'm telling the audience that we're taking the show on the road. We're getting out of this stale studio for the summer because my new intern is putting it down."

3
FAST TRACK

Morning, Marí. You ready to work?" I asked when I saw my new intern walking down the hall to greet me.

"Yes, and here's the blog responses that came in overnight. Erica showed me how to pull it. I really appreciate all those nice things you said about me on Caroline Tells All."

"What did the viewers think of taking the show on the road?"

"They've given you," she looked down at the paper and said, "about seventy or so suggestions about where you should go."

"We're going to blow this thing out of the water! I hope they're ready."

"Your girl Nikki V. is gonna eat her heart out."

"Right again, Marí."

"Morning, E, what's up?" I asked Erica, who was already opening my office door.

"Brad and Sharon have been here since eight meeting on the road trip."

"Really? By the way, have you met everyone yet?" I asked Marí as I sat down at my desk.

"I took Marí around this morning and introduced her to everyone," Erica said.

"Good, because we have a long ass day ahead of us. So maybe the three of us need to talk first."

"Good idea," Erica said. "I reviewed your calendar with Marí so she could get an idea of what your day is like."

"I hope you wore comfortable shoes." I looked down at Marí's feet, seeing she had on gray and yellow Pumas. "You'll need them."

I turned on my computer while Marí used the remote to turn on the television.

"E, do we know what cities we might go to? I was thinking about it last night. Without a doubt I want go to New York, maybe Houston, Miami. Hell, let's fly all summer."

"We'll have a better idea later this afternoon," Erica said, "after we've discussed locations, clubs, and the format of the shows."

"Cool. Let's see what this looks like," I said, then rewound the video to replay last night's show.

"Marí, you know, once you're on point with everything you'll be able to free up Erica to work on special projects she's been dying to do, as well as planning this crazy road trip."

"Please, Marí, get on point soon because I'd like to go home on time at night," Erica added with a pleading look.

"I'm a quick study, Erica, so don't worry," Marí said.

It was about twelve-thirty when the three of us headed to the conference room for our daily production meeting. The main topic of discussion was our taking the show on the road.

The meeting was already in progress when I opened the conference room door and saw the publicity director, our vice president, camera and sound engineers, along with a few other studio heads that didn't generally attend our daily meetings. There was no doubt; we were going on the road.

"Afternoon, everyone. This is Marí, my summer intern with the brilliant idea."

They all greeted Marí and we took our seats at the table.

"Caroline, we really believe that your going on the road will be great for you and the ratings," Sharon said, at the head of the table in a boring bone suit.

"That's what I'm hoping, but I don't want people to think we've turned into some fake-ass reality show. I want to keep it real," I said, glancing around the table to make sure everyone understood.

"And you're right," chimed in Brad from where he stood over the lunch spread, fixing himself a plate.

Sharon leaned across the table and jotted notes as she talked. I noticed Marí was doing the same. That was a good sign.

"This is how we'll do it," Sharon said. "We're selecting specific cities that have hot clubs or maybe some that need some attention, and that's where we'll hold the show. We'll still do our video countdown and celebrity interviews, the same as if we were home that will be shown at the same time, except it'll be a live audience on the road with the clubs as a backdrop. And you'll get the celebs on location or interview ones that are willing to travel to do your show."

"Which we're hoping is going to happen," the director of PR added.

Erica spoke up. "It's definitely going to happen. I've already received a few calls. My plan is to tell all artist representatives they can get an interview at any of the clubs for their clients but there's gonna be no preset questions. It's all freestyle, especially if we're keeping this real, right, Linney?"

I nodded yes.

"I'll do your version of editing, then I'll send it to the studio for final edit," Brad said.

"What about my approval?" I asked to make sure nothing went out before I signed off.

"We'll shoot it back to you for approval and then we'll air it the next day. That way we'll always be a day behind you," Brad said.

"What are the clubs expecting to get out of all this free publicity? I mean, they're going to make lots of dough with us in the house," I pointed out. "Shouldn't we be getting something extra out of this?"

The vice president then spoke up. "Caroline, if this goes off the way we're thinking it might, this could put you and *Top of Da Charts* in a whole other category, with some built-in bonuses for yourself."

"Not bad," I nodded, my excitement growing. I glanced over at Marí, who was still taking notes. I had no idea what she was writing.

"You keeping up with all this?"

Marí looked up from her notebook. "Yes."

Sharon continued. "The finance guy is in the process of approving the budget I dropped off on his desk last night. Once we have that, then we can move forward."

"What about sponsors? Are the advertiser rates going up?" I asked, squeezing lemon into my glass of water.

Brad spoke up after he washed down his tuna with coffee. Yuck, I don't know how anybody kissed him. "Damn, Caroline, what are you now, an agent?" he asked.

"Not exactly, but when your man represents millionaire athletes you learn to think like one," I offered.

"Just so you know, I put a call in to your agent about an hour ago and we're working on some sponsorship deals that'll get you a nice percentage," Sharon added, making sure all the legalities were handled.

I winked at my intern and said, "See, Marí, just because we're young don't mean we gotta be slow."

"I see," Marí answered.

"Yeah, Marí. I meant to tell you, if you come up with any other ideas, please don't hold back, just shout them right out," Brad said, giving Marí a big smile.

"I will," Marí said, shying away from him.

"All right, let's come up with a list of cities," Sharon continued. "Erica, did you have a chance to pull the viewing audience stats by city and state?"

So this was it, I thought. This was what would take me beyond being the host of a music video show. What was next I wasn't quite sure, but I knew exposing myself on the road could open lots of doors—and oh how good that would look on the cover of *People*.

"If you don't need me anymore, I'm out. I have to get over to wardrobe. Marí, you can hang with me."

The first thing I had to focus on before going anywhere would be my wardrobe for the show that evening, so I went to see Raphael with Marí following close behind.

"Raphael, have you met my intern?" I asked as we entered his large office, which also served as makeup and wardrobe.

"Yes, I saw the little doll face this morning, already working too hard," he said, then posed in front of the full-length mirrors.

"I tried to warn her this place is crazy, but she still wanted the job," I joked, looking at Marí.

"Marí, Ms. Linney here is gonna work your little butt off," Raphael told Marí while giving her the once-over, and doubtlessly not approving of her army green cargo skirt and top.

"I'm ready for whatever this job brings," Marí said, an eager smile spreading across her face.

"In that case, doll, can you call Barneys and ask them what the holdup is on my order. The number is in my book on the desk."

While Marí was on the phone, Raphael and I began looking through the racks for what I'd wear on the show that evening. While I tried on a few things, none of which seemed to please him, Erica burst through the dressing room door.

"Ms. Thang, why the hell are you tearing the hinges off my door?" Raphael demanded.

"It's nothing but good news. Listen up. Sharon asked me to come up with a preliminary list of cities, right? Well, here it is. Tell me what you think."

"Please don't let them be anywhere boring," I said, slipping off my skirt in front of the three-way mirror. In wardrobe I always felt like a little girl playing dress up in my mother's closet.

"Not at all," she said, then started counting off with her fingers, "How's Vegas for number one? Second will be Denver, then third will be Topeka, Kansas. . . ."

"Hold up, you gotta be kidding me. Who the hell is in Topeka, Kansas?" I asked while standing there in my panties and a halter that I'd just tried on. These guys had seen me damn near naked on plenty of occasions when they'd burst into my dressing room with ideas.

"Dorothy and the munchkins are there," joked Raphael, passing me a pair of hip-hugging jeans.

"You'd be surprised how many folks tune in from Kansas," Erica said.

I hadn't seen Erica that interested in anything since we'd gone to the Grammys. I was glad Sharon and Brad were allowing her to organize this show on wheels idea. Hopefully Marí would relieve Erica of my day-to-day stuff.

"Yeah, right. Go on," I said, about to step into the True Religion pedal pushers until Raphael motioned that I had to remove my panties. He always wanted me as close to naked as possible.

"Anyway, then you go to St. Louis, up to Chi-town, around to Columbus, Ohio, and then you'll roll into your hometown of Philadelphia with a big party to wrap up the tour."

"That's awesome!" I heard Marí say while making another call for Raphael and jotting in her notebook at the same time.

"What happened to New York? Shouldn't we be stopping there?" I asked.

"Brad figured rather than do the expected and go to the Big Apple, why not take you home to Philly and tie it in as your homecoming."

"My Linney, the homecoming queen! I love it," screeched Raphael.

"Oh, you love anything to do with queens."

I saw Marí chuckling at our banter. I'm sure she was thrilled to see her idea coming to life.

"All right, I'm feeling it. So when do we fly out?" I asked.

"That part I'm not sure of yet, but it'll be soon. We don't want any other network to get a head start on us."

Standing in front of the mirror, smoothing out my outfit to see if it really worked for me, I turned to Erica and asked, "My intern's coming along, right?"

"I would guess—it was her idea," she said, adding "I gotta go, lots and lots of work to do."

"I'm down, Kansas and all!" Raphael yelled after Erica.

I hadn't asked Marí, but I could tell by the way her face was beaming that she too was ready for a road trip.

Erica turned around and left.

"I'm telling you, the fans are gonna love it." Marí said. "You've only just mentioned it on the blog and Ms. Gwen already has a sheet of calls from people wanting to know the details. Oh yeah, before I forget, Julius called and he wants you to meet him for a late dinner tonight. Here's the info," she said, handing the slip of paper to me."

"Linney honey, those little bad boys and girls are going to be sweating you to death," said Raphael as he whipped out a sexy red Tracy Reese dress for me to try.

Traveling to different cities with *Top of Da Charts* was

starting to sound appealing no matter what city we were going to.

I bobbed my head up and down and said, "I'm feeling it.
Yeah, *Top of Da Charts, Top of Da Charts,* we coming at ya!"
and they both joined in with me.

Raphael was settling me down and had draped an apron
around me to begin applying my makeup when Marí took
a call from Brad.

"Brad says he needs you in the recording studio to shoot
a teaser for the road trip."

"Already? Damn, this thing is moving like the Con-
corde."

"We'll be right back," I told Raphael as I grabbed Marí
and pushed her out the door in front of me.

I couldn't believe this was all happening so fast. But I
loved it and all the buzz it would create around me and my
show.

At 5:45 I was standing behind the curtain pumped up
and ready to face the camera. I could tell that my little intern
was a bit tired, though, as her pace had gradually slowed
down. I was sure she hadn't expected such a busy first day
and she'd been here since 8:00 A.M., while I'd arrived closer
to noon.

I turned around and said to her, "Marí, you sure you
don't want to go home and get some rest? You've been here
all day."

"No, I'm fine. I have to see the show. I always like it when
you do the top ten countdown."

"Okay, don't say I didn't offer. It might not ever happen again," I said, hoping she'd be ready for whatever might
come next.

"No, really, I'm good. You do your thing," she said, moving aside so Raphael could dab at my lipstick.

"You gonna view the show from back here?" I asked her.

My music was blending into the last commercial and I felt my adrenaline rush. I started clapping my hands, getting myself pumped up. I was ready.

"I'd really like to sit in the audience if I could. That way I'll be able to get the vibe of your audience plus it'll be interesting to listen to their off-camera feedback."

"Another great idea, go ahead," I said, and stepped around the curtain to start the show.

"*Top of Da Charts* with Linney, y'all. Let me hear you!"

I left the studio that evening too early for my dinner date with Julius, so rather than go back to my condo, I phoned Kia to see what she was up to. As I expected, she was hanging out shopping on Rodeo. I was on my way.

I valet parked beneath Two Rodeo Drive and walked out onto the street, which was streaming with luxury cars, beautiful people, and tourists who gazed at all the expensive stores, and I felt good that this was a part of who I was.

More than that rusted Hollywood sign, being on Rodeo Drive let you know that you had arrived in Beverly Hills. I mean, where else can you find Armani, Gucci, Cartier, Neiman's all in one strip and surrounded by such an affluent neighborhood? I couldn't remember ever being on Rodeo when the sun wasn't shining.

I tiptoed up alongside Kia, who was standing in front of Jamba Juice running her mouth on the cell phone, cursing someone out. She broke from her conversation when I pinched her on the neck.

"Damn, who pissed you off?"

"That stupid ass BMW dealer. I told him I needed my car today. I'm tired of driving this piece of shit rental."

"Um, well, if you took some driving lessons . . ." I started to say, considering Kia had a fender bender every other month, and according to her, always the fault of the other person.

"Linney, don't you frickin' start that shit. I know how to drive. It's these people out here."

Kia locked her arm in mine and we began our stroll down Rodeo, which always helped me to wind down.

"What's up with you going on the road, Linney girl?"

I stepped back in shock and said, "What? You actually watched the show?"

"It was on in my dressing room when I was changing. Hey, I've got a shot at a five-page layout for *In Style* in a few months. And Ms. Tyra has selected me as one of her judges for the new season of *America's Next Top Model*."

"That's excellent news, Kia. Sounds like a party to me," I said, as if I needed a reason to celebrate.

We stopped at Cartiér and I picked up some Délices perfume.

"Like I said, where are you taking your butt on this tour? Any place exciting?"

"I hope so. Vegas is first and for real. I can't wait to be jetting all over the place. The more I think about it, Marí was right. The studio had stagnated my growth. This tour is gonna bust my show through the roof."

The guard opened the doors of Stuart Weitzman for us.

Kia turned her head and asked, "Who the hell is Mari?"

"She's my new summer intern. Wait a minute. I thought you said you watched the show. I have been talking about her for two days. I knew your ass was lying."

Kia pointed to a pair of shoes and nodded to the saleslady, who already knew her size.

"I mean, I don't get to see it everyday, but when I'm—"

"Cut the bull, Kia. I'm supposed to be your girl and you ain't even checking me out."

"Come on. Don't get all bitchy with me or I'm going to hold back your backstage pass for fashion week this year."

I turned from the boots I was considering buying. "You wouldn't dare."

"Maybe . . . But if you promise me we'll go out for a real lunch next week I won't."

"Kia, don't start," I said, being the stronger of the two when it came to watching my weight. In the business of Hollywood neither one of us could afford to gain a pound.

"Please, Caroline. I'm dying for some fried chicken."

"All right. But listen to this, I think Julius just signed his first basketball player."

"Who? Who?"

"I don't know. Some seven-foot rookie straight out of high school. For all I know he's probably twelve years old."

Kia and I spent the next hour doing some power shopping, our favorite sport. A man had his sports and we had ours. Afterward I headed down Santa Monica Boulevard to the Belvedere, where I was meeting Julius for dinner.

The Belvedere was a classy restaurant located inside the Peninsula hotel, which is what Julius preferred. Myself, I liked the chic and trendy places that served sushi and the things that

weren't fattening. Most of the time when we went to those places I ran into fans and sometimes it was distracting. This was
Julius's way of having me to himself without interruptions.

Julius didn't see me enter the Belvedere because he was
busy writing something on a napkin and talking on his cell
phone. I could never get really jealous of the time he gave
to his clients, but what kind of woman would I be if I didn't
pout just a little. Wasn't that what he expected me to do?

I tilted my head to the side and let a smirk form on my
lips. Julius stood up and kissed me while he listened to whoever it was he was talking to.

"Julius," I whined.

He shook his head yes and ended his call.

"I got him, baby, I got him! Damn it, we're celebrating
tonight!" he exclaimed, then motioned for the waiter.

"Basketball player?"

"You know it! If this boy goes high in the draft, then I'm
going to be the top dog, right up there with the Jew boys."

"You're so full of yourself, Julius Worthington, but I love
you anyway."

The waiter came back with a bottle of Laurent-Perrier
and took our dinner order.

"How was work today, baby? I didn't get to see much of
the show. I was at the gym working out with a client."

"It's cool, no guests, just me and . . ."

"Right, right countdown. But what was that red outfit
you were wearing? Whoever sent you that should dress you
all the time."

We clicked glasses.

"Oh, so you liked that little piece," I said, wishing I
would've worn it to dinner. But rarely did I wear anything in
public that I'd worn on the show.

"Damn right. Did you bring it home?"

"No, I passed it on to Erica."

"Guess I'll have to take Erica out then!" he joked.

"Sorry, brother, but nobody else could put up with you."

I began updating Julius on the tour that still didn't have a date. He in turn told me more details about his player contracts, which I wasn't always able to comprehend because of the glut of information he passed off to me. I'd even relented to watching games with him to learn more about his business, even though most of the time I was sure I was more of a nuisance.

It wasn't until the waiter sat our entrées in front of us that I realized we were popping the cork on our second bottle of champagne.

"What am I supposed to do while you're bouncing from city to city with all those brothers drooling over you?"

"Jules, why can't you fly in to see me somewhere?" I asked, picking up my fork to taste the raisin couscous.

"If that's what you want me to do, I have no problem with it. Maybe I can meet you in Philly."

He poured me another drink, then cut into his filet. I was beginning to get the impression that he wanted me a little tipsy.

"But you know I'll be keeping it warm for you," I said, referring to the warmth between my legs.

Julius leaned over and gently placed his hand on my cheek. "Yeah, yeah I know. But I'm telling you, don't be letting them brothers be hugging all over what's mine out there on the road."

I grabbed his fingers and kissed them. "Never, ever! You know I love you."

"Looks like you're loving that champagne right now."

"I think I've had enough," I said, realizing that I was close to being drunk.

"That can mean only something good is about to happen for me."

I might've been close to drunk but I knew exactly what Julius was referring to. When I was under the influence Julius had no problem getting me to give him as much slow neck as he could handle. And now, after two bottles of champagne, I was sure he'd fill my mouth with, as he referred to it, his love juice. Needless to say, we didn't linger around the restaurant for dessert.

In the morning when I heard ringing, I was sure it was part of my hangover, that is until I heard Julius saying hello. I peeked over at the clock radio and was able to read its digits: 7:13 A.M.

Who the hell was calling him? Did athletes even get up that early? I turned over and closed my eyes.

"Baby?"

I didn't answer right away; it was too early to talk. I just buried my head under the covers.

"Linney baby, here. It's for you," Julius whispered, tapping me on my back.

"What? Who is it?" I moaned, a little too hungover to really care.

"The studio," he said, putting the phone to my ear.

Reluctantly I took the phone under the covers with me. "Hello," I groaned into the receiver.

"Caroline, it's Brad. I need you to wake up. I have some good news."

"What time is it? Did I say I was coming in early?" I asked, still not wanting to open my eyes.

"Time to put *Top of Da Charts* on the road."

"Wait a minute. . . . What the hell are you talking about, Brad? It's Saturday," I said as Julius scooted closer to me.

"I know, but listen. Here's the deal, we've decided to put you and the show on the road today."

Now I was waking up. "You're kidding, right?"

Julius was definitely fully awake because his hardness was poking me in my back. I reached behind me and playfully slapped him away. He snuggled up closer, wrapping his arm around my waist, pulling me into him.

"Caroline, we have to do this right away. Everybody knows about it and I don't want any other networks to have a minute to sneak in their crews. Plus the bonus is there's a championship fight in Vegas this weekend and parties all over the place. I want you there. Sharon's on the phone with Club Pure putting together the details."

"I can't leave yet, I'm not ready," I said, my voice trailing off as one of Julius's fingers slipped inside me.

"Raphael's working on your wardrobe and the RV will be ready in about an hour, and that thing is equipped with everything you'll need."

I was ready to hang up because I was dying to have Julius inside me, but the word RV brought me back into the conversation.

"Wait a minute. Did you say something about an RV?" I turned now and looked at Julius.

"Where's Erica?" I continued. "I can't do this without her. And what about the intern, Marí?"

"Erica's already at the station and I called Marí. She'll be ready at noon, so we need you here around three."

"I guess I don't have a choice," I said as warmth spread

through me from Julius's touch. He began nibbling on my stomach.

"You gotta be crazy if you think I'm traveling across country in a trailer, sleeping in dirty ass trailer parks," I said, my attention going in two directions.

Brad started laughing so hard he almost choked on the coffee I was sure he was drinking. "If it's a road trip, then you gotta be on the road. And believe me, this thing is more than a trailer. Wait till you see it."

"For some reason I'm not excited. Brad, are you sure we can't just fly over to Vegas and meet the crew? I mean, how would I shower, eat, and have any privacy? Who's going to be in the trailer besides Marí and me? I hope you're not sending us out on the road with a bunch of strange men," I babbled, wondering who would be driving me and who would be traveling with us. The station didn't own an RV. I needed details.

"Slow down, Linney. You won't be with strangers. It's going to be me, Raphael, and Juan. Just get yourself together and have your skinny little ass here by three o'clock."

After hanging up, I sat up and said, "Jules, you ain't gonna believe this shit."

"Linney. Before you start telling me about an RV and a road trip, can you take care of this?" he asked, pointing to his dick that was jutting out.

"I will, baby, but can you listen for a minute, please?"

"Aww man," he said as he grabbed my hand to stroke his dick while I talked.

"Remember I was telling you about the intern and the show going on the road and how it was a great idea?"

"Mmm-hmm," he moaned, covering my hand with his to slow the pace of my stroking.

"Well, that was Brad, and he wants me to leave today to go off in a trailer."

"I think he said RV."

"Trailer, RV, what's the difference? I don't do the open road thing. I'm calling him back and telling him—"

"Linney, Linney, shut up and listen to me. I'm talking to you as an agent, not as your man." The more I stroked, I could see he was beginning to drip with a little precum.

"You're going to go on the trip, do what you gotta do, and when you get back, your ass will be so big, you'll have the pick of what your next job will be."

"You sure, Jules?"

"Positive. Now, this is what I need you to do." He said no more, just pushed my head under the covers.

By 11:00 A.M. I was leaving Julius's en route to my condo in Beverly Hills, cursing all the way that the studio expected me to drive across country in a funky ass RV. I began to second-guess the trip. Had it really been a good idea? I'd seen strange stories about people who traveled across country. Had I ever taken a road trip? As a little girl, when I went somewhere with my parents, we always flew.

I had no idea what to pack but decided I really didn't have to bring much from home because Raphael would be taking care of my wardrobe. But if the show was truly going to be a road trip, hell, all I would need was a few pairs of jeans and some sweats. So I packed a suitcase full of lingerie, toiletries, and sweat suits. If these designers and boutiques wanted me to wear their clothes, then damn it, this time the wardrobe was entirely on them. But then that also threw me into a panic at the thought of leaving Raphael behind, so I called him.

"Raphael, Linney here. Please tell me you're going on this fuckin' road trip with me," I pleaded, while looking around my apartment and remembering I needed to cancel the housekeeper.

"I'm already packed and so are you. Plus you know there's no way a diva like me would miss this excitement!"

"But it's a trailer."

"Look, Ms. Thang, obviously a sistah has not been watching her own show. Have you not seen these RVs your rapper boys are traveling in?"

I thought about it and realized he was right. Some of them had real luxury motor homes.

"It better be phat, I know that."

Next call I made was to Kia, who I knew would agree with me because she detested anything dirty. By the time she answered I didn't even wait for her to say hello before I started ranting about how Brad and Sharon were out of their minds if they thought I was gonna be some damn Thelma and Louise.

Once Kia finished laughing she wasn't nearly as agreeable as I'd hoped she'd be. She was more concerned about borrowing my convertible Benz.

"Kia, do you hear what I'm saying?" I asked her, while locking the door to my place.

"Yeah, but look at it like this—the show's ratings are gonna go crazy, you get more money, maybe a few magazine covers, definitely *People*, and boom, you're the hottest thing in the country."

"Kia, that's not going to make me say yes to your holding my fifty-thousand-dollar car."

"Linney, please, you know I'm driving a rental and that is

not cool. I need to be wheeling that SL 55. Please. I'll take care of it, I promise."

"All right, all right," I said, giving in to her. "I'll pick you up on my way to the studio."

"I love you, Linney."

"Yeah, yeah, just be ready at three o'clock."

4
SIN CITY

I arrived at the studio around three thirty. The parking lot was crowded with the station staff and everyone was surrounding the monstrous RV in which we'd be traveling.

When Brad and Sharon saw me enter the lot, they came rushing over to my car. I'd never seen them so excited, which made me realize that they were depending on me to make this trip a success. Needless to say, not only were they giving me a big responsibility, but the future of my career also depended upon the trip's success.

When I climbed out of the car Sharon sidled up next to me and draped her arm around my shoulders. Now I knew this was serious—she'd never shown me any affection. Meanwhile Brad was already lifting my two bags out of the trunk.

"Looks like you guys are trying to put me outta town," I said while reaching in the backseat for my purse and backpack.

"Caroline, I know this is spur of the moment but sometimes it works best that way. Plus the responses we've gotten in just two days means we have to do it while it's hot," Sharon said in reassurance.

Marí and Erica walked up and interrupted.

"Caroline, wait till you see the RV. It's beautiful," said Erica.

"What's up, Marí? Is the thing really all that? Am I gonna feel like a rapper on the road?"

Erica answered for her. "Linney, you know I wouldn't lie to you. This thing is like the Four Seasons on wheels."

I almost forgot about Kia until she poked me in the side.

"Marí, come here and meet my girlfriend, Kia."

"Hello, Kia."

"Hi," Kia said, paying Marí no attention, "Linney, you straight?"

"Yea, I know your ass can't wait to pull out of here," I said, moving out of her way as she got in the driver's seat.

Erica leaned over and said, "Kia, how you doing?"

Kia adjusted the seat as I closed the car door. "I'm great," she said, "but I'm also outta here. See y'all later."

"Please return my car in one piece," I begged.

"Call me! Luv ya!" she hollered back. She turned up the volume on the steering wheel and made a U-turn out of the lot.

I now faced the group, giving them my full attention. "All right, let me see this thing."

The company who was sponsoring the RV had sent a salesman who took us on a tour of the huge red, gray, and white motor home so we'd know how it worked. According to Sharon, traveling with me would be Marí, Raphael, Brad, and Juan, who was our tech guy. Anybody else they needed they'd just hire on the road.

"Look at this shit! This thing is so phat!" exclaimed Juan as he opened his arms to take in the width of the forty-foot-long RV. He'd been packing the equipment in the side storage compartment. For real, I ain't never seen a tricked out camper. What kind of wheels are those?" he asked as we climbed on board.

I'd never been inside an RV before, so I was quite surprised at how spacious it was when I stepped inside. It looked as good as my condo. The furniture was all tan leather with Viking kitchen appliances and state of the art computers that included monitors that would feed our tape back to the studio.

The vehicle comfortably slept six people on bunks that were hidden in the extended sides of the camper. Lucky for me I had my own bedroom in the rear of the cabin. But Brad had promised me that all of our nights would be spent in hotels.

There were four captain chairs, four flat-screen TVs, including one hidden from view on the outside wall so we could watch if were relaxing outside. Maybe the ride wouldn't be so bad after all, especially since the salesman said it drove like a car.

Erica was bouncing all around the cabin and as much as I wished she could go with us, I realized she had a husband and a two-year-old son. I also needed someone to be back in the studio who I could depend on. Plus she was probably glad to be rid of me for a little while.

"So, what do you think, E?" I asked, lying back on the leather sofa.

"I think you should hear the sound system. Check this out," Juan said.

All of a sudden Elton John's "Rocket Man" came banging out of the surround sound throughout the RV. I was sure that came from Raphael's collection, but nonetheless it got me pumped up and ready. Maybe this trip would be the excitement I needed to put a boost in the show and in my career as well.

It took us over an hour to finally pull out of the parking lot. As the studio crew filmed our departure, we toasted with Moët and set out for the *Top of Da Charts* road trip.

Marí, Brad, and I kicked back in the captain chairs, while Juan took the first leg of driving with Raphael as his cocaptain. The three of us tossed around ideas for the layout of the upcoming road shows—there was more spark in the RV than in any of our recent production meetings. It wasn't long before I was stretched across the bed for a nap.

When I woke up I searched the panel for the intercom and called out for Marí. I pulled up the miniblinds and saw that it had gotten dark out.

"Yeah, Caroline. You need something?"

"Nothing, I'm good. What are those guys doing up there?" I asked, playing with the buttons and gadgets on the wall.

"Raphael's on the phone, Juan's still driving, and Brad is asleep."

"How much further do we have to go?"

"To be exact, we've been on the road two and a half hours, so if we keep at this pace we should be to Vegas in another two."

"You hungry?" I asked, realizing that I hadn't eaten.

"I could eat. You want me to fix something?"

"I'm getting up. I'll help."

I knew I'd better watch my eating habits on the road or nothing would fit. I freshened up and met Marí in the kitchenette, where she'd begun preparing turkey burgers with all the trimmings. With the smell of food throughout the RV, everyone began scampering about to eat.

Brad, Raphael, and I were seated at the table while Marí fixed our plates. I told her it wasn't necessary but she insisted.

"I can't wait to hit some of these restaurants in the different cities we're visiting," Brad said.

Why'd he have to say that, I thought, then reached over to steal two French fries from his plate that I shouldn't have been eating.

"Hey Brad, help me understand something. If you know so much about food and claim to be a restaurant connoisseur, then why the hell are you always eating those stinking ass tuna sandwiches everyday?" Raphael asked then flung open a cabinet that contained at least twenty cans of Chicken of the Sea.

"Yeah Brad, what's up with that?" I asked.

"Your asses get stuck on this road, you'll be begging for one of those cans. Plus tuna is good for you," Brad shot back.

"Hey, Marí, you think we could drive this thing?" I asked, feeling full of energy after having eaten a decent meal. "The guys can probably use a break."

"I used to drive my brother's four-by-four all the time," she said as she sprinkled pepper on her salad.

"Come on, let's do it!"

After we'd eaten, Marí took the wheel while I changed from my jeans to a pair of shorts and a baby tee.

As I was about to go up front I looked out the rear window and noticed a black Hummer behind us that was actually riding up on our bumper. Obviously we'd been driving too slow.

I skipped past the guys, who were watching *Two for the Money* and popped into my seat, content to ride shotgun until I could see how Marí made the thing move. I leaned back against the headrest and turned on the chair massage.

I admired the way Marí drove the RV with ease, especially rounding the mountains. I hoped I could do as well. The girl had really been a plus. I was glad I hadn't let anyone else do the interviewing or I would've missed her. Marí was smart but pretty plain, so maybe over the course of our trip Raphael could doll her up a bit.

"Marí, how's it feel to see your little idea turn into a big one?"

"It's still kinda unbelievable. I mean, I never expected all this," she said as she glanced out the huge side mirror.

"To tell you the truth, I wasn't really feeling the RV thing, but it's nice. You want something to drink?" I asked her.

"Bottled water is good for me."

I went to the refrigerator and got the water, and that's when I noticed the Hummer again, this time riding alongside us.

"Marí, have you checked out that black Hummer that's been keeping pace with us?" I asked, uncapping her bottle.

"I wasn't going to say anything, but it has been riding our ass. Every time I slow down they speed up."

"Maybe some fan who knows it's us."

"I don't think so. It's like he doesn't really want to pass us, yet he keeps trying."

"Shit, it's not your fault the highway is treacherous through here," I complained, looking out my side mirror at the mountain we were cruising down.

At that moment the RV shook as the Hummer bumped us from the passenger side.

I held on to the dashboard to brace myself from the jolt. "What the fuck?"

I pushed on the panel of buttons until I found the one to let down the window. The Hummer, on the shoulder of the road, was revving its engine almost like the driver wanted to race. Its darkly tinted window came down.

"Yo, this ain't no place to be playing," I shouted.

"Get that piece of shit off the road!" the driver yelled out.

"Fuck you. Get off our ass!" I yelled back.

"Caroline, please don't egg them on. They could have a gun," Marí said.

"They don't have no damn gun. They're just a bunch of drunk and crazy hillbillies."

Brad heard the commotion and came to the front. "Who the hell are you yelling at?" he asked, leaning over me to see out the window.

"These simple asses next to us are trying to run us off the road," I told him.

Brad tried to be diplomatic. He leaned over me and said, "Hey, man, why don't you chill out. We'll slow down if you want to pass."

The hillbillies yelled, "What I want is for you to get off our road," then tossed an empty can of Bud our way that missed coming through my window.

Just then Juan came to the front with the video camera. Now this was gonna be a show.

"We're grabbing some footage of this shit. Come on, Caroline, mike up. No better time to get this road trip started."

I snapped the microphone he handed me onto the collar of my shirt. "Heard that," I said.

"Linney, be careful. These boys are drunks," Brad warned.

"Oh, c'mon, let's have some fun," I urged.

Juan had taken to trading obscenities with the men, and I could see it was making Marí a little nervous.

"Just keep the RV steady, Marí," I said.

"I'm good, but I don't think you're supposed to mess with folks with road rage. They could be dangerous, Caroline."

"I'm gonna show their asses some road rage all right."

"Linney, I am not letting you go on camera without makeup," Raphael said.

"Oh please, we ain't got time for that," I said, then I turned on my microphone and began to comment on the ordeal.

"It's Linney here, y'all, coming to you from the mountains of Nevada. I got some real live road rage going on. Take a look at this."

Juan panned the camera at the Hummer while simultaneously holding the large microphone out the window so he could record their ridiculous remarks.

"So this your road, trash boy?" I yelled back out the window.

It was funny until I heard one of them yell, "How 'bout y'all send us some of that black tail over here."

"Did I hear y'all say sumthin' bout wantin' some of this here black tail?" I asked with my best country drawl.

"Yeah, black girl, come suck on this."

"Oh, I got something you can suck on, watch this," I said, and with no hesitation I pulled down my sweat pants and mooned them.

The two rednecks were so stunned that they lost control of their Hummer and careened off into a ditch.

We were falling over each other with laughter. Later, when Juan played back the footage mixed with a Tim McGraw song, it was even funnier. If this was how this trip was starting, I was curious as hell at what might lie ahead.

Thirty minutes later we could see the lights of Vegas on the horizon. I'd been to Vegas several times but it was always by air, so the skyline was different coming over the mountains. The view was just breathtaking. I could see all of the hotels that were along the strip.

We made our way down the boulevard and pulled up in front of the Wynn. The car port was crowded since the fight was in town.

"Look at all the people. C'mon, let's go get the cameras," Juan said as we began gathering our things.

"I don't think they're here for us," I said, somewhat disappointed.

"Who cares? C'mon, Caroline, we gotta take advantage of it, especially for our first stop," Marí said.

"You're right, Marí. I'm ready."

Everyone began to scramble and get cameras and equipment. This was our first stop and we hadn't given much thought to how we'd set up for our arrival because we'd been more concerned with the layout of the actual shows.

I was about to climb down from the cab when Raphael stopped me.

"Oh no, honey, you cannot arrive in Sin City looking all tired. Come back in here."

"What are you talking about?" I asked, slinging my backpack over my shoulder, still trying to go out the door.

"That face, girl. You gotta look just a little tired but glamorous before you step outta here," Raphael insisted, pulling me back into the RV.

After spending twenty minutes at Raphael's makeshift makeup table and having Brad go inside to set things up with the hotel manager, we were ready. Raphael had been right; I was television glamorous, yet I looked like I had been on the road. Juan stood waiting with his video camera and I snapped on my microphone. We'd finally arrived. The majority of people outside the Wynn had no idea who we were, but the few people who did helped us to ignite the crowd. Their enthusiastic reception helped set the tone for the show. I was glad Raphael had polished up my look, if even just to make a quick appearance.

Marí went with me to my room and informed me that we had two hours before we had to be at Caesars for the party at Pure. Once I had showered I stretched out on the chaise in my suite and put a call in to my parents, whom I'd forgotten to tell I'd be traveling.

After reassuring my father that I was not in Vegas to elope, I called Julius.

"Baby, I was just about to call you," he said.

"We just checked in and I'm supposed to be resting before the show, but I wanted to call and tell you that I miss you already."

"Yeah, I'm smelling the sheets. Now get to work. Call me later."

Around midnight Marí, Raphael, and I were climbing back into the RV to head over to Pure. For the few minutes I was outside, the 102 degree desert heat attached itself to my skin. I had no idea how people survived outdoors during the day in this climate. Raphael had put me in a studded vest acting as my shirt and a pair of low riding jeans, with chunky jewelry. Brad and Juan had gone ahead to set up for the show.

The place was just filling up when we arrived. The club was really sleek. The floor we'd be filming from was decorated in shades of white, ivory, and silver. While we waited for management to finish setting up our spot, I was surprised to find myself getting nervous. I'd been in front of that studio audience for so long that a live audience, which I had less control over, was a totally different experience. I noticed that in Vegas people came out to drink, party, and get loose, while LA people came out to be seen.

The crew was set up in the main room, where they played hip-hop. Raphael noticed I was somewhat jittery, so he insisted we have a glass of wine. I knew the fight was over and my guest had arrived when I heard the crowd hissing. Anaconda was in the house. We made it over to our area. It was time to open the show.

"Linney here in Sin City with *Top of Da Charts*! Can we let 'em know where we're at?"

"PURE, PURE, PURE," the audience chanted, and then I began my monologue before sitting down with Anaconda. He sat among three young barely dressed girls.

"Everybody's been waiting on this showdown and I see you gave them what they wanted," I said to him.

"They should've never doubted me," he replied.

"But you don't fight that often. How do you do it? You know how to win everytime with a knockout?"

"I can fight when I want 'cause my money is long and so is my reach."

We talked for another thirty minutes when I saw Marí sprinting her way through the crowd from the direction of the ladies room, waving at me frantically.

"Caroline, hurry up. You gotta see this!" she shouted above the noise of the club when she reached me.

"What, what is it?" I asked, standing on my toes attempting to see across the jam-packed room where a crowd was gathering near the bathrooms.

"Come on, hurry up before you miss it!" she said, nearly dragging me from my seat.

"But I have to finish here."

"Bring him with you. You have to get this. They're about to throw down."

"Who? Who?" squealed Raphael, who was on my heels, along with Anaconda.

"Shareese and Baby Beef. They're in the ladies room fighting over Sugar Ray."

Sugar Ray was a new rapper from the Derrty South. His single had been number one for two months. I'd just interviewed him a few weeks ago. Supposedly he had a son by Baby Beef but he also had his own harem of women.

Shareese was New York's one-hit wonder, an R & B singer. She now sang the hook over rappers' lyrics, but word on the street was that she also took the hook from them, mostly from the backdoor. Baby Beef, on the other hand, was a foul-mouthed rapper chick with a baby face who had been known to go toe to toe in a freestyle rap competition against man or woman.

The place was so packed I was surprised the fight didn't incite a riot. I couldn't believe it. Our first night on the road we were getting live coverage of a girl fight. You couldn't get this in the studio.

"Wait a minute, tell me what happened," I said to Marí.

"It's like this. Shareese was giving head to Sugar Ray in the men's room but he'd come here with Baby Beef. And what happened was Baby Beef caught them while they were getting it on."

"Juan, bring that damn camera over here and hurry up," Brad ordered.

By the time we reached them they were both rolling on the floor with Baby Beef on top pulling out Shareese's weave. Before security could separate them, Beef had busted Shareese's top lip wide open.

"Linney here, y'all. They're mixing it up out here in Sin City and Anaconda ain't the only one kicking ass. The chicks are wilding."

Juan began taping—nothing like getting it when it's hot.

People were clamoring to get in front of the camera.

"Now try sucking dick with that, bitch!" Beef shouted.

"You getting this? You getting it?" I asked Juan.

"I got you! Go on, keep talking," he said.

"It ain't over, bitch! I'm coming for you!" Shareese yelled as security dragged her out the door.

Once things calmed down, Juan and Brad were dying to get back to our hotel to edit the tapes and send them off, but we couldn't leave just yet because Sugar Ray wanted to see me. I was hoping he wasn't going to ask me not to show it, because I wasn't about to let anyone dictate to me what to put on my show, especially something that happened in public.

I had Marí go with me over to his cordoned off VIP section, Juan following with the camera.

"Yo, sit down, Linney girl, you all outta breath. Here," Sugar Ray said, offering us a glass of cognac.

"What's up, Ray? Sorry about what happened with your ladies."

"Ladies? Hey, bitches don't mean shit. Look, a brother can't help it if it taste like sugar. Now git dat on *Top of Da Charts*," he said as he stared straight into Juan's camera lens.

Sugar Ray was clearly fucked up, and it was more than cognac that had his eyes half closed. If I didn't know any better I would've thought he'd been drinking cough syrup. It was only so many things that made you look like you were asleep when you were clearly awake. He didn't say much but that sound bite was all we needed to close out our night at Pure.

Before I could thank Marí for catching that full-scale brawl, she came up with an even better idea as she suggested overlaying the fight with the old Brooke Valentine song, "Girlfight."

"Marí, girl, you have to keep your eyes open for all this type stuff, especially when I'm caught up in interviews."

"I know, I know. It don't get no better than this!"

5

ON THE ROAD AGAIN

This afternoon I was behind the wheel as we headed toward St. Louis. Initially it had been a little scary being so high up in the air, but after weaving across the yellow line a few times I finally got the hang of it. The longer I drove, the more I realized what a calming affect it had. Not a lot of traffic, just me and a long stretch of highway.

We'd been on the road for over a week. So far we'd hit Vegas, Denver, and Topeka, Kansas, which had the biggest crowd waiting for our arrival. I'd thought that Topeka was going to be a bore, but it proved to be the total opposite. The club where we were supposed to do the show had an electrical outage, so we had to do it from a nearby park. It turned into a block party, making it the first time we put the TV screen on the side of the RV in gear. The momentum was building faster than we could imagine.

Brad and Juan had to sleep in the RV one night for what they said was security reasons. But then Marí found the videotape of what they were really doing. Hell, they'd even gotten the girls to sign releases. Now they had groupies. The real challenge was how we could possibly edit it for broadcast. I was sure Brad and Sharon would find a way to intersperse it into my footage.

As for the ratings, well, we'd only been to three states and the show had been repeated several times. Viewers even wanted to know if they could buy the DVD of the road trip. Of course I had my agent all over that.

"Caroline?"

"Girl, you scared me. I thought everybody was a sleep."

"I'm too excited to do that, so I pulled the responses to Caroline Tells All and I couldn't even get through all of them," Marí said.

"You know what, Marí?"

"What's that, Linney?"

"You should get in front of the camera too; I mean, the audience should get to know all of us."

"That would be awesome. Are you serious?"

"Wait and see when we get to St. Louis."

We rode along for a while in silence, me thinking about how much I missed Julius and becoming curious if Marí had someone back in California.

"Marí."

"Yes, Linney."

"Your parents know you're on the road, right?"

"My parents?"

"I know you're an adult, but you did let them or somebody know."

"Oh yeah, they know everything I'm doing."

"And so what about your boyfriend? I know you got one."

"Who, me?"

"Yes, you, Marí. Don't be trying to play all innocent."

"Well, I date quite a bit, but I'm not dedicated to anyone in particular. I just like to have fun. I never found one man who held my interest long enough, especially not those college boys."

"Funny."

"What's that?"

"My friend Kia is always telling me I'm going to get bored with one man."

"Were you a virgin when you met him—Julius, right?"

"He's the only one. I mean my wheels were well greased when he came along, which wasn't totally true since none of my previous lovers had been able to take me to the heights that Julius has."

With things settling down in the RV I could see Marí beginning to nod off. She was such a trooper. I knew if I told her to go to bed she'd refuse, but still I insisted that she take my room and get some sleep.

It was nice getting to know Marí. I guess I'd never been a mentor to anyone, at least knowingly. I'd actually begun to consider her more of a friend, especially since she and I were the only females along for the ride. I mean, Marí wasn't perfect, not that I expected her to be, and she could certainly use a little fine-tuning when it came to her wardrobe. It consisted of cargo pants, cargo jeans, and cargo skirts; she had a pocket for everything. I also didn't understand with that thick, wavy hair she had why she only wore it in a ponytail, and a crooked one at that.

But what kind of irritated me was her obsession to keep the RV clean. It was like she was our own personal maid service. I repeatedly told her to stop picking up after us, but she wouldn't listen. I think Marí thought being on the road with us was another college course, the way she took notes. I figured she was keeping a diary of our trip. I understood her wanting to be efficient and take notes, but it was almost as if she wrote things verbatim. And maybe it was minor, but the drumming thing she did with her fingers on everything could be a bit annoying.

"Stop it," I said to myself, laughing as I imagined just what Marí thought about me.

I brought my thoughts back to business and began wondering what would be my next career move. I couldn't stay at *Top of Da Charts* forever. But I had no idea what my options were; maybe I really did need a college degree.

The best person to talk to about business was my brother. I put a call in to Maurice, but his voice mail said that he was out of the country. I didn't know what was up with that so I called my mother on her cell.

"Mom, it's Linney. Where is your son?"

"Honey, I can't talk right now. I'm in a meeting with the party planner."

"For whose party?"

"Your father's. It's the retirement party. Please don't tell me you forgot. You will be home in time?"

"You know I will!" I said, not recalling the details.

"I'll call you later. Be safe out there, dear."

It was nearing sun down and as the radio had predicted, it had started to rain. The back and forth of the big windshield wipers was hypnotic, so I turned the radio on to one of the local stations. No better way to get into the mood.

I'd been so caught up in my thoughts that somehow I'd exited I-670 and was on an alternate route. Foolishly I'd turned off the navigation system because I found it way too distracting. I knew I couldn't have gone too far outta my way, but rather than wake anybody, I wanted to figure it out on my own.

Realizing I was somewhat lost, I turned the system back on and tried to follow the directions, but obviously I'd screwed something up because now I was on a back road to nowhere. But still I didn't want to wake anyone because I wanted to prove to my crew that I too could handle the road just as well as them.

As I was attempting to type in the directions to St. Louis with one hand and keep the other on the big steering wheel, I noticed through what now had become a steady rain that someone was standing in the road next to a blue pickup truck with its hood up. I would've kept going if it weren't for the fact that it was raining.

When my headlights began to bring him into full view I noticed it was a white guy with his thumb out. Did people really still hitchhike? Well, I wasn't about to stop and pick up a strange man, even though he looked harmless. I began to pass him but then felt bad when I saw him drop his thumb. How much harm could it be? There were five of us and one of him, plus the guys didn't know it but I'd seen that little pistol Juan had in his bag.

I slowed the RV down. Maybe I was tired, or had seen *Two For the Money* too many times, but the closer I got the more he looked like Matthew McConaughey.

When I pulled the RV to a stop, I shouted at Brad to wake up so I could let him know what I was doing. As grouchy as he was, Brad got out his camera and filmed the guy getting on the camper. It never ended.

"Hey, what's this all about? What are you, some reality show?" he asked, hesitating before stepping into the RV.

He wasn't a scraggly hitchhiker at all. He was what my friend Kia referred to as a dirty boy, which meant he was a clean-cut guy trying to look dirty. He had a heavy five o'clock shadow going on, needed a haircut, and wore jeans that could've used a wash. But something about him still looked fresh. And it was no doubt that he'd been working out somewhere, all of which made him kind of sexy.

"No, come on, it's safe. We're just giving you a lift. Don't you want to get out of the rain?" I asked. "You can sit up front with me."

He reached out to shake my hand. His didn't feel dry, as I'd expected.

"I'm Vin, and you?"

"Caroline Isaacs from *Top of Da Charts*. This is our road trip," I said, thinking McConaughey or not, this white boy was fine, and to tell the truth, I was excited about having him ride alongside me.

"I saw it on the side of the RV."

He leaned back, then stared at me again, "Oh yeah. I've seen you, but you look different somehow."

"I hope that doesn't mean I look bad out here," I said, typing into the navigation system to recall the directions.

With his eyes still taking me in, he said, "No, Caroline, not at all. But what are you doing out here?"

"Our show is on a trip cross country doing stops in different cities. It's been unbelievable," I said, my eyes now taking him in like we were playing a game.

"You like it? You know, your job, the trip."

Pulling the RV back onto the road, I said, "Most definitely, I love it. I've met so many people."

"What about a boyfriend? You have one of those back in California?"

"Sure do," I said, happy to talk about Julius so that I could calm the quick fantasy I was having of being with a white man—first time for that.

"What's your story, Vin?" I asked, taking my eyes off the road for a minute to sneak a quick look at him again. Vin had propped his feet on the dashboard, allowing me to see the thick muscles in his thighs that pushed against his Levi's.

"You might not believe it, but I've been kind of a corporate guy for the last five years. Worked for my father's commercial real estate business."

"And what happened, your daddy fired you?" I asked.

"I wish. No, I just left. Couldn't take any more of that day-to-day robotic life. I hated having to live my life by somebody else's rules, somebody else's clock."

"But it was your father, it couldn't be that bad," I said, and at the same time realized how I would not want to work for my meticulous father.

"It wasn't him—it was the clock, the work environment, not enough personal time to think your own thoughts. Everything had to be about business. It picks at your personal life until you can't distinguish one from the other. I mean, look at you out here on the highway. Would you trade this for an office job?"

"Not quite," I said. I wanted to know more about him. "And now you're on vacation?"

He pushed his hand into the waist of his pants and I could see that his crotch was slightly bulging. I turned my head and kept my eyes forward.

"Yeah, an extended one. For real, I quit, left."

We were silent for a moment as I contemplated how easy it had been for him to make that decision. Had I wanted to, I could've quit and lived on my daddy's money. I knew plenty of people who did just that. But how boring that would have been.

"I realized, Caroline, that I was a free spirit and the corporate life, well, it was stunting my growth."

"What did your family say? Didn't you have a girlfriend or anything?"

"I was working a job I hated and engaged to a woman I couldn't stand. So I stuffed two grand in my pocket and hit the road to wherever it took me. Shit, I don't even have a cell phone."

Vin closed his eyes like he was enjoying his freedom already, which made me more curious about the life he'd left behind.

"Damn, don't you think your fiancée is worried about you? What about your family?"

"Family's cool. Girlfriend don't matter. What about you? You satisfied with that boyfriend of yours?"

"I love Julius; he's been so good for me," I answered, wondering if I'd somehow given him the wrong impression, if he'd seen through to the rise he'd gotten out of me.

"I see, so then why are you out here like me?"

"I told you, this is for work."

He shook his head as if he didn't believe me. "You could've flown if you'd wanted to, I'm sure. So I'm thinking if that's the case, then what are you missing at home that your man Julius isn't giving you?"

I took offense to what he'd suggested. "Nothing. Our relationship is fine. I think we'll probably wind up getting married in another two years."

He shook his head again and turned in his seat to face me, his legs stretched out between us. "Let me put it another way," he said, his voice this time lower and so damn sexy that I had to readjust myself in my seat.

"Linney, that's what they call you on your show, right?"

Was it me or did the L in my name roll off his tongue differently?

I nodded yes, then asked, "I thought you hadn't seen the show."

"What are you missing, Linney, when you're making love? You know that you're not getting something you want out of it."

My palms began to tingle with perspiration. "I'm not missing anything. It's all good with me and Julius. I love having sex with him."

He chuckled, then said in a whisper, "Sex, huh."

I decided it was time to pull over and take a break from driving and a breather from Vin. The more I thought about it, I wasn't sure if it was me or Vin that was horny. Both of us had been on our own individual road trips and this wasn't the type of conversation we should be having.

Before we could find a place to stop, it started to rain harder. I didn't realize the road we were on was flooded until the front tires began to hydroplane. Vin must've noticed I was getting nervous. He rose from his seat and kneeled beside me. I smelled his day-old cologne mixed with the rain and his sweat. Now my thoughts were muddled and my ass was wet.

Calmly he said, "I wouldn't advise you to put your foot on the brakes."

"I'm not. Please just shut up and let me drive this thing."

The water resistance was so strong that I couldn't imagine what New Orleans went through, because this was no comparison. But it was Vin's voice and his hand on my thigh that both soothed and excited me at the same time.

I'd gotten the vehicle under control but not my body, which seemed to have a mind of its own. But it made me think about what he said. What was I missing with Julius? I didn't think I was missing anything. I'd never even given it any thought. It was Kia who'd kept telling me I needed to venture out. Even Marí said she'd been having fun juggling men. Was I the only one?

There was no doubt Julius loved me. We practically lived together and the only thing that was stopping me from giving up my condo was that he wanted us to get married first. I agreed because I knew my parents weren't going to go for that living together thing. But somehow I didn't think that was what Vin was referring to.

I figured he was nodding off by the way he was slouched down, his head against the window and arms folded across his chest like he didn't have a care in the world. Curiously I looked down, and from the light in the cabin I could see the outline of his dick. Why was I even looking? I hadn't been with another man since I'd first slept with Julius. That had to mean he satisfied me, right? If so, then why was Vin's question bothering me?

"Vin?"

"Yeah, Linney," he answered, yet not opening his eyes.

"What do you mean about being satisfied?"

"Some women think they're satisfied until they've had something else, then they realize what they've been missing. It's not about size, not about love. It's all about technique, all about finding out how a woman likes to be fucked."

His words startled me.

"Excuse me, but Julius and I make passionate love, so if that's what you mean, then yes, he knows what I like."

"Look, Linney, that's good for you. But I'm not the type of person that's going to make love, so maybe that's why I'm on the road. I mean, if that's the kind of man you want, then, yeah, you're satisfied and you should go back home and get off this road. But if you want to be fucked and fucked right, then I'm the one you want to see."

The arrogant white bastard. I couldn't believe he'd said that. How dare he have an opinion on what satisfied me? But if he were so wrong, then why wasn't I defending myself against his insult?

I couldn't fool myself anymore, especially with the slickness that was now on my thong. This man was turning me on; no, he was making me hot. What was I going to do? I couldn't put him out of the RV because I was a little horny; no, make that a lot horny. Any woman would be—just look at him. Kia was always telling me I needed to try something different.

At that moment Marí came to the front and informed me that the crew wanted to stop at the next rest stop for food.

"That'll be where I get off," Vin said, straightening himself up in the seat.

"You're leaving?" I said too quickly, like I didn't want him to go. "You don't want to ride all the way into St. Louis?"

"Big towns don't excite me anymore. I'm going to be a small town guy from now on."

I was disappointed that Vin didn't want to ride with us any further, because I wanted to keep talking with him to see if in fact I was missing something in my life.

A few miles down the highway I saw the sign that a rest stop was ahead. I almost didn't want to stop because I didn't want Vin to leave me. But that was foolish thinking. I pulled off when I saw a flashing red and green sign that read "Thelma's Diner" and EAT HERE, GET GAS.

We piled out the RV, three white boys, two Puerto Ricans, and one black woman. I'm sure we were an interesting group. The seven of us walked into the silver and black half-filled diner. All the patrons turned our way. I almost wished Brad hadn't brought the video camera in with him, because they weren't giving us a big welcome.

We seated ourselves, sliding into a large circular booth with me on one end and Vin on the other. Surprisingly the redheaded waitress was pleasant. I guess if nothing else, she hoped we'd be big tippers. While she was passing out the sticky menus I excused myself to go to the bathroom. As I was walking away I heard Vin tell the crew he'd be right back also.

I passed the counter where the cook stood at the grill flipping pancakes with a food-stained apron. And I could've done without seeing the dead fly smashed against the refrigerator glass where the pies and cakes were stored.

Stepping inside the bathroom, I slipped and almost fell from the muddy, wet footprints on the floor from people trekking in from the rain. This was nasty, but it was a road trip, which made me think of the digital camera Marí had stuffed in my pocket after our last stop. It had both photo and video modes. I took it out and snapped a few photos for the album.

I checked the first stall, which was filled with graffiti: "Kim loves Ron" inside a heart; "for a blow job see your mother;" and a pretty good picture of two people having sex, well, more like just the vagina and the penis. Another shot there for the album.

The second stall wasn't any better, because not only was the toilet overflowing but also there was a used tampon floating on the top. Maybe I should've just gone back to use the bathroom in the RV, but it was dark out there.

I peered into the last stall and took a chance even though the lock was broke on the door. I was pulling my pants down so I could situate myself over the toilet without sitting on it when I heard someone go into the stall next to me.

I didn't know who'd gone into the stall, but since there wasn't any toilet tissue in mine, I did what most women do. I called over to the next stall and asked if someone could pass me some tissue. I didn't expect the response I received.

"You don't need any tissue, I'll lick it dry," Vin said from the next stall, where he was peeking at me from under the divider.

"What are you doing in there?" I asked, feigning surprise that he'd followed me.

"I'm coming in, Linney."

I must've suffered from temporary insanity because I didn't stop him, just stood where I'd squatted with my pants down to my knees. When he stepped into the stall he didn't say anything, didn't even ask if I wanted him, because he was confident that I did.

Vin took charge. He spun me around and slammed me up against the door of the stall. His strong arms kept me from falling on the dirty floor. He put his hands down my pants and yanked them all the way down to my ankles. It was all happening so fast. He did like he'd promised as he licked me from the back, long strokes until I practically fell to my knees, and instead of licking me dry, I was soaking wet. Julius had never made me cum just from oral sex. I didn't even realize I was screaming out until he put his hand over my throat and began talking to me.

"This is how you want it, ain't it, Linney?"

"Don't do this. I gotta go," I cried to him.

"Lovemaking only happens on TV, baby. You wanna be fucked, don't you?"

He grabbed hold of my breast, flipped it out of my shirt, and squeezed so hard I screamed out in pain or pleasure, I wasn't sure which. The digital camera I'd been carrying fell out of my pocket and onto the floor.

I wanted to reach down and pick it up but Vin had my body bent in half as his dick penetrated deep into my belly. Then I heard the toilet flush and I thought he'd done it accidentally, but obviously there'd been someone in another stall.

He reached down, picked up the camera and started snapping pictures of his dick going in and out of me. I knew I should've stopped him, but right then I didn't care because something unbelievable happened. I actually saw myself cumming. It wasn't just running down my legs either, it was squirting onto the graffiti-ridden bathroom door like a water fountain.

"Look at you cumming. That man ain't never fucked you like this."

"Yo, who's in here? What's going on?" someone yelled.

I scrambled to get my pants up. When I turned around I didn't even get a chance to glance at all that dick he'd put inside me, but I did realize that he hadn't cum. How had that been possible with the way he'd fucked me?

When we stepped out of the stall, we were facing a big, hefty, redneck cop.

"What are you two doing in here? This lady said it sounded like someone was getting assaulted." The officer snorted as he stood there chewing on a cigar and swinging his nightstick.

"No, officer, I'm fine," I answered, my legs wobbly as I tried to tuck in my T-shirt that was too short to be tucked.

He gave Vin a grin of confidence, proud maybe that his fellow white boy had scored a black girl. "I can see what you've been doing and this ain't the kinda place for that, so I suggest you get back up in your fancy trailer and hit the road."

"Officer, what are you talking about?" I asked.

"I'm talking about that," he said, and pointed to my left breast, which was sticking outside my shirt.

I glanced at myself in the cracked mirror. I definitely had a deer-in-the-headlights look. My hair was tossed all over my head. What had Vin done in so short a time?

"Now both of you get your asses outta here."

Vin and I both scurried out of the bathroom. We hadn't been in there that long, I knew, because the crew was just beginning to eat. But I pondered how the hell Vin could've done so much damage in just a few minutes.

I wasn't hungry anymore and all eyes were on me. I heard Brad say, "I guess we're taking this to go."

The patrons were all looking at us and whispering as we exited the diner. Had I been that loud?

Raphael was right behind Vin and I.

"What you been up to in the bathroom, Ms. Linney?" he asked in my ear.

"I don't wanna talk about it," I said, trying to catch up with Vin, who was crossing the parking lot ahead of me.

"Vin, wait, where you going?" I asked.

"I told you. This is where I get off, Linney."

"Why? Where are you going?" I pleaded, mad at myself for asking.

"Wherever the road leads me. Free spirit, remember?"

I wanted to ask Vin to ride with us at least until we got to St. Louis. I wanted to see what about him had made me do what I'd just done in that bathroom. I also wanted to know why he hadn't cum.

He leaned over and kissed me on the forehead. "You take care of yourself, sweet Caroline."

"But wait, you left your bag in the camper and I thought you said you wanted to take a shower," I said, still desperate for him to stay.

"Hell, you're right, a hot shower would be good."

We went into the RV and I was hoping that Vin wasn't finished with me, because I wanted to be able to satisfy him too. But he was totally focused on getting back on the road. So while he showered I sat in the cabin and fiddled around with the monitors. The rest of crew dallied outside. Finally he was done and the crew was back also. Try as I may, I couldn't convince Vin to ride with us into St. Louis. But I did have a question.

"Vin, why'd you make love to me so fiercely like that?"

" 'Cause you needed it."

"What do you mean?"

He smiled, kissed me on the forehead again, and said, "You take care of yourself, sweet Caroline."

I showered the smell of Vin off me. I wanted to go to sleep but now the shame that I'd cheated on Julius began to gnaw at me. Plus I looked like hell. Looking at my face in the mirror, I could see that my forehead was bruised, probably from Vin banging my head up against that stall door. But even twinged with guilt, I had to admit that I'd never had love made to me like that. Actually, making love wasn't what Vin had done. Vin had fucked me. With that thought I fell off to sleep.

It wasn't until Marí woke me up to tell me it was time to get prepped for our arrival in St. Louis that I realized how sore I was. My thighs hurt so bad, as did my back and my head from Vin pulling my hair. I could barely get out of bed.

"You all right?" Marí asked, standing in the doorway.

I couldn't help but giggle. "A lil' sore." I sat up on the side of the bed and threw my legs over.

"Caroline, that hitchhiker didn't hurt you in that bathroom, did he?"

"Between us girls, Marí . . . wait a minute, here, let me show you something."

I stood up and went over to the closet where I'd stashed the digital camera.

I wanted to show Marí the pictures he'd taken before I could delete them, because there was certainly no way I was keeping that kind of evidence around. Vin had been a one-night stand and that was the end of it. I reached into my pants pocket that hung from the hook on the closet door and felt around. No camera. I checked the other three pockets. Empty. I tried to remember if I'd even gotten the camera back from him.

"What are you looking for?"

"Pictures. I had some . . . I mean, Vin took some pictures of us."

"Not in that bathroom I hope," she asked, sounding as disgusted as it probably was.

I stopped searching and nodded my head yes.

"Caroline, we have to find that camera. Don't you remember where you put it?"

"I put it in my pants. Marí, you didn't happen to see it when you were straightening up?" I asked, remembering that I'd simply tossed my clothes on the floor when I'd gotten undressed.

"No. I just picked up your stuff and hung it up. I'm sorry."

"It's not you, it's me. Can you just please help me look for it?"

"Sure, of course."

"It just has to be here," I said while tossing things around in my room. But as I tried to locate the camera I noticed something else missing. Raphael had gotten a bejeweled bustier from Gaultier for me to wear for our wrap party in Philly, and the box it had been in was open and the bra was missing.

"What is it?" Marí asked, peering around me as I bent down on the floor.

I looked down at the empty box. "I don't believe this shit. . . ."

"What is it, Linney?"

"Not only did that bastard steal my digital camera but . . ." I threw the empty box across the room. "My fuckin' bustier."

"Caroline, are you sure? Come on, let me look."

The room wasn't that big but Marí and I unsuccessfully checked again. We were making so much noise that Raphael came to the door.

"What the hell are y'all doing in here, rearranging the furniture?"

Both Marí and I stared blankly back at him.

"Damn, y'all done tore this room up. You got shit everywhere. I know this ain't Marí's doing."

Neither one of us answered. I was sure Marí was waiting to see if I would fess up.

"Come on, what is it?"

"Vin, I think . . ." I plopped down on the bed and tears started falling down my face.

"That hitchhiker stole Caroline's digital camera and the Gaultier bustier you got for her."

If I thought I was distraught, well, Raphael was ballistic.

"No. Uh-uh. No he didn't. Turn this mothafucka back around. I ain't that much of a bitch. I will kick his ass," he yelped, his hands flying every which way.

Juan came to the back and wanted to know what was going on. Brad was on the intercom.

"Yo, what's the problem back there?" Brad asked.

"That bitch ass white boy turned out to be a thief," Raphael said.

"Linney, don't worry about it. You can get a new camera. All he's gonna do is post the picture from our trip on the Internet. What's the big deal?" Juan asked.

I looked at Marí for support.

"What?" Juan asked.

"Linney, girl. Don't tell me you had no damn kinky shit on there," Raphael said.

I couldn't bring myself to say yes because I felt so stupid.

Marí saved me by saying, "No, it wasn't that bad." But my crew knew better.

"Oh, what if he sells them to the tabloids for money?" screeched Raphael, hopeful, I'm sure, of forthcoming gossip.

"He wasn't broke. Vin had money. He had at least two grand in his pocket. I saw it," I said.

"I don't think that's what you were looking at, if you know what I mean," Raphael teased.

I started to laugh because crying certainly wasn't going to help. God forbid they'd start taping that.

"Look at all the celebs whose porn has hit the airwaves. All their careers skyrocketed, even those who didn't have one," Marí said.

"I know you mean well, Marí, but you gotta understand that boosting my career is one thing, but hurting Julius and embarrassing my family is another."

"I'm sorry."

"It's all right. It's my own fault."

"If anything he'll probably sell them to you first," Juan said.

"He's probably wearing that bustier, right now," Raphael said. "I'll bet he's a cross-dresser, which means we'll never get it back."

The crews making light of what I'd lost made it sound easier to deal with, and I prayed that that was the end of it.

June 2006

Unbeknownst to everyone else, Erica had called and told me it was Marí's birthday. I could already tell Marí kept her personal business to herself, so I didn't blab to the crew, just decided I'd make some plans for the two of us. We'd reached St. Louis early and as the guys unloaded the RV and Marí and I checked into the hotel, I had the concierge reserve a table for lunch at B.B. King's Club. Marí was too happy to accept the invitation.

Between the upscale restaurants and the meals we'd cooked in the RV, both of us were ready for food as close to home-cooked as we could possibly get, especially the spicy gumbo they served up.

After lunch Marí and I ventured out to a mall where we

watched a woman get a tattoo from the front of Rose's Tattoos and Body Piercing.

"I've been wanting to get another tattoo. Do you have any, Linney?"

"No. I've always wanted to get one but I'm too scared."

"Come on, let's take a look," she said, and we stepped inside.

The place was small and the walls were full of every design imaginable, some a little scary.

"This is it, ladies. Take a look-see up on the wall and pick out your tatt."

"You wanna do it?" Marí asked, her eyes hopeful.

"Marí, I don't know. I've never done this before."

"I'm not going to force you, Caroline, but don't worry, it's not going to mess up your skin or anything. You're still gonna be beautiful."

I pushed her playfully and said, "I'm not worried about that. I just don't want it to hurt."

"I'll be right here with you. I'll get one too. How 'bout we get them to match?"

"Okay, okay, I'll do it."

We'd chosen a black orchid with a pink inside, resembling a vagina, as I'd told Marí. We were behaving so silly from all the beer we'd drank at B.B.'s that they probably thought we were lesbians. I made Marí hold my hand throughout the process. There were two artists who worked on us simultaneously, because if I'd watched her first, I would've changed my mind.

The artist cleaned up the area, then shaved around my ankle. The procedure tickled at first, but once I took a look at those needles, it felt like a hot knife.

By the time we returned to the hotel, Raphael was waiting in the lobby for us. It was time to get ready.

We arrived at Toxic nightclub, and the place was so small
that they had to set us up in the middle of the floor. The
place was packed and really benefited from the attention we
brought.

As with previous club stops, Marí kept me abreast of
things I wasn't able to see, like when she saw two celebrities
wearing the same outfit. They probably hadn't wanted that
on camera but we got it anyway.

My guest for that night was Brick, a hardcore rapper from
New Jersey who I actually enjoyed talking with because he
always seemed a little more versed in lots more than just the
rap industry. But tonight for some reason I sensed he had
something on his mind. He sat there sipping on Hennessey,
his signature drink, and of course was having a little more
than that. I never knew how folks could stomach that stuff,
but tonight he and Marí convinced me to do a few shots.
And I'm sure Marí was still trying to calm me down from my
tattoo experience. It was working.

Once Juan had the audio and video feed hooked up, we
were ready.

Marí sat on one side of the booth and I on the other, with
Brick in between. Initially we talked about the industry, his
latest album, and his new protégé—a rapper from St. Louis.
The last thing I expected was for him to open up about his
personal life.

"This is a shout out to *Top of Da Charts* and my girl
Linney, and yeah, here's one to you too, Marí, her hot Hispanic sidekick," he said, as we became engaged in conversation.

As we were talking with Brick, a few brothers walked by deep in diamonds and platinum and all the typical hustler gear.

"Wow, he was fine, did you see him, Linney?" Marí asked.

I wasn't sure but I thought I heard Brick mumble, "You right about that."

When Marí's head peeked around the back of the booth, her brown eyes wide with surprise, I knew I'd heard right.

"I'd like to check out that little honey. Do you know him, Brick?" Marí added.

"Me too, me too," Brick murmured.

I knew what Marí was doing but wasn't sure I wanted to go there. Brick was a gangsta rapper on tour in St. Louis, and if what he was alluding to was at all true and we put it on the air—he'd be a gangsta rapper no more.

He slid further down in the booth and did his trademark thing for which the women and now apparently men loved him for: licked his lips.

"You want another shot, Linney? What about you, Brick?" Marí asked.

Slowly he nodded yes and I did the same. But as much as I didn't want to see any harm come to him, I couldn't begin to imagine what an outing like this would do for our ratings. If we exposed this clip to our audience, to the world, then our ratings would be off the charts.

Halfway through our third shot, I took a chance to see what I could get. I decided to try to dig a little deeper.

"So what rapper you think makes the cut in this business as being hardcore? I mean everybody can't be as gangsta as they look," I suggested.

"Yeah, you right, you right," he said, his eyes taking in the crowd.

"That's what I always thought too. Some of them seem, well, you know, not quite what they appear to be," added Marí.

Brick's watery eyes took in Marí for a moment. I thought he'd caught on to what we were doing. "What's your name again?"

"Marí."

"Marí, these mothafuckas ain't shit in this game. I done had the best of them," he said, slamming his shot glass on the table.

The waiter rushed over to wipe up the spilled contents.

"Shit, we know you can outrap them, Brick," I said, giving him yet another chance.

"Yeah, that ain't all I done did to 'em."

Brick was sinking, but Brad had the camera steady and was catching every minute, and so was the microphone. Raphael stood grinning beside Juan, probably hoping if he played his cards right, he too could get a piece of Brick.

"What you saying, Brick? You done took some shit from them?" Marí asked, sounding just like she was in the street game herself.

"I'm saying these niggas is taking dick and I'm giving it to 'em."

I paused and took another swig of the strong brown liquid; I needed it as much as he did.

"Aww, get out of here. Not these hard ass niggas. Brick, that ain't you."

He draped his arm around Marí, while talking to me. "Linney baby, I can give you names of who's taking dick, who's giving it, and who's the best at it."

This was getting good, but I was also nervous. What if we aired this and Brick sued us or tried to have me killed? Anything was possible when you were about to put somebody on blast.

"Brick, I need to ask you this. Why are you putting yourself on blast?"

"Tired, Linney, tired of being somebody I ain't. Tired of being with these bitches when I really want to be out with my nigga. So fuck it, I'm one and done," he stated, followed by his tongue making circles around those thick wet, juicy lips of his. I could only believe that he was good at what he did.

I put my hand up for the cameras to stop rolling. I turned Brick's face around to look at me even though I was sure he wasn't seeing straight.

"Brick, the camera is on. Are you sure you want to talk about this?"

He looked at me, his eyes soft from the liquor, but also soft with the desire to be honest with himself. He then turned around and looked at Marí.

"What you think, girlfriend?"

"I say talk about it. Free yourself, Brick."

And that's exactly what he did. He gave us every name, even most incidents down to the detail. I wasn't sure how I was ever going to air this, but Marí reminded me that he'd given his approval when he'd signed the release to go on the air.

When we were finished with him and all his graphic details, he had to have his boys carry him out of Toxic.

Juan was itching to get back to the RV to begin working the film. He included Raphael because this was his kind of thing, someone outing themselves. We all met back in the RV.

"Guys, I don't know. This could blow up in our faces," I said.

"Linney, he signed the release, so it's a done deal. We gotta do it," Raphael pleaded.

"You're right, but what about the people he named? This ain't R and B we're fucking with."

"Nobody is airing anything until I review it with Sharon," Brad said, just as concerned with any consequences that might follow.

While Juan and Brad edited the tape, Sharon called and we listened to her on speaker.

"Brick's personal life is fair game, especially since he'd been well aware that he was on camera," Sharon said. "My suggestion is that we don't air the other artists' names, since they haven't agreed to have their personal lives exposed. So we'll have to think of something creative."

Marí was the first to speak up. "What if we overlaid their names with their music. You know, edit out the name, blend in the music as if it's just a part of the show."

"And if the audience gets it, they get it," Sharon said.

"Oh, they're gonna get it," Raphael said.

"And those artists who've got a beef with us, well, we'll just show them a copy of the raw footage and see if they'd prefer to have that version aired," I said.

It was confirmed. We were putting Brick on blast.

That night we checked out of our hotel early because we didn't want anybody looking for us to get that tape back.

7

INTERCOURSE, PA

The headlines were everywhere: "Linney outs Brick."

The Source, XXL, the *Post,* and *Daily News* were strewn all over the RV, with journalists comparing me to Barbara Walters and Oprah on the basis of my ability to get people to open up and tell their secrets.

After the show on Brick aired we rarely had a peaceful moment. The only peaceful time we did have was in the RV, and then everyone's phones were constantly ringing. Marí had practically taken over answering mine.

No longer did artists wait for their publicists to call me. They wanted to refute Brick's outing of them themselves. We hadn't given up anybody's name, just played the appropriate song over the name. I hadn't received any threats, but I can't say the same thing about Brick. Supposedly he was lying low in Puerto Rico. So the artists he'd mentioned just showed up at our show and did impromptu appearances and performances.

Erica was telling us that *Top of Da Charts* was at the top of everyone's lists. I was almost tired of hearing about the lists and then realized how instrumental Marí had been in making all this happen. I also knew that the measly amount we'd been paying her as an intern wasn't enough. I put a call in to Sharon and insisted that she get a raise to that of a full-time employee.

I looked around the bedroom that I'd been living in for the last month and wondered just how much longer I could stand being on the road. After covering almost twenty-five hundred miles, I had to admit the RV, even with all its luxury and high-tech conveniences, was starting to feel just a little tight.

We'd gotten more footage than we'd ever use. We'd just left Ohio, and it was nothing but four hundred miles between there and Philadelphia. I assumed from the pace the RV was moving that Juan was driving.

The clubs we'd visited in Chicago and Columbus, Ohio, had to have the streets barricaded because of the swelling crowds. So we in turn went into the streets to interview folks.

In Chicago I attended my first professional baseball game, seeing a Cubs day game at Wrigley Field. But at the seventh inning stretch Marí and I skipped out to go shopping on the Magnificent Mile. We covered so many miles walking and shopping that we had to have Juan come pick us up in the RV because we couldn't carry our bags.

We were about five hours outside Philly and had been making good time coming in from Ohio. I couldn't see Marí from my room, but I could hear her. She must've run out of things to do, because the only sound was the drumming of her fingers on the recliner that she was sitting in.

Thinking of her, I glanced down at the tattoo we'd gotten. It really was beautiful, but I wasn't sure if Julius and my parents would feel the same. Nor would Sharon like the five pounds I'd put on, which on camera would look like an extra ten.

"What's on your mind, Marí?" I asked as I scooched up beside her on the couch.

"I don't know. I was thinking about Philadelphia. I heard club Teaz is pretty hot on its own, but with you coming it's about to catch fire," she said, making a notation in her notebook.

"It's not just me anymore. They look forward to seeing all of us now."

"You think so?"

I looked around the RV. Raphael was giving himself a pedicure and Brad was at the counter dicing up onions for tuna salad, stinking up the entire cab.

"E called last night and said the joint's been sold out to capacity. They've even put up tents in the parking lot and are blocking off the streets," I said.

"That's awesome. I can't wait to get to Philadelphia," she said, then took out a jar of Vaseline to apply to her tattoo.

"Here, you're going to need some of this so your tattoo won't get dry," she offered.

"Shit. I keep forgetting. I'll use it when you're done."

"No, just put your leg up, I'll do it," she said, then lifted my leg on top of her lap.

"Only fair if I do yours too," I told her.

"Y'all two are so gay," said Raphael.

Marí continued to talk as she gently massaged the orchid with the Vaseline.

"According to our itinerary we're to go straight to the Ritz-Carlton, who've had their hotel lobby on lockdown with the exception of the hotel guests because the fans are out of control. Sharon has a media room set up where you'll do your interviews upon arrival. Then you'll have a few hours to relax before a big dinner with the execs from VMT and some other honchos they've invited. After which we'll do wardrobe and head off to Teaz."

"Marí girl, you got that shit together," Raphael said.

"Marí," I said, "make sure you squeeze in that schedule that I'm going to be hosting a party in my suite tomorrow night for my friends, okay? But y'all know I've only got one thing *really* on mind, and that's—"

"JULIUS!" Marí and Raphael both screamed.

"Oh, I see y'all got jokes. I'm crashing holla!"

I squeezed into what now seemed to be a very narrow shower stall. I think the longer we'd been on the road the smaller it got. I'd been talking a lot about Julius in the last two days so the crew all knew how much I missed him. A lot of that was overshadowed with what I'd done with Vin, however I just prayed the stolen camera with us having sex wouldn't resurface. Part of me wanted to be honest and tell Julius about my infidelity before he found out some other way, but Marí thought that was absolutely the worse thing I could do. The other part of me simply wanted to forget the whole incident. I stuck my head under the showerhead.

None of that negated how Vin had ravaged my body in that dirty bathroom. I'd never forget the way he'd made me cum, but for now I'd have to store that memory far in the back of my head and only recall it when it was safe. What scared me was the prospect that Julius couldn't satisfy me after having spent those brief moments with Vin. That seemed impossible because I loved Julius and Vin had only been a one night stand.

I was falling off to sleep when I heard it.

"BAM!"

The huge camper wobbled off balance. I jumped off the bed and ran to the front of the cabin. "What the fuck was that?" I asked Raphael, who was now driving with Marí seated beside him.

"The frickin' tire blew out," he said, trying to gain control of the RV.

"Raphael, do something," I said as he screeched the RV to a stop.

"I don't know what we're gonna do now. I ain't changing no tire on this big ass thing," I heard Juan say from over my shoulder.

With all five of us jammed into the cabin, Raphael let down his window.

"It's dark as shit out there."

I looked over at a frightened Marí, who was gripping the arms of the chair while she asked, "Where are we?"

Brad spun his watch around on his wrist. "It's gonna be light soon. It's four-thirty."

"Turn on the navigation system. It should show us where we are," Juan said.

"System's saying something about intercourse." He looked down at his cell. "There are no bars on my cell phone."

"Get the hell outta here," I said as I pushed the button to dial my own cell phone. But then I noticed I too had no reception.

"We might as well see what's out here," suggested Juan, who stuck that stupid twenty-two in his pocket, then unlocked the cabin door.

"Hold up. I can't go anywhere without this," Brad said, picking up his video camera from the floor.

"Brad, this shit ain't funny," Marí told him.

"Hell, I'm a man, I'm going too!" Raphael said.

Apprehensive, I went along with everyone else, stepping out behind Raphael with Marí on my heels.

I never knew what pitch black was until I stepped into the total absence of light outside the RV. I could barely see the people around me. The chilly air made the area even more eerie.

"Shit. We can't see to change the thing even if we knew how," I said.

"I'll get a flashlight," Brad said. A moment later, sure enough, the first sign he shined it on said Intercourse, PA. Where the hell were we?

"Oh, no. This is some real *Children of the Corn* shit," Raphael said.

"What's out here?" I asked.

"How do I know? I can't see shit." Brad replied.

"Marí girl, let's go back inside," I urged.

"Let's stay together," she suggested sensibly.

We all followed behind Raphael like a chain gang. I don't think anybody wanted to be left alone in that darkness. But Raphael just walked in a circle and ended up back at the RV.

"I suggest we wait until it's light, then we can walk somewhere," I said, tripping as I went up the steps.

Back inside Brad put on a pot of coffee, Marí made us tea and decided to make an early breakfast while we waited for the sun to come up. I began to wonder if I was ever going to get home. The guys were trying to decide who would walk to find a gas station when there was a knock on the RV door. We looked at each other to see who was going to answer.

"Who the hell is knocking?" Brad got up and peered out the peephole. He turned and said to us, "Now this is really funny."

When the door opened we were caught off guard by two bearded white men dressed in black and white who stood peering back at us. I now knew exactly where we were. We were in Amish country.

"Umm, good morning," Brad said.

"Good morning to you folks also. I'm Jacob and this here is my son Luke. You ladies and gentlemen look like you could use a hand," the man said. He was dressed in overalls, a black hat, white shirt, and a long narrow beard.

I couldn't imagine how they were going to help.

Marí stepped in front of Brad and asked, "Is there a phone anywhere around—we can't get any service."

"Oh, those things won't work around here. We don't have enough wiring," the man said.

"Do you live near here?" I asked.

"The farm is about ten miles up ahead. If you'd like we could take you up there. But if you gents have a jack, why don't you let us give you a hand with changing the tire."

We went out into the road, and sure enough there were two horse and buggies with a woman sitting in each passenger seat. Now this was something that needed to be filmed. Brad carried the video camera with him but I made him wait until I asked them if it was okay.

This would definitely give the audience a laugh, if not the studio. Here we were stuck in Amish country with Raphael, Brad, and Juan, none of whom had ever attempted to change a tire, and now they had to stand there like choir boys while our new Amish friends did the work.

As if their helping us with the tire wasn't enough, they offered us fresh bread and cinnamon buns. Brad wasted no time making another pot of coffee.

An hour later we were back on the road and our cell phones were operable. We went into action. I called my parents and Marí phoned the studio, letting them know we were behind schedule. But her jumping into action also made me wonder if that girl ever talked to her family.

8
HOMECOMING QUEEN

We passed the King of Prussia Mall around 11:00 A.M. and I began to get anxious to be in Philly. I'd never looked forward to going home so much. Riding along the Schuylkill, I was in the cabin while Brad drove and Marí sat beside him, running down a minute-by-minute schedule that had been faxed to us. For some reason all the details were too draining. I just wanted to get there and make it happen. I knew I couldn't shortcut anything, especially the media session. But getting out of the RV was going to be the biggest relief. I hadn't told anyone but I was planning on hanging out at my parents for a week or so. After this trip I needed a quiet vacation.

Since we were three hours late in arriving and everything had to be moved up, it promised to be hectic prior to the show that night. We'd been told that there already was a throng of fans waiting for us, but I figured since we were late, most of them would be gone.

As we exited the Vine Street Expressway onto Fifteenth Street, traffic started to back up. It got even worse as we rounded City Hall, and that's when we saw the reason. The fans were there.

When Raphael started fiddling with his makeup case, I told him to forget it because my hometown was going to see me au naturel. It took Brad thirty minutes just to safely park in front of the stately Ritz-Carlton that sat on the Avenue of the Arts, behind two huge cement columns and two doormen.

From what I could see out of the RV window there was now a Borders across the street whose second-floor windows were filled with onlookers, and a Tower Records one block up on the corner of Chestnut where the line of fans extended. Fans held posters with my pictures and those of the crew—all of us, it seemed, now had fans. It brought a surprising rush of tears.

People and cameras were everywhere. It was as if the entire city had come out to greet me. It truly felt like a homecoming.

"You okay?" Juan asked.

"How you wanna play this? It's your show, Linney girl," Raphael said, handing me a tissue.

"Just as I am. I'm home," I said, for the first time not even caring what I looked like. I stood in the mirror just to check myself, which gave Raphael ample time to smooth my hair back in a ponytail. I hoped at least it wasn't crooked, and then he dabbed on a little lip gloss.

"That's it, that's enough. I gotta get outta this thing," I said impatiently.

Brad stepped out of the RV first, then Juan, Raphael, and Marí. The cheers got louder each time someone exited. I came out last and, had it not been for the police barricades, I would've been mobbed. But still, I stopped to sign autographs and take pictures.

Inside the lobby of the hotel was a large rotunda with a high vaulted ceiling. We gathered there and the studio heads and additional film crews followed us. Juan was glad to hand the RV keys over to one of the PAs who'd come out to assist us. He was taking it to get fully serviced at a local dealership. Sharon and Brad were soon deep in conversation. Juan rushed off to his room to get freshened up because he wanted to hang out in the lobby where all the action was. The concierge informed Marí that there were thirty-two boxes of apparel that had been shipped from various vendors and he needed to know whose room they should be taken to. We both pointed to Raphael.

Next we went up to the media room and I interviewed for about an hour or more. All the while I could feel my energy beginning to drain, but I knew once I saw Julius, all that would change.

Finally Raphael, Marí, and I were able to take the elevators up to our rooms. I leaned against the wall as we rode up to the tenth floor.

Raphael put his arm around Marí. "Peach, if it wasn't for you, we'd still be sitting back in that drab ass building in Beverly Hills, huh, Linney?"

"You're right about that—Marí's our hero," I said, then put my arm around her.

"Stop, guys. It was no big deal."

"It is a big deal," I said. "Our going on the road has turned us into a phenomenon. Just goes to show you how if you give something small a chance it can turn into something big."

When we reached the tenth floor Marí and Raphael stepped off and I stood between the doors so they wouldn't close.

"Raphael, you know I have to look outstanding tonight."

"Linney girl, you ain't got to tell me, 'cause when I finish with you, you're gonna be polished, sexy, flirty—"

"Enough, enough. I already know you're the best. I'll see you later," I said, kissing him on both cheeks.

I wasn't about to leave Marí out. "And you, Marí, I don't know what to say."

"It was nothing. Just some silly idea I thought up."

"Marí, your silly idea is what got us here. Thank you so, so much. Now give me some love," I said, and wrapped my arms around her.

"The fun is just getting started, Caroline."

I was staying in the Presidential Suite, which was located on the club level of the hotel. When I pushed open the double doors the room was filled with multicolored roses, some in vases, and petals just tossed around the room. The scent was heavenly. This beautiful and sensual welcome was all courtesy of Julius Worthington, who was stretched out in a white seersucker robe on the couch smoking a big fat cigar.

"Julius, Julius!" I screamed out, and ran to him, knocking over flower vases and damn near falling over myself to reach the couch.

"Wait a minute, baby. Slow down. You're going to hurt yourself," he said, trying to keep me from diving on top of him.

"Oh my God, Julius, I love you, I love you. I missed you so much," I mumbled as I kissed all over his face, with tears streaming down my own.

Julius laughed, stubbed out his cigar with one hand, and brought me to him with the other.

"Welcome home, Linney," he said.

"I can't believe you did all this! How much did all this cost?" I asked, looking around the room at the dozens and dozens of roses.

"I spare no expense when it comes to you—never again. I'm set, baby, we're set. You and your little road trip just made me the hottest agent in the country."

I had no idea that traveling across country with my show would have an effect on Julius's career.

"Well, you got the hottest woman in the country right here. Now what you gonna do about that?" I asked, and then began planting kisses on his chest.

"Is that so?" he said, and opened his robe to expose his beautiful hard dick.

I went right for what I wanted, probably being a little wilder than either of us could recall.

"What you doing, girl?" he asked, playfully pulling himself out of my mouth. "Come on now, don't you have autographs to sign, some interviews to do? Your cell phone is ringing like crazy."

"Right now all I have is you," I said, then pulled the cell from my waistband and turned it off. "To hell with that damn phone."

I got to my feet and started stripping off my clothes. This afternoon I was going to please my man, as I'd never done before. My mouth was about to be filled with his love juices.

"Wait a minute, hold up," he said as he sat up. "Let me get your ass in the shower, get all that road dust off you."

I didn't want to waste time showering, but I knew the way Julius liked things . . . nice and slow.

He took me by the hand and said, "Follow me."

He turned on the water and began peeling off my clothes.

"You ready?" he asked. " 'Cause I got something special."

Julius stepped into the shower stall and pulled me with him.

Using the wand he wet my skin, then he lathered a sea sponge with mint chocolate chip shower gel. Briskly he washed me, front, back, and doused water in between my legs.

"Julius, you know I love you, right?"

"You tell me anything when I got you naked."

"Sure will, and I'll do this too," I said, and slipped onto my knees. The only thing between my mouth and his dick was the water as it splattered in my face. I took it deeper and deeper, moving it around the back of my tongue until I gagged from the water and the thickness of his dick.

"Whew, baby, you need to take your ass away more often. Now get that ass out of the shower and let me see what you're really working with."

I walked out of the shower in front of him and instead of getting in bed, I ran into the living room.

"You want it, come get it."

He caught me by the couch and said, "Bend over." Then he rubbed his hands over my ass and across my hips. "I like all this," he said. "You filled out."

As good as our lovemaking had been from the living room to the bedroom, I still couldn't sleep after two hours of trying.

"Did I wake you Linney?" Marí asked when I answered the ringing hotel phone.

"No, I wasn't a sleep," I said. "I can't sleep—too many things on my mind."

"I know me too. It's almost six o'clock and we have dinner reservations for seven-thirty. Raphael called my room and he's dying to get started."

"All right I'm going to wake up Julius, so we can get ready. Tell Raphael to give me thirty minutes and he can come up to dress me."

I nestled beside Julius until he woke up.

"Baby, you gave it all you had today," he whispered, and pulled me close.

"It was good, wasn't it?"

"When did you say you were going away again?"

"Jules, stop playing," I said, and lay my body on top of his.

He smoothed back my hair and his eyes penetrated mine. "I love you, Caroline, you hear me? I missed the hell outta you."

"Jules, I love you too."

There wasn't much time for a drawn-out lovemaking session to quench his growing manhood. I made it my business to tease him with my tongue, enough that by the time I swallowed his dick fully in my mouth, he had no choice but to explode. That Negro was knocked out again, and looked like he might not ever wake up. It really was time to get ready. I went into the bathroom and picked off the rose petals that were stuck to my ass and thighs.

With my towel wrapped around me, I opened the door for Marí, who damn near knocked me off my feet with the pencil skirt and loose fitting off the shoulder Versace blouse she was wearing.

"Hot momma, look at you!" I screamed. "I love it!"

She shrugged self-consciously. "I feel like I've been playing dress-up."

"You put all the other Latina divas to shame. Eva Longoria can kiss your ass."

"Stop it, Caroline. Now what's all this stuff?" she asked, looking around the room that Julius and I had destroyed. "You had a busy afternoon, huh?" she asked, beginning to pick up things.

"Marí, you fuckin' stop it right now. You're a diva tonight. Stop it!"

"Okay, okay."

"And my other suggestion is that you get yourself some while you're here."

"Linney, please. I'm not even thinking about that."

"Look at your hair," I exclaimed, turning her around to see the sexy updo Raphael had given her. "Marí, you're gonna kill 'em tonight."

"Linney, you're embarrassing me. Please stop."

"All right, I'm just saying. . . . So where's Raphael?"

"He's waiting for the bellhop to help him bring your stuff up."

"Then we have time for a toast between us girls," I suggested, and went over to the bar.

"Where's your boyfriend?" Marí asked, uncorking the bottle of Moët.

"Shit, that's right, you haven't met Julius yet. Plus he needs to get his butt up anyway so he can get in the shower."

I went into the bedroom and woke Jules, who began trying to lure me back into bed. After wrestling myself away I went back to the living room with Marí, who'd poured us two glasses of champagne, compliments of the hotel.

"You make the toast," I said to her when she passed me my glass.

She held my eyes for a moment, then said, "Here's wishing that this trip gives us both what we deserve."

"Cheers!" we both said, and clinked glasses.

Then the whirlwind began when Raphael came barreling through the door with two racks of clothes and too many boxes of shoes. It was on.

Julius hearing all the noise came to the door of the bedroom. "Sounds like a party in here."

"Jules, come here. I want you to meet Marí."

I introduced the two of them, and the only comment Julius had before getting ready for dinner was to tell Raphael that for tonight's show he wanted me to look hot and nasty. Raphael had no problem filling that order.

Instead of having to climb back in the RV, Juan, Marí, Raphael, Julius, and I were driven by limo over to Seventh and Chestnut Streets to the restaurant, Morimoto. A separate room had been reserved for our privacy, because there was a throng of fans inside and out. I was beginning to think they were following us everywhere we went.

Our entourage entered through the neon-chartreuse glass doors to a welcoming crowd and a celebratory atmosphere. There was a table spread with all the food that I loved: eel, salmon, tempura, lobster salad. All of this was at the expense of the restaurant because they too wanted to be part of the tour. The event was sort of a meet and greet for the media and the folks who'd sponsored the tour. Every time I turned around Julius had his eyes on me, but I'm sure he was talking up business in reference to his own clients, as well he should. He was right; this trip had been advantageous for both of us.

Multitasking was what I did at Morimoto as Sharon and Brad whisked me from one exec to another sponsor. Everyone wanted to say hello and to thank me. Some guests invited their children. In between it all I somehow managed to talk, sign autographs, and pose for pictures. *Top of Da Charts* had set Philly on fire.

"Caroline, I know I've been hard on you but I'm really, really proud of what you've done on this tour. So please don't let anybody steal you away from us," Sharon pleaded as she pulled me off to the side.

"That's not about to happen. I love it at *Top of Da Charts*."

"No, you're not getting me. We've been in talks with your agent for days and you've got some big things ahead."

"Really? Well, I'm all for that."

"Good. Now enough business. Go enjoy yourself." And then she hugged me.

Maybe it was all the excitement, especially mixed with the champagne toasts and the flow of sakura, which was the bartenders' take on a cosmo mixed with sake. But somewhere in between our entrée and dessert my stomach started to feel a little queasy. I didn't mention it to anyone, just figured I needed to cut back on the drinking.

All night Marí wasn't far from reach as my personal assistant, taking all the business cards that were handed to me and giving out ours.

When we got back to our suite at the Ritz it was about ten-thirty. Not only was I still a little nauseous but I was beginning to feel light-headed. Instead of complaining, I slipped in the bathroom and drank a glass of Alka-Seltzer, hoping it would settle my stomach. I figured once I showered and had a chance to breathe I'd be okay. That moment never came because Sharon and Brad forgot to inform me that they wanted to video my getting ready for the show, so there went the moment of privacy I'd been hoping for. I wasn't sure how Julius would feel about so many people in our room, but he loved it and even posed in a few shots with me.

The suite was a swirl of activity. I knew I'd be glad when this night was over. As Julius had requested, Raphael dressed me in a sexy and revealing midnight blue Roberto Cavalli dress and a pair of Manolo Blahnik heels.

Finally, around midnight, we headed out to Teaz, this time in the RV, which had been washed, polished, and was dazzling. Its outside screen played footage from our road trip as we drove through Center City.

The area around Eighteenth and Walnut had been blocked off and the RV and the caravan of cars following were the only ones allowed down the block. The RV pulled up in front of the club to screaming fans. I was almost scared to get out. Cameras were flashing everywhere.

Before disembarking Brad wanted to give a short speech while Julius poured champagne for everyone.

"I want to say congratulations for a successful tour, and I pray *Top of Da Charts* and Caroline Isaacs always remain at the top of the charts."

Then I added, "Thank you to my friend Marí for her brilliant idea."

We clinked glasses and everyone drank except me because my stomach was flipping. It was showtime.

When we got inside Teaz it was swelling with people. The light show caused me to sway till I got myself adjusted. Brad and the club's manager led our entourage through the crowd and up to the stage.

Then I heard my music, which seemed louder than usual. I was able to make out every instrument and on cue I stepped in front of the microphone.

"Linney here y'all with *Top of Da Charts*! *Top of Da Charts*, y'all! Linney's bringing it to your right here in my hometown! Is Philly in the house?"

The audience roared in response. I'd never seen or heard anything like it. This was definitely the pinnacle of my success at VMT. I had no idea how we could ever top this.

But for me the music was way too loud. It was hurting my head and the champagne was turning to acid in my stomach. The crowd looked like a pack of lions coming at me. I had to focus.

My head was pounding so bad I was forced to end my monologue sooner than scripted, which caused a scowl from Marí. Not knowing why, but sensing something was wrong, she instructed deejay Chocolate Charmer to take over.

"Caroline, you okay?" Marí asked.

I felt behind me for someplace to sit and found the couch. "I don't think so; I feel woozy," I said, still holding my head.

Julius came from the side of the room where he'd been standing. "What is it, baby? What's wrong?"

I fanned myself with my hand. "I don't know, I just feel sick. I started feeling it at the restaurant. I think it's from all that champagne."

"Exhaustion, that's what the hell it is," he said.

Brad and Sharon came over. "What's going on, Linney? I hope you're not sick," Sharon said.

I closed my eyes and didn't bother to answer. Wasn't it obvious to everyone that I was dying? At least that's what it felt like.

"I'm taking her back to the hotel," Julius said, guiding me up from the couch.

"No, I can't. I gotta do the show," I said, pulling away from him.

The audience couldn't see what was going on behind the half wall, but with everyone hovering over me I felt like I had to do this show. This was my big moment.

"She'll be okay. Give her some air," Sharon told everyone.

They all stepped back except Julius and Marí, who brought a trash can, holding it up in front of my face.

"Not like this you're not," Julius said, whipping out his hankie to wipe my mouth, which was wet with saliva.

With my body trembling against his, I said, "Jules, you don't understand. Everyone's here. . . . I can't let them down."

Both Marí and I were watching the clock on the deejay booth. I had two minutes before I had to get back on the microphone in front of my audience. I stepped away from Julius to stand on my own, but I was too weak.

"That's it. Let's go!" Julius demanded, totally disregarding my responsibility to the show.

I knew he was right. I couldn't go on, at least not right then.

"Wait . . ." I said to Julius, then turned to Marí. "Marí?"

"What is it? What do you want me to do, Caroline?"

"You gotta do the show. You gotta take this one for me."

She backed away from me. "Caroline, I can't. This is your show, and this is the finale."

I shook my head no. "I can't do it—Marí, you have to."

Marí looked down at the crowd, then over at Sharon and Brad. There were thirty seconds left. Juan was holding the microphone out for one of us. I nodded my head toward Marí and let Julius and Raphael lead me down the back stairway.

We followed Missy, the clubs' manager, to her office, where they sat me down on the couch because I refused to leave the club. Plus I didn't have the strength to walk. What the hell had happened to me? Had I really had that much champagne? Regardless, I had to see Marí do the show. Unable to control myself, I'd thrown up in the trash can but insisted they let me lie there under a blanket until Marí's first set was over.

I tried to focus in on my surroundings, the desk, chair, cabinet . . . but everything was blurred. Missy came back with some ginger ale and turned on the monitor. There was Marí, who'd watched me long enough to know how to handle the crowd. They were amped up and so was she. Plus she looked gorgeous. I knew that it had been my good fortune for Marí to have walked in my office with a desire to be my summer intern. Not only had she brought new life to the show, tonight she'd saved my ass. Yes, Marí was more than an intern, now she was my friend. And once I got myself together from whatever the hell was wrong with me, I was going to see if she too wanted to hang out with me in Philly for a while. At this point I didn't know how I'd survive without her.

9
RECOVERY HOUSE

I'd stayed in bed all day Sunday at the Ritz and Julius refused to give anyone access to me. The kitchen staff kept me supplied with soup, tea, water, and whatever Julius called down for. Unfortunately that night he was driving me out the Schuylkill to my parents' house in Villanova as he'd convinced me that was where I needed to be, since he was leaving town. When we pulled up their winding driveway it was no surprise to me that they had a doctor waiting to examine me.

He offered no real explanation except what I already knew—too much champagne, exhaustion, and possible food poisoning. His diagnosis and recommendation was rest and plenty of fluids.

"Julius, would you care to stay for dinner?" my mother asked him.

"Thank you, Mrs. Isaacs, but I have a flight to catch."

"I appreciate your bringing our Caroline home. She needs a break from that lifestyle."

Julius gave me a kiss good-bye and I trudged upstairs and climbed under the covers. I not only felt miserable but I missed Julius already.

I slept the rest of the night and most of Monday. When I woke up my mother was in my room unpacking my suitcase.

"Caroline, honey, what happened to you?"

"I'm all right, Mother. You didn't need to call Dr. Emerson," I told her, referring to the man who'd been our family doctor since I was a child.

"Well, I wanted to make sure nothing was seriously wrong with you. Now that you're home Gladys and I will see to it that you get better."

Gladys had been our housekeeper since we'd moved into the Isaacs estate when I was five years old. I noticed since the last time I'd been home my bedroom had been painted and my mother had added new furniture, with the exception of the bed my father had custom made for me when I was in high school.

"You get a bath and something to eat," my mother said. "I have to go out. I'll see you when I get back."

My mother was right. I was a mess. My hair was matted and my underarms were a little funky from sweating out that fever. I pulled my hair back into a ponytail and had to laugh at how I'd just gotten Marí to let down her hair and now I was doing the exact opposite. Next I took a long soak in the Jacuzzi.

I pranced throughout my parents' home, which my mother had dressed in its summer décor. Light colors and calla lilies throughout.

Monday night my parents went out so I hung out in my father's study, where I'd often played doctor as a little girl, imitating him on the phone with his patients. His office was always an adventure to me and still was. On the walls were black and white family pictures and and his high school diploma. Of all the degrees he'd received it was the only one he'd ever hung because he said that without that one he wouldn't have gotten the others.

Sitting in my father's high-back leather chair, I logged on to his computer to check my blog comments and my e-mails. It was nice to see the outpouring of get-well wishes from everyone. It also was no surprise that Marí had received so much support for taking over for me at Teaz. I couldn't wait to tell her. I decided it was time for me to update my blog.

> The banging success of the road trip, in addition to all the celebrating once we reached Philly, wiped my butt out. I'm so sorry I missed everyone who came out to meet us at Teaz over the weekend, but I'm glad that my girl Marí had a chance to show off her skills and hold it down (pssst, you'll be seeing more of her).
>
> I never doubted that the girl could pull it off! Believe me it pays to be good to your intern. They are a hot commodity and will look out for you, if you look out for them. So stay tuned 'cause we're going to have some hot things jumping off in the upcoming weeks!

As I perused through the e-mails on the business side I noticed one announcing that in a month a new nightclub and casino would be opening in Philly called Hustler's, down on Columbus Boulevard. I'd heard mention of it back in the winter but wasn't aware that it was that close to opening. It appeared that Hustler's was to be the scene of a new pop culture television show similar to the format of *Top of Da Charts*. I clicked through to their Web site to see who was behind it, and what I found interesting was that they were in search of a celebrity to host their opening night along with someone to be the permanent host of their show, *Hustler's Live*. I thought how cool it would be if I could land the job of hosting its opening with all the glamour and red carpet celebrities. As the idea began to sink in I realized that if this role of hostess for the opening of Hustler's didn't conflict with my hectic veejay schedule at *Top of Da Charts*, I might well be able to land the job. It was only for one night. With that in mind I made a mental note to discuss it with my agent so that she could pitch it for me, especially since I was the hometown favorite. Who better for opening night than Linney?

With two days of rest behind me, when I woke on Tuesday morning I called Marí before I got out of bed.

"Linney, how are you? I tried to reach you yesterday but your phone was turned off and Julius wouldn't let anybody bother you."

"I know. He's so protective of me. I'm out at my parents' now. I've been sleeping. I slept most of the time anyway, but I'm good as new now. So what's up? Tell me what I've missed. I know you've heard how much people loved you at Teaz." I could hear Raphael in the background shouting hello.

"Yeah, I read your blog. Thank you so so much," she said. "The guys wanna know when we can come see you. I mean, if you're feeling up to it."

"Please come. I'm dying for some company," I pleaded, glad my parents weren't home, because there was no doubt in my mind that my mother would've wanted to throw a full-blown luncheon for them.

"Okay, give me the directions."

After hanging up with Marí I showered and got dressed, finally free of whatever had ailed me. It was going to be good to be home and be spoiled.

Around one o'clock that afternoon Sharon, Brad, Raphael, Marí, and Juan showed up at the house. They obviously hadn't had a problem following my directions from the city out to my parents' Villanova estate. When I heard the doorbell ringing I came out from the family room to greet them.

"Linney here, y'all!" I said when I opened the door, so they could see I was back to myself.

Raphael and Marí hugged me at the same time.

"How are you feeling, Linney?" Sharon asked.

"I'm fine. Whatever it was has moved on. Come on in," I said, leading them through the house, forgetting this was their first visit until I heard Raphael gasping.

"What is your problem?" I asked before I turned and saw him ogling over the house.

"Girl, this house is fab-u-lous. Can I please live here?"

"Raphael, you're right. It is beautiful. I wanna live here too," Marí exclaimed.

"Thanks, guys. Feel free to take a look around," I said, hating to give tours of the estate.

"I've just never been in a house in Villanova," Marí said.

I guess had I not grown up here, I would've been impressed with my parents' estate also. It was a 1922 colonial that sat on three acres of land. The grand entry had a three-story staircase under gilded ceilings. Off the center hall and dining room there were French doors that led to a patio that overlooked a heated pool and lighted tennis court, all surrounded by hundred-year-old trees.

We stepped outside onto the patio. Gladys came out behind us and placed a serving of ice tea and lemonade onto the glass table.

"What happened to you the other night, Linney? Did you eat some bad food or something?" Juan asked.

"I don't know. Probably too much drinking, but I'm cool now. I could use some sunshine and fresh air."

"Good, because we have some news I think you're going to like," Brad answered.

"All right, give me the scoop," I told them, my eyes going from Sharon to Brad to see who would speak first.

Sharon stood up behind my chair. "We've decided to keep *Top of Da Charts* in Philly, for a while that is, instead of going right back to LA. There are a lot of New York and DC folks I'd like to bring in to get on the show, and of course some local talent here."

I spun around to face her. "That's awesome, Sharon. I mean, at least I think so. But what about everybody else?" I asked, mindful that Philly wasn't home to everyone.

"Well, everyone?" Brad asked.

"Hell, you know I love exploring new territory," Raphael said, probably drooling at the idea of exploring Philly's gayborhood of Thirteenth and Spruce streets.

"I'd love to be here a little longer!" said Marí, who was sitting next to me.

"Excellent, because I've already gone ahead and confirmed it with the owner of Teaz. The plan is we'll tape the shows from their place around noon. We'll use a studio audience most days, except when we have our countdowns or if we go on location around the city."

"Maybe Marí would consider cohosting a show with me."

"Why would I do that? It's your show, Caroline," Marí said.

I slapped her on her thigh. "Girl, after you saved my ass I'll be repaying you till the end of the year. Sharon, Brad, you're okay with it, right?"

"Like Marí said, it's your show, Linney—whatever you want," Sharon said, Brad nodding his agreement.

"Damn, look at that pool," Juan interrupted, from where he stood against the wall of the patio. "Does anybody use it?"

"My dad put that in for me when I was learning to swim," I said, then turned to Marí and asked, "Marí, what do you say?"

"Well, uh, I'd love to."

"I got a question," Juan said. "Do we get to keep the RV while we're here?"

Sharon sipped on the minted lemonade and shaded her eyes from the sun. "For a little while. But we're going to set you all up with some leased cars to share, and for now you'll stay at the Ritz."

Right then I heard my mother coming in and realizing, I'm sure, as soon as she saw the big RV in the driveway, that I had company. Before I could warn everyone, she'd made her way onto the patio.

"Good afternoon," my mother said, standing there in her white tennis skirt and top. I know no one except my mother who actually wore a tennis bracelet when playing tennis.

I got up and stood beside her to introduce everyone. I could tell she was slightly annoyed that I'd had guests and hadn't informed her. She always needed to be prepared.

"It certainly is nice to finally meet everyone my daughter works with. Caroline, did you ask Gladys to make sure your friends had something to eat?"

"Oh, they're cool. They ate before they came out," I said, hoping they had.

Mother put her arm around my waist. "I'm sorry, you'll have to excuse my daughter, but a good hostess she's not."

"Mom, they're fine, right?" I asked, giving everyone the evil eye that said they'd better agree with me.

"Yes, Mrs. Isaacs, we're fine, but thank you," Marí said, speaking for everyone.

"I pray you're not here to whisk my daughter back to Hollywood. Who was the person responsible for bringing her home anyway?"

"That was Marí. Remember, Mom, I told you she'd come up with the road trip idea," I answered.

She looked at Marí without even having to guess which one she was, probably because she was the only Hispanic female in the group, then reached out to shake Marí's hand. "Marí, you're the one I should be thanking for bringing my daughter cross country?"

Marí smiled demurely and said, "It seemed like it would be a great idea at the time, but I'm sorry she took sick."

"No dear, it was an excellent idea and I thank you very much. My daughter here"—she patted me on the shoulder—

"just needs to take better care of herself. And she needs to spend more time with her family, so they can make sure she does."

"Mom, you're going to be able to do just that. We're planning to tape the show from Philly for a while."

"That's wonderful. You can help me get ready for your father's retirement party."

"Oh yeah, right," I said, not only having forgotten all about the party, but dreading having to tag along with her to prepare.

"So folks, when would be a good day for everyone to come out for a home-cooked meal?"

"Mom," I said, thinking about how much she was going to be a pain in my butt.

"Thursday would be a good day, if it works for you, Mrs. Isaacs," Brad offered.

"Okay, day after tomorrow it is. How's six o'clock? I'll see you then. Nice meeting everyone," she said, and then disappeared back inside the house.

10

BACK ON TOP

On Wednesday I was my old self again and ready to get back in front of the cameras. I needed to be at the club early because I was scheduled to do a walk through of the setup with Marí and Tiffany Johnson, the owner. As much as I dreaded it when my alarm went off at 6:30 A.M., I climbed my butt out of bed, showered, and dressed, all to have breakfast with my parents.

"Morning, Mom, Dad," I said, kissing both of them after I entered the breakfast room.

"How are you feeling, honey?" my mother asked.

"Good, really good. I think all that excitement mixed with a little too much alcohol must've knocked me off my feet," I answered, and then sat down to the big plate of food Gladys sat in front of me.

"I'm sure you needed the rest," Dad commented.

"Linney, I wanted to talk to you about the menu for tomorrow night," my mother began.

"Mom, I told you that you didn't have to go all crazy. You can just have something light and easy. These aren't Main Line kids. They don't want crumpets and caviar. They'll be happy with some hoagies and cheese steaks."

My father chuckled from behind a copy of the London *Financial Times* he was reading and said, "Caroline, when have you ever known your mother to do anything the simple way?"

He was right. My mother was the queen of party planning and had been ever since she'd begun giving me and my brother birthday parties.

"Whatever you want, Mom, do your thing," I told her, giving an approval she didn't need.

"Perfect. Now do me a favor and call your brother today. I want you to invite him out tomorrow night to meet your friends. He's been off on another business trip in Brazil and he could use a good home-cooked meal too."

"I doubt if that boy's on business," my father mumbled.

I stuffed my mouth full of another one of Gladys's hot blueberry muffins. It was definitely going to be hard to maintain my weight while staying at my parents'.

"No problem, Mom. I'm sure Maurice will add some excitement to the evening."

I stood up to leave before my mother gave me another assignment. "I have to go or I'll be late. Dinner at home tonight or are we going out?"

"You're on your own tonight, sweetheart. Your father and I have an engagement to attend," she said, removing the napkin from her lap to follow me.

I stood behind my father's chair, my hands on his shoulders. "Okay, have fun. I'll probably hang out in town for a while, so I won't be in till late," I said, and kissed him on the top of his head and started out of the room.

"Caroline?"

"Yes?" I paused and turned around, recognizing by the tone of my father's voice that he wanted my full attention.

"Remember, this isn't California, Caroline. This is our home," he stated, not even looking my way.

I didn't respond to his statement. They believed that just because I worked in the entertainment business and what's more lived in Beverly Hills that my lifestyle would do something to embarrass them. I had no plans to do anything different in Philly than I did in LA.

"Which car am I driving?" I asked as my mother walked me to the garage.

"Take my Benz wagon, dear. I had it cleaned up for you. It's gotten a little dusty with no one using it."

I went out to the three-car garage and first saw my father's Bentley, which I would've much rather been driving. I got into the drivers' seat of my mother's Benz wagon. I knew that, depending on the length of time I'd be in Philly, my brother would make sure I was driving something fly.

After familiarizing myself with my mother's car and pulling out of the garage, I tuned the radio to the Beat, where the station was announcing the opening of Hustler's. I again made a mental note to call my agent. My first call, though, was to Julius.

"Jules, baby, where you at?" I asked into his static-filled phone.

"Dallas."

"Does that mean I won't be seeing you anytime soon?" I asked as I drove around the circular driveway to get through the iron gates.

"You don't know that, baby."

"Yes, I do, because I'm not coming back to LA for at least another month—they wanna tape some of our shows from Teaz."

"That's good news. Then you'll get to spend some time with your family."

"Yeah, but I won't get to see you," I complained as I sat behind a bus depositing students in front of Villanova University.

"You know I'll come out. Remember I have quite a few clients on the East Coast now."

"Yeah, but Jules, my dad is already complaining about me hanging out. You know, the whole speech about how to conduct myself. 'You're not in California, Linney.'"

"If you're talking about hanging out, then your ass must be feeling better," he joked.

"I am and I want to have some fun while I'm home, You know, show the town that I'm back. People are going to expect to see me at the clubs and stuff."

"All right, stop whining. I got an idea. You remember that condo I leased at the St. James?"

"What condo? When did you get a condo in Philly? You never told me about that," I said, as I made my way onto the crowded Schuylkill Expressway, toward Center City.

"Girl, you're something else. You know I've got that running back on the Eagles. He used it until he got a place, and my lease isn't up for another year."

"Does that mean we're going to be living together? Because Mr. and Mrs. Isaacs aren't going to like that at all, especially right up under their noses. I mean, it's not like we're planning to get married or anything."

"Who said we weren't?"

"Julius Worthington, don't play with me."

"Ain't nobody playing. Now listen up."

Julius went on to give me the address to his place at Eighth and Walnut, and the entry code to his condo. But I was barely paying him any attention. All I was thinking about was his having hinted around about our getting married. I was already wondering if he'd let me pick out the ring or if he'd do it himself. I'm sure he knew it had to be big.

After hanging up with Julius I did as my mother told me and called my brother, Maurice, who was stuck in customs at Philadelphia International Airport.

"Maurice, hey, it's me."

"Hey, baby girl, who's the prettiest girl in the all the world?"

"Me, me, me," I screamed back to him, responding to the game we'd been playing since I'd been a not so pretty little girl.

"I hear you and your show are in town."

Nearing the Museum of Art, I was none too thrilled to be stuck in traffic. "Yeah, I got in over the weekend," I said.

"How was your road trip? It looked pretty exciting from the highlights I saw on VMT."

"It was awesome, but listen, I'll tell you all about it when you come out to the parents for dinner tomorrow night."

"Huh, already? Come on, I'm just getting in," he complained.

"Sorry, but Mom insisted I call you to invite you out to the house to have dinner with the crew from my show. You know how she likes to show us off, especially you. Plus it'll be fun."

"All right. For you, baby girl, I'll come out. What time you want me?"

"Standard Isaacs dinner time, six o'clock."

"I'll be there when I get there."

We both laughed and hung up. Yes, it was going to be great being home for a while. I turned up the volume on the steering wheel and popped in the promo copy I'd received of Beanie Siegel's comeback CD.

About twenty minutes later I pulled into the crowded parking lot at Teaz. When I went inside it was bustling with people cleaning and putting together the stage for today's taping.

Teaz was nothing like I'd remembered. It had been so packed that night; I'd not noticed the color contrasts and the whole lounge affect. Now I knew why we were taping here.

Tiffany Johnson, who I'd not met the night of the show, met me at the top of the ramp. "Welcome to Teaz, Caroline. I'm glad you're feeling better," Tiffany said, extending her hand.

"Thanks, Tiffany. I think I had a little too much fun on the road," I said as I glanced around the brightly lit club in search of Marí.

"Excuse me a minute, Tiffany," I said, looking around among the workers for Marí. I spotted Juan and yelled over, "Juan, have you seen Marí?"

"Not here yet," he shouted back across the dance floor.

"She's the one who stood in for you, right?" Tiffany asked as she led me toward the stage.

"Yes, Marí Colonado. And from what I hear she had this place in high gear. I'm sorry I missed it," I said, wondering where Marí might be.

"A natural, I would say. So are you ready to take a look around?"

"Sure but, Tiffany, you didn't happen to get a call from Marí, did you?"

"There weren't any messages on my service, but I can check again."

"No, that's all right. But that girl is usually on time for everything. Well, come on, let's get started."

We began walking through the first floor of the club. "Okay, let's see," Tiffany began, "the entire club, including the three VIP rooms, can hold about five hundred people, eight hundred if the police don't find out. You'll see that we've closed off the upstairs suite for you to use as a dressing room."

I saw where she was pointing but my eyes were checking out the dance floor. "Wow, I must not have noticed this glass floor," I commented, looking down at my reflection.

"Actually, it's a very thick frosted glass and when the lights are set on it right, it's almost like you're dancing on air."

"I can believe it," I said, doing a spin move across the floor.

Just as Tiffany was showing me the office space we'd be using, I saw Marí come running up the ramp into the club.

"You're a little late, aren't you, missy?" I said, teasing her, my hands on my hips.

"Linney, I'm so sorry. I got lost trying to get here from the hotel. I think I turned—well, I know. I turned the wrong way on, what is that, Logan Circle? And wound up in some-body's frickin' hood," she blurted out all in one breath.

"Whoa, slow down. How'd you get lost? You've been to Teaz before, on the night of the party, remember? And aren't you still staying down at the Ritz?" I asked, surprised to see her so breathless, almost like she'd ran here.

"I know, but I wasn't driving myself. Philly is an entirely different city than LA. It's so complicated and I . . ." her big brown eyes were like saucers.

"No big deal. Calm down, it's not that serious. But listen, we've got some work to do. We have to come up with some ideas for the show while it's here in Philly, and I know that's your specialty."

Tiffany interrupted our banter. "Ladies, listen, I have to take a call. Can you excuse me for a minute?"

"Sure, Tiffany. And thanks again for the use of the club. We're really going to try to make some things happen here."

I picked up two bottles of water from the table that had been set out for the crew and we walked over to sit in a booth. As Marí gulped down her water I began to share with her some of the ideas I'd come up with.

"I was thinking, Marí, that initially we could do some sort of show to recap the road trip. You know, highlighting the things that were really hot. But I'm also thinking about a Philly theme. What do you think?" I asked, noticing that she seemed distracted with the people milling about the club.

"Maybe one or two shows to wrap the road trip, but that should be all. We don't want people to think that's all we have. But I do like the Philly thing. I mean, it's your home and everyone would come out for you."

Marí was a little jittery, I noticed, rapping on the table with her knuckles.

"You're right. We could highlight different areas of the

city," I said as I watched her glance at the caller ID on her ringing cell.

"Didn't I read somewhere that Philadelphia is a city of neighborhoods, each with its own unique culture?" she asked, recapping her empty bottle of water.

"Now you're onto something. We could highlight each neighborhood, South Philly, Germantown, West Philly, then tie them together."

"It's your town, Linney. If anybody can make it work, you can," she said nonchalantly.

"Good. So today for the countdown we'll hype up the club, sort of a Celebrities at Teaz theme, and play music videos of artists who've visited here, in between the countdown videos."

She rose from her seat. "You want me to check with Tiffany and see if they have some footage?"

That girl was antsy about something. I knew if I asked her she'd tell me it was nothing. But then when I thought about it, I hoped maybe she'd met someone who'd stirred some excitement in her.

"Perfect."

While Marí worked with our crew and Tiffany's staff, I went off to the dressing room when Raphael arrived to see what I'd be wearing.

Since the success of the road trip our wardrobe had been flooded with top designer apparel, shoes, bags, and even makeup. Everybody wanted their brand on the credits of *Top of Da Charts*. Raphael couldn't have been happier that now we had so much to choose from. I must've changed clothes four times before he was satisfied. Even though she wasn't interested, I insisted Marí pick out some stuff for herself and

also had her pack up a box to send back to California for
Erica.

When it was time to go on the air that afternoon my
adrenaline rush was back. The club looked great and just
from the sight of things, I knew that hosting the show from
Teaz was going to be a big hit! The curtain pulled back and
I was on!

"Linney here, y'all, from *Top of Da Charts*!"

I couldn't lie. By the end of the show I was exhausted.
But still it felt good to be back. There'd been a few glitches
that afternoon, some audio, some with lighting, but all in all
it went well, with Teaz adding the perfect backdrop. When
we wrapped up I took a rain check on having dinner with
Marí and Sharon. I wasn't about to get burnt out anymore.
But I made sure to remind everyone that dinner was at 6:00
P.M. the following night at my parents.

11

BREAKING NEWS

July 2006

Thursday afternoon the show went much smoother. We had a great studio audience who fed into the hype of our being in Philly. Also it didn't hurt that our surprise guest that afternoon was Butta, who was in town filming a commercial.

I was more excited, though, that I'd be able to stay at Julius's apartment in the city, which I planned to move into over the weekend. That way I could quit all the back and forth driving in the bumper-to-bumper traffic from the suburbs to the city. I hadn't yet figured out how to drop that bomb on my parents, but I'd get it done and soon.

I phoned Maurice on my way home to remind him of dinner. He tried to weasel out of it, until I assured him that there would be women; however I didn't bother to tell him that it was only two and that I didn't think either one of them were his type. The other bug I planned to put in his ear was that I needed a car to drive while I was in town. My brother owned two Mercedes-Benz dealerships, one in Lower Merion and the other in Voorhees, New Jersey, and if I was going to be staying in town, then my brother needed to make sure I was driving the hottest thing popping on the lot.

Back at my parents' that afternoon I changed into shorts and a tank and assisted my mother in putting the final touches on the formal dining room for the dinner. She was so particular about where every little thing was placed. I'm sure more than anything else she annoyed the hell out of her house staff by getting in their way. But they'd all been with her long enough to know all her little nuances. It was my belief that if my mother had had to work, she could've easily been in the party planning business.

"How was your day, honey?" she asked as she followed the florist into the dining room with a handful of fresh lilacs.

"Not bad at all. We're gonna focus on some Philly stuff, so it's going to be pretty busy over the next few weeks."

My mother didn't answer right away. She was switching the linen napkins from a striking blue to a bright yellow to match the new dinnerware. She'd wanted the table setting less formal.

"Are you going to have time to see some of your old friends?" she asked. "There are also some engagements I've been invited to that I'd like you to attend with me."

"I don't know, Mom. If I have the time I will," I answered as she handed me the napkins to fold.

She stopped what she was doing for a minute and put her hands over mine. "Linney, listen to me. I understand how important your job is, and you've been blessed with success at a young age, but you must remember, honey, with all that working, you still have to make time for your family. You know how important that is to me and your father."

"I know that, Mom," I said, realizing how pissed off she was going to be about my moving into the city. Since this wasn't the time for that, I decided to steer the conversation elsewhere.

"What did you wind up putting on the menu for tonight?"

She clapped her hands together and exclaimed, "You're going to love it! Gladys fixed some of your favorites, and I helped her."

I looked over my mother's shoulder at Gladys, who playfully rolled her eyes. I knew she hated it when my mother got in the kitchen beside her—we all did.

"We're having a southern menu—fried chicken, barbeque chicken, pork chops in gravy, about three different salads, fresh green beans, collards, and yams."

"I don't even wanna know what's for dessert. I knew you were going to overdo it, but I can't wait to eat," I said, certain that if I stayed at my parents my wardrobe wouldn't be fitting in a few days.

"What about Dad's retirement party? How's that coming along?" I asked to sound interested, yet not really wanting to get involved.

"Now, that's what I call hectic," she said, placing the glasses at the right spot above the plates.

"I told you I'd help out."

"Good, because your father and I want you to invite your friend Julius to the party. You're going to need an escort, unless you'd like me to pick someone for you," she said, sheepishly grinning.

"That's quite all right, Mom. I'm sure Julius will be able to make it," I replied, hoping that he could.

"I mean really, Caroline, we would like to get to know him a little better. We've only met him a few times."

"Cool, I'll call him now. If you don't need me anymore, I'm going upstairs to shower and change."

"Go right along, dear. I don't want you to keep your guests waiting when they get here. Nothing worse than an unprepared hostess."

"Mom, how many times do I have to tell you that this isn't formal?"

"I know. Now you go get dressed," she said, waving me away.

Around 5:30 P.M. everyone began arriving. Juan and Raphael were the first to arrive, and they wanted nothing more than a cold Heineken and to sit in front of the high definition television to watch the Phillies and Dodgers game. I directed them to the media room. Shortly after my mother made them comfortable, Brad circled the driveway with Sharon behind him in their rentals. I'd thought Marí would've been with her but she was alone. I stood outside while they parked.

"Hey, Sharon, you found your way all right."

"Yes, I just followed the guys. I have to tell you again that this place is beautiful. How the hell could you ever have left here?" she said, surveying the perfectly manicured grounds the landscaper had touched up that day.

"Girl's gotta grow up sometime. By the way, where's Marí?"

"I don't know. I called her like three times and just figured maybe she'd rode home with you this afternoon."

"That's weird. I haven't heard from her either."

I showed everyone into the family room to meet my parents. My father couldn't stay for dinner because he had a hospital board meeting, which seemed pretty convenient to me.

My mother insisted I give them a tour of the house. Raphael and Sharon were the only ones interested enough to join me. I took them upstairs to the second level first to see my parents' master suite but didn't waste time on the other five unused bedrooms. Then back downstairs through the main floor of the house and out to the pool house and exercise room, Dad's library, and study. Seeing the way Sharon had lusted over the swimming pool, I promised them that before returning to the West Coast I'd host a pool party. Hell, maybe we'd even tape a show on the patio. I laughed as I realized that maybe I did possess some of my mother's party planning genes after all.

We'd all moved out onto the patio to have hors d'oeuvres. Raphael was engrossed in conversation with my mother. I was surprised that she was so knowledgeable about couture fashions here and abroad. Meanwhile Brad and Juan were discussing how they could do a show from Love Park or Penn's Landing.

I was getting a little worried that Marí hadn't arrived yet and was just about to call her when the doorbell chimed. I went to the door to greet her. The first thing I noticed was how refreshed and relaxed she looked. This girl was definitely getting some and it was working wonders.

"Hey, girl, what's up with you? Are we boring you at *Top of Da Charts* or did your butt get lost again?" I asked before she gave me a hug.

"No, not all. It's just that I lay down to take a nap and before I knew it I looked up and the clock read five-thirty."

"Really, now? Who might you have been laying down with . . . ? Sharon said she tried to reach you a few times."

"I guess I must not have heard the phone ringing. Is everyone here?"

"Whatever. I'm just glad you made it. Come on, everyone's out back at the pool."

At exactly six-thirty my mother was ready for us to be seated. I knew her delay in serving was because she'd been waiting for my brother. I also knew that if the guys didn't eat soon, they were going to be drunk. The seven of us all gathered around the huge oak table that sat at least twenty people, a table that my father had had custom made for parties just like this.

We'd started on our appetizers when I heard the loud voice of my brother teasing Gladys in the kitchen.

"Good evening, everyone," Maurice said as he sidled up next to my mother, giving her a big hug and kiss. "I'm sorry I'm late, Mom, but my meetings today were back to back."

"Hello, son. Caroline, can you please introduce your brother to everyone," my mother said, ignoring his lame excuse.

But before I could do that he just had to embarrass me in front of everyone. Maurice came over and nearly lifted me off the floor in a bear hug.

"Linney, Linney, who's the prettiest girl in all the world?"

"Stop playing, Maurice. Put me down," I said, my legs dangling beneath me.

"Come on now, don't show off, tell me," he said, squeezing me and making me blush. "Who is it, baby girl?" he asked again.

I knew he wouldn't stop until I answered him. "It's me, it's me," I squealed in embarrassment.

Everyone got a kick out of that and I knew they'd be teasing me at work from here on out.

As I introduced Maurice to everyone, he walked around the table to shake hands. My brother looked exceptionally handsome, which I'm sure was due to his recent vacation. He was the only person I knew who could party all night and still look good in the morning. It was almost like partying rejuvenated him.

"Linney, you didn't tell me that these lovely ladies were going to be here."

"Yes I did. Stop lying."

I watched him as he kissed the back of Sharon's hand. And poor Marí, she barely wanted to let his hand go. Most women found my brother irresistible. He was handsome, rich, and his body well toned from his personal trainer. But my brother was a bona fide playboy and at the age of twenty-nine he had no plans of slowing down.

As Maurice took the empty seat at the other end of the table, he said to no one in particular "My sister likes to keep all her beautiful girlfriends away from me."

"Maurice, what line of business are you in?" Marí asked casually.

"He's a used car salesman. Can't you tell from all the BS he talks?" I joked. "Now pass me the greens."

"Caroline, that's not nice," my mother said, realizing I was only teasing, yet she proudly took up for him. "My son is the owner of two Mercedes-Benz dealerships and some other commercial properties as well."

With the exception of Marí, I was sure everyone was well aware of who my brother was. There weren't many African Americans with that kind of clout, especially at his age.

"See, my sister's got it all wrong. I'm the more debonair one of the family," Maurice said as he bowed his head.

"Please. You weren't always debonair; you're the one who got suspended from school on a monthly basis with all your pranks. Mother never had to come up to Branfman for me."

Everyone laughed at our sibling banter.

"Yeah, but I was the one who went to college and, um, how many degrees do I have," he asked, always teasing me because I didn't go to college.

"Don't matter, you're still a knucklehead," I said. "Seriously, Marí, my brother was in *Black Enterprise* last month as their Young Entrepreneur of the Year—that is under thirty—for now, I might add."

"Impressive," Brad said, "and Mrs. Isaacs, this food is superb."

"And Maurice here has his MBA and real estate licenses for Pennsylvania and New Jersey. He is Mr. Intellectual, he thinks," I added, without feeling any jealousy over my brother's success. I probably was more proud of Maurice than anybody.

Sharon spoke up. "Caroline, what about you? Look at what you've accomplished. Who would've thought at twenty-four you'd be one of *People* magazine's most beautiful people for the fourth year in a row?"

Maurice wiped his mouth of barbeque sauce, then said, "Yeah, that's right, sis. Because of you these young girls now know that they can do more than shake their ass to make it in the entertainment industry."

"If they don't keep shaking them, we'll all be out of job," Juan joked.

"I know one person who's been glad to have a job under you, right, Marí?" Brad asked.

Marí seemed to be noticeably smitten with my brother's charm, as she'd barely touched her food and sat there rapping her knuckles on the table.

"No doubt. Seriously, Linney, you have taught me a lot about business and about being prepared for opportunities. So much so that things are beginning to happen for me," she stated, and then pushed her full plate away from her.

"I knew they would. You're a go-getter Marí. And let's not forget all that great stuff you keep coming up with," I said.

Marí glanced around the table at each of us as if she wanted to say something, then pushed back her chair and stood up to get everyone's attention. I couldn't imagine what she needed to say that could be so serious.

"There are many things I could say about my friend Caroline. She really gave me the biggest opportunity I could ever hope for the day I came into her office. She's been so patient with me and willing to try my ideas that I . . ." She paused, then continued. "Because of you, Caroline, I have something I'd like to share with everyone."

I was beginning to feel uneasy about wherever it was that Marí was headed with her speech.

"Because of Caroline," she said, pausing to look into my eyes, "I've been offered an opportunity that most interns only dream about. I've been offered the chance—now it hasn't been confirmed yet—but the chance to host the opening night of Hustler's nightclub and casino."

All eyes immediately turned to me.

"Well, do tell," Raphael mumbled, all the while rolling his eyes.

"Very nice, Marí," Brad added.

"Yes, congratulations, Marí," Sharon said.

I still hadn't responded because I was undoubtedly in shock.

"Sounds like you deserve a toast," Maurice said, then walked over and stood beside Marí's chair, insisting everyone stand up.

I cleared my throat. "Yes, Marí, you deserve a toast," I repeated, yet wondered why I felt like the rug had just been pulled from underneath me.

After dessert and having to listen to Marí's excitement about her opportunity, I was glad when everyone left. I couldn't stand much more of it, especially the way she kept directing all her comments and gratitude toward me. I knew I should've been appreciative, but something just didn't feel right about the way it had all gone down. I hated to think I was just jealous.

Even after everyone left I still had to endure another twenty minutes of listening to my mother tell me what great coworkers I had and how generous it was that I'd inspired a nice college graduate like Marí to follow in my footsteps.

Finally, when I made it to my bedroom, I put in a call to Kia.

"Hey, girl, what's up?" she asked.

"Nothing," I answered, then lay back against the mound of pillows on my bed.

"What's this I hear, that you're not coming home until September?"

"Yeah, something like that. How'd you find out already? I know you ain't been watching the show, Kia."

"You know how fast shit travels in this business. But why are you sounding so damn depressed? Is it that bad out there? I mean, it's not cold or anything, is it?"

"It's July, Kia. Don't act like you never lived on the East Coast. Are you taking good care of my car?" I asked, not sure if I really had something to complain about.

"Yep, and you don't have any dents or dings. But seriously, Linney, I know you. What's up?"

I caught a glimpse of that stupid tattoo that I'd let Marí talk me into. Thank God my mother hadn't seen it.

"What's up, Linney? Spill it."

"It's probably no big deal, but you remember my intern, Marí? You met her when we left to go on the road."

"Yeah, the one who did the show from Philly."

"Well, she just got an offer to host that new casino and club opening here."

"Hustler's? Wow, that is big for an intern. Yeah, I can see why you'd be pissed."

"I mean, I should be happy for her, right?"

"Please, girl. Don't even sweat that shit; it happens all the time in the modeling industry. You befriend someone, then they get the cover or layout that you wanted. Remember, though, that little Ms. Marí would be nowhere without you. Take the credit you deserve for getting her career going. And for being able to spot her talent in the first place."

"You're right. I did give her a chance, didn't I?" I said, telling myself that in no way should I have felt undermined.

And anyway, I hadn't even been in the running for the job because I'd never called my agent.

"You damn right," Kia said. "But listen, on another note, I wanna come out. Let me know when you're doing something big, you know, with all the players."

I got up from the bed and started taking off my clothes, then turned on the water in the Jacuzzi. "All right, girl, I will. Oh yeah, guess what? I'm going to be staying with Julius."

"Huh? What are you talking about? Julius is here. I saw him last night with one of those little boy clients at Spago's."

"He has a spot here in the city," I said.

"You're a lucky girl," Kia said, "with that guy and your job. Don't lose sight of that."

"You're right," I said. "Thanks for listening, Kia. Now I'm going to bed. It's late here."

I hung up with Kia, grateful for her sanity and her support. But I think a part of what bothered me about Marí was that if I were truly her mentor and we were friends, then why hadn't she bothered to at least seek my advice and opinion? Something about this whole Hustler thing, about that girl, seemed suspicious.

12
CLEAN SLATE

The next morning I woke up late for breakfast. I washed my face, brushed my teeth, and headed downstairs. I'd finally gotten up the nerve to tell my parents about my plan to move into Julius's apartment.

"Morning, Caroline. This is a surprise, you joining us for breakfast so early," my father teased as he poured himself a cup of steaming coffee.

"Very funny, Dad."

"It's nice of you to join us, honey, but you should've at least gotten dressed."

I shook my head at my mothers comment. Growing up, Maurice and I were not allowed at the breakfast table in our pajamas. The only exception was if we were sick, and then our meals were delivered to our room, We had to be fully dressed for every meal, which was exactly one of the reasons

I couldn't live there for the duration of my stay in Philly. I don't know why they couldn't just be glad I'd gotten up at the crack of dawn to eat with them. I mean, it wasn't as if the appearance police were peering in the windows, checking on me.

"What are your plans, now that you're going to be home for a while, besides working?" my father asked.

"That's what I wanted to talk to you about. I'm not exactly going to be home."

He folded up his paper to give me his undivided attention. "What do you mean? Your mother told me that you were staying for the remainder of the summer," he quizzed.

"Yes, Caroline, what do you mean? Has your producer changed her mind?"

I knew they weren't going to like what I was about to say, but I was an adult and had a right to do what I wanted.

"I'm going to be staying at Julius's place at the St. James down on Washington Square," I answered, my eyes looking inside my coffee cup instead of directly at them. Some adult I was.

"Julius? You mean you're going to be shacking up with him?"

"Dad, it's not like that."

"I'm very disappointed that you've made that decision. How do you think that's going to look, you living with a man and not being married? You're better than that, Caroline."

"Dad, Julius is rarely even in Philly. His permanent residence is in Malibu. We don't even live together out there. I'm only going to be using his place while I'm here. I mean, with him being a sports agent, he travels all the time."

By this time my mother had taken herself out of the conversation and I'd lost my appetite.

"By the way, how is that going? Is he even able to support himself?" my father asked.

"Dad, I am not supporting Julius. He makes out very well for himself," I said, almost yelling. I really resented the fact that he'd think I'd take care of any man. "If you actually knew Julius, you'd see that he's not that kind of man."

I directed my attention to my mother. "Anyway, Mom, like I said, he'll rarely be there, so we can still have dinner together or I can come out to lunch, whenever you'd like."

"I guess your father and I don't have any say-so in this. You're going to do what you want anyway."

I now looked fully at my father. "Dad, I'm only moving there so I don't have to commute so far everyday."

"Philadelphia isn't the same as California, Linney. This city is a little more conservative, or should I say a lot more conservative."

"Dad, I understand what you're saying, but I swear he's not going to be there like that," I answered, when what I really wanted to say was that they were the ones who were conservative, them and all their snotty friends.

I was sure they were ready for me to be married to a lawyer or doctor, like all the other girls I'd gone to private school with, but fortunately for me I had a career. My plan was to enjoy my life before I started having anybody's children, unless of course Julius did actually propose.

In order to appease my mother once my father was out of the house for his eighteen holes of golf, I spent the rest of the morning discussing with her my father's upcoming retirement party. She'd made all the plans and had hired a team of people to carry them out. The event was to be held on our estate under a huge tent in two weeks. While she went to walk the grounds with the landscaper and florist, I headed upstairs to find Gladys.

"Gladys, do you think you could get my things packed up and have them sent over to this address?" I asked as I scribbled down Julius's address for her.

"Sure, Ms. Caroline, I'll get to it this morning."

"Thanks," I said, and went into the second-floor sitting room to phone Julius.

"Jules, where are you?" I queried, which was the norm these days since he traveled so much.

"I'm at LaGuardia about to board a plane to LA. Can I give you a call later?"

"Yeah, but I wanted to tell you—"

"Linney, I gotta run. We're about to take off. I'll call you tonight when I get home."

Since Julius didn't have time to talk, I took time out to lay by the pool while looking through a stack of fashion magazines. I couldn't help but think about Marí and her big announcement. My guess was that she'd probably been interviewing for the job all along—that's why she'd been late all those times. I knew how interviews went—the folks wanted you to meet everyone from the big honchos to the office staff. They would do photo shoots, have you submit reels of yourself, and there were on-camera tests to see how you came across. I simply didn't understand how she'd done all this right under my nose in such a short time.

Thank God I hadn't mentioned to anyone my interest in the job at Hustler's, because I would've felt like a fool. Oh well, I wasn't going to let that come between us. I guess

Marí felt she'd handled things in the way that worked best for her.

Later that afternoon, strolling into Teaz, Marí was the first one to greet me.

"Here you are, Linney," she said as she cheerfully handed me a cup of hot water and lemon. It had been a while since I'd had that.

"Thanks, Marí. You didn't have to do that," I said, feeling like a jerk for being jealous.

"Listen, I'm really sorry about not telling you about the job offer before I blurted it out at your parents'. But it all happened so fast, and I just knew you'd be proud of me," she said as we made our way into the office for a morning meeting.

"Marí, I *am* proud of you. Girl, you deserve it, as hard as you've been working," I responded.

"No, I should've discussed it with you first. I hope you're not mad," she said, so bouncy that I really couldn't help but be happy for her.

"Why would I be mad? Marí, I'm happy for you. This is going to be great."

"You sure?" she asked, blocking the door so I couldn't get into the meeting.

"Marí, I could never be selfish like that," I said, and kissed her on the cheek.

She moved away. "Thanks, Caroline. Your support means a lot."

Before I went into the office, I turned and said, "You know what, why don't the two of us go on a tour of the city this afternoon?"

"Linney, would you really take the time to do that with me? It would be so much fun."

"Yep, and if you're going to be working here, you're gonna need to know your way around. We wouldn't want you running late everywhere," I said, and took a seat beside Brad.

"Great, I can't wait." Despite the fact she'd taken the job I'd wanted, Marí seemed back to her old self.

Countdown Fridays were always the easiest day on the show. No guests to interview, just me and the audience, who were always at their liveliest—which was good 'cause my ego needed a boost. And Marí was there making sure the crew and I had everything we needed to make things run smoothly.

By the end of the show I'd forgotten all about my being envious of Marí's job at Hustler's. There was surely enough room in the business for the both of us. Plus I was more than ready to hang out.

"You ready, Marí?" I asked after I changed out of my stage clothes and we got into my car.

"Absolutely! Where are we going first?"

"This might be corny but I don't know anyone who hasn't come to Philly for the first time and not wanted to visit this place," I said as I pulled up in front of the Philadelphia Museum of Art steps.

"This is it, Philly's number-one landmark."

"We're going to get out, aren't we?" she asked, her face beaming with excitement.

"You wanna run up those steps like Rocky, I'm guessing?"

"Yeah! Come on, Linney," she said, pulling on my arm.

"I'll probably get a ticket for parking here, but let's do it."

We climbed out of the wagon and, standing at the bottom of the steps, I said, "Ready, set, go!" And we went running up the steps, laughing and soon out of breath.

After we caught our breath we got back in the car and I took her for a ride along Kelly Drive, past Boathouse Row, and then over the bridge and down the West River Drive back into the city. We then traveled down to Old City, where I pointed out the various restaurants I'd been to when I'd come home. I even showed her where I'd be staying at the St. James.

"You wanna go have a drink?" I asked her.

"This time of day? It's only three o'clock."

"Oh, come on. We're celebrating your new gig."

"Sure, whatever you say but not around here."

"Let's ride out to the hood," I said. "I have the perfect bar out there." I headed out Walnut Street and over Thirty-eighth Street toward an area referred to as the Bottom. I parked on the corner of Thirty-eighth and Lancaster and we went inside Scooter's.

"This doesn't look like the type of place you'd go to, Caroline," Marí commented as we went inside and our eyes adjusted to the dimly lit bar.

"Come on, it's cool. This is the bar where my brother took me at sixteen to have my first drink," I said, and then ordered us two wine spritzers.

"By the way, I meant to ask you who's your brother's girl-friend? I'm sure she's somebody really hot, or is she a celebrity?" Marí asked with curiosity.

"My brother with a celebrity? No, never. The boy has got

to be the only celebrity in a relationship. Maurice T. Isaacs is the man."

Graciously we'd accepted a few complimentary drinks as people began to take notice that I was Linney from *Top of Da Charts*. As the men began flirting with us, I could see Marí was getting uncomfortable.

"Okay, Linney, there is something else I want to see."

"Just tell me and we're outta here."

"Where or what the hell is Belmont Plateau? You know, the one Will Smith raps about in his old "Summertime" song?"

"You are too funny, but that was another hot spot when I was a teenager. That's where I lost my damn virginity. Come on, I'll take you."

Before leaving Scooter's I took a picture with the barmaid for them to post on the wall along with other celebs who had visited.

I made my way up Lancaster Avenue to Forty-fourth Street and out to Belmont to Montgomery Drive. Belmont Plateau, a grassy area in the park that overlooked the city, was a spot where young lovers often parked to do their thing. During the day especially on the weekends, people went there to picnic and show off their rides. We got out of the car and stood at the top of the hill.

"This is it, the famous Belmont Plateau, and that's the Belmont Mansion over there. It's not too crowded today, but on a Sunday, oh girl, it's off the chain."

"Really?"

"Yeah, and right over there"—I pointed to a spot behind a bunch of trees—"is where I let some boy from Frankford convince me to do the nasty for the first time, and I been doing it ever since."

"You're crazy, Linney."

I pointed across Belmont Avenue to the Mann Music Center. "My parents used to force us to go there for what my brother and I called old folks' concerts. You know, jazz, heavy R and B. It was 'part of your culture,' they said."

"I gotcha. Come on, where to next?"

"I know. Let's drive out to Branfman. That'll be fun. I haven't been there in a while."

"Branfman . . . that doesn't sound like any place fun. What's out there?" Marí asked as if it were something contagious.

Her response put me on the defensive. "It's where I went to high school, that's all. No big deal."

"Oh no, it's okay. I'm with you."

It took us about half an hour getting through traffic to get to Lower Merion and onto the campus of Branfman. I noticed that Marí was somewhat tense.

"This place looks like a college campus—it's beautiful," Marí exclaimed as I announced to the security guard who I was. Slowly I drove the winding roads across campus.

"It's the closest I'm ever gonna get to one. Marí I told you before, I never went to college—not that I couldn't have gone—but my job at *Top of Da Charts* just fell into my lap," I said, remembering my time at Branfman.

"How'd that happen, Caroline? Was it something you always wanted to do, be a television veejay?" Marí asked as we drove past the main office and I pointed out the baseball and football fields.

"No, actually what happened was I was in my final year of high school when VMT came out here to film a reality segment on wealthy suburban kids. When we all met with them in the auditorium for interviews, I wound up getting chosen as the spokesperson. That put me on the road to being the host of *Top of Da Charts.*"

"Wow, it really did fall in your lap. There aren't too many women your age making big money and having the celebrity status you do," Marí said, then rolled down her window.

We parked to watch a group of football players doing calisthenics. I noticed Marí drumming her fingers on the armrest.

"Marí, I'm sorry. I must be boring the hell out of you."

"Oh no. Please go on. I love it," she said with not much conviction.

I pointed across the field. "Over there in that building is the gymnasium. That was my favorite part of going to school. It really was the best of times for me there."

"You played sports? I thought that would be too physical for you."

"Did I? Girl, I was an all around athlete, especially in lacrosse. I loved my coach, he was the best," I said, remembering my coach as I sat staring at the gym that held my not so long ago teenage memories.

"You want to get out and walk around?" Marí asked.

We strolled over to a clump of trees and sat down among them.

"Did your brother go to Branfman too?" Marí asked, feigning interest. I noticed that her eyes were focused on a distance point, sad even.

"Hell, yes, and probably screwed every girl in his class. But I bet it wouldn't surprise you that he was also president of his class," I said, pulling up blades of grass.

"I still can't believe some woman hasn't snatched him up yet."

"My brother? Please, he loves himself too much to share the spotlight with anyone."

"Maurice is handsome and quite a catch for some lucky girl."

"Maybe one day. According to my parents, it's his duty to keep the Isaacs lineage going."

"And to keep the Isaacs good looks going too," Marí added, and I shrugged dismissively.

"But being beautiful, Linney, is what keeps you on the cover of *People* every year," Marí said.

"Marí, I wasn't always beautiful," I said, plucking a stray dandelion from the grass.

"You had work done by your father?" she asked with some distaste.

"I didn't have a choice. I was still in high school when he did some laser stuff to my eyes and got my overbite fixed. Until I got that stuff done all the kids thought it was funny that my father could make everyone else beautiful while I was looking like hell. So I begged him to hook me up and he did. And a little boob job didn't hurt either."

"Caroline, you're too much. You're so funny. I can't imagine you any other way than you are now."

"Yeah, well, it was all for the best," I said as I began to realize that I'd been monopolizing all of Marí's time talking about myself.

"I've just been yakking it up all day about me and my life. Marí, tell me about you, how it was for you growing up. You're quite a beauty yourself, you know. You have that whole Hispanic J. Lo thing going on."

I could see Marí's jaws tighten. "No big deal. My childhood was pale in comparison to yours. But I love hearing your stories, Caroline. Keep talking, it's nice to get to know the other side of you."

"Marí, how come you never want to talk about yourself? I mean, we've been hanging out for two months and not once have you mentioned your family. Isn't somebody wondering where you are?"

"My family is small. They're back in California. Believe me, there's nothing exciting in my past."

"All right, don't let me find out you got some deep dark secret."

She laughed. "No secrets here. You ready?"

I headed back down Lancaster Avenue and into the city. The mood in the car had changed to a somber one and the drone of the afternoon deejay's voice wasn't helping. I was almost sorry I'd tried to pry into Marí's personal life.

"I have another idea, Marí. Tell me what you think. Julius isn't going to be coming to town this weekend, so why don't you stay with me. We could have a girls' weekend, go to the spa, do some power shopping and a lot of partying."

"Really? You want me to stay with you at Julius's? I'd love that," she said, her mood getting lighter.

"Yeah. He lives right downtown and it would be convenient for both of us. There are restaurants all over the place, we'd never have to cook, and you'd never have to clean up because he has a housekeeping service."

"Good, because I could use a break from the hotel. By the way, Linney, does your brother live in the city too?"

"Last I heard that Negro had a loft somewhere on Twenty-ninth and Locust, but I haven't seen it yet. He's got a house out in Wayne too."

"And no girlfriend. Isn't that amazing?"

"Marí, don't go getting no ideas. That boy is way too fast for you."

"Are you saying he's out of my league?"

"No, Marí. What I meant is he's not good enough. You deserve somebody who wouldn't cheat on you. I just don't see you with a playboy."

"Oh," was all Marí said.

"All right, so it's set. We'll go down to the Ritz, get your stuff, then do some shopping down on Second Street and charge that shit to the show."

"Can we do that?"

"Hell, yes! I get an allowance every three months for clothing and I haven't used it in almost a year."

"But, Caroline, I don't think I can do that like you can. Plus what about all that free stuff you gave me?"

"Marí, don't worry about a thing. I got you on this one."

"If you say so. But are you sure? I have some money. At least let me pay for the spa."

"Please, Marí, keep your money. My brother has hook-ups all over this city. Plus I'm dying to go to this spa my mother told me about, someplace she went a few weeks ago on Twentieth Street called the Body Klinic. I'll make an appointment for us while I'm waiting for you to get your stuff." Just then the chirping of my cell phone interrupted us.

"Linney here!"

"Is this the prettiest girl in the world?"

"Yes it is, big brother. What's happening?" I looked over at Marí and said, "It's him, the playboy."

"I want you to come out to a party some of my frat brothers and I are having tonight."

"Really?" I said, nodding over at Marí and turning the radio down as I pulled the car to a stop in front of the Ritz.

"Yeah. A few of them are in town and we're throwing something together at the Marbar. You up for it?"

"Mmm, I don't know. Let me ask my girl," I said, kidding with him. I turned to Marí and asked, "My brother wants to know if we want to hang out with his horny friends tonight at a bar where they'll be doing a lot of drinking and taking advantage of young women like us. You up for it, Marí?"

"Is your brother going to be there?"

"Without a doubt."

"Okay, if you're there, then I'm there."

"Alright, Mo, we'll see you tonight, but I'm inviting some of my girls from the Main Line to get down too."

"Not a problem. See you around eleven."

This would be my first good Friday night hanging out in the city and I planned to make it a big one. While Marí went to her room inside the hotel to pack her things for the weekend I began dialing and leaving messages for my friends, telling them the party plans for the night, and suggesting they first meet me at the St. James.

13

NIGHT ON THE TOWN

Later that evening Marí and I were settling down from shopping and having just plain girl fun—the stuff that only women knew how to do. We'd been up and down South Street, visited the vintage boutiques in Old City, and were loaded down with bags when we got back to Julius's place.

Julius had leased a two-bedroom furnished apartment on the penthouse floor of the St. James. The lobby entrance was long and sleek. His place was a corner unit on the eleventh floor. It was easy to see that nobody lived there, as all the closets were empty and there was absolutely no food in the refrigerator or pantry. To the right of the entrance was the kitchen. The master bedroom and living room were surrounded by a terrace. At the end of the hallway was the second bedroom, where Marí would be bunking for the weekend.

While Marí unpacked the clothes we'd picked up from her hotel and the many new things we'd splurged on, I ordered takeout from El Azteca, as suggested by the doorman. Julius's bar stock was low, so I paid the doorman to get us some liquor from the Wine and Spirits store. My mother surely wouldn't have approved of the fashion in which I threw a party together.

After the food and liquor arrived Marí and I sat down in the dining room and started grubbing on the mix of food I'd ordered before my friends arrived. I don't know why, but I still felt the need to pry.

"So, Marí, tell me, do you have any siblings?" I asked, propping my feet up on the chair across from me.

"Two brothers, that's it, no big deal. You want one of these Coronas?" she asked, pulling one from the carton.

"I probably shouldn't. Beer is so fattening, but pass me one. So do your brothers live in Los Angeles with your parents?"

"I don't know what they're doing. Hey, don't you think we should get ready?" she said, getting up to start stacking the dishwasher.

There she was again, dodging personal questions. I watched her as she moved about and wondered if lil' ol' Marí had something to hide, or was she simply embarrassed that her childhood might've been a rough one? I'd been to the proverty-stricken projects in Del Rey but looking down on people less fortunate is not what I did. I just wanted to get to know her better.

"How about your mom and dad, do they know you're in Philly?" I asked, reaching across the table to dip my tostada in salsa.

"Here you are," she said, holding up the container.

My guess was she wasn't comfortable discussing her family, so I chose another topic. "Did you always live in LA and go to high school there?"

"Just public school, nothing like Branfman. But did I tell you I'm entering my senior year at Loyola? I told you that in the interview, right?"

"Yeah, you told me. So how do you like it—you know, college?" I asked, always curious because I hadn't gone.

"It's great, and now I have so much to go back and talk about."

"You know, I often feel like I've missed out on something by not going to college. I know my parents wished I would've gone. It's like I skipped a big chunk of my maturity. Julius is forever telling me that one day I'm going to be forced to grow up," I said before chugging down the last of my beer.

Marí stood up and started wiping the table around the containers. I was used to it now.

"Linney, believe me, you haven't missed a thing. Do you know how many women wish they could be you? Women who've gone to college don't have half of what you've got."

"I just got what I got. I didn't work hard to get it," I said, sometimes wishing I hadn't been born with a silver spoon in my mouth.

"And you think that's a bad thing?"

I stirred my fork around in the refried beans. "Maybe, maybe not, but it is what it is."

"Caroline, my only wish is to one day have what you have."

"Marí, from the looks of things, you're on your way. The

opportunity you've been offered at Hustler's is fantastic."

"They haven't given me the go ahead yet and I don't want to presume anything."

"I guess you're right. But you have told your family already, haven't you?" I asked, not really intending to bring up her family but it only seemed natural.

"I'm going to wait. Now enough about all that. I'm taking my shower so I can get ready. You should be doing the same so we won't be late when your friends arrive."

Marí had briefly talked about her family yet she really hadn't told me anything. It was obvious that my friend definitely lived a very private life. Mine was the exact opposite and I was willing to respect her differences, but I hoped she realized that the moment she stepped into the limelight her private life wouldn't be private any longer.

I heard my cell phone ringing in the bedroom. "Let me get this," I said.

"You want me to open you another beer?"

"Sure, bring it in."

I'd missed the call but went to use the bathroom instead, and when I came out Marí was there with beers for the both of us.

"What are you going to wear tonight?" she asked.

"Nothing special, jeans probably."

"Linney, there's your Corona," she said pointing to the dresser. "I'm going to get ready."

Around nine-thirty Marí took a call from the doorman, who informed her that we had guests in the lobby.

"We're not even dressed yet," she said, referring to our lounging around in our robes, me putting a coat of gloss on my toenails.

"My friends from school don't care; they're just going to have a couple of drinks while we get ready. It's just a little impromptu thing. This is how we do it all the time."

"You want me to get out some ice and stuff?"

"Good idea. I'll get the door. Marí, look over there and see if you can figure out how to turn on that stereo."

At the door were Alexis, Alvin, Kim, Hasaan, and P.S., all friends of mine from out in the suburbs with whom I'd attended Branfman. I hadn't seen any of them since I'd gotten back into town and we rarely saw each other when I visited during the holidays. But these guys had been my crew throughout high school and before I left for California.

I introduced Marí to everyone right before she ran off to get dressed. I sat there in my robe drinking and catching up with them. I was so glad I'd invited everyone over. It was really helping us to get loosened up, and I was grateful that I'd be able to enjoy myself tonight without being in front of the camera.

When Marí came out of her room I was astounded to see her in a Betsey Johnson dress with her wavy hair hanging on her shoulders. I didn't even know she knew how to style it without Raphael.

"Oh, shit. You doing that outfit justice. Let me get my clothes on because you are showing my ass up."

I was in my room squeezing into a pair of Rockin Republics I'd gotten that day when Alexis came in.

"What's up with your girl?" she asked as she dabbed on one of my perfumes.

"Who, Marí?"

"Yes, the chickie is out there blabbing away."

"About what?"

"I don't know—you and her this, you and her that. Then I asked that heffer which room was yours and she says 'You can wait here, I'll go get her.' What's up with that shit? I might not see you all the time, Linney, but I for sure don't need anybody running interference."

"Stop being so jealous. She didn't mean any harm."

"Whatever."

While I was finishing my makeup I had the doorman call a car service to taxi us around rather than taking the chance of any of us getting busted with a DUI. We could've really had our own party right there at Julius's, the way the music was blaring and the drinks were flowing. If we didn't get out of there soon I'd be too tipsy to go anywhere.

The Marbar was located at Fortieth and Walnut streets in University City. When the bouncer recognized my face he let us right in past the waiting line. We made our way up to the second floor, where the place was crammed with people and loud with music. My brother was standing in the midst of it all in an icy blue button down shirt, off white drawstring linen pants, and a pair of Prada driving shoes.

"Oh yeah, this might be better than I thought. Look at all these fine ass men," Alexis determined after she ordered us a round of key lime pie martinis.

"Linney, I don't know anybody here, so don't go too far," Marí added.

"You'll be fine, just go with the flow," Alexis told her.

"Wow, your brother really looks hot. Look at all those women swarmed around him," Marí said.

I sent Hasaan over to get Maurice because I could've never gotten his attention from where I stood. As my brother strolled over to us I was sure every woman in the Marbar wanted his attention.

"Good evening, ladies. Glad you could come out. What's up, sis?" he said, then kissed me on the cheek.

"What's up, Mo?" Alexis asked him. "You're looking dapper, as usual."

He grabbed her by the waist for a hug. "Lexi, Lexi, I swear, one of these days."

I thought I noticed Marí throw a piercing gaze toward Alexis.

"Shut up, Negro, and get us some drinks," Alexis said, flipping him the bird.

"Maurice, you remember Marí, right?" I asked, holding up Marí's hand to his.

"Yes, I certainly do," he replied, carefully checking Marí out. "But I don't think she looked like this when we met the first time," he said, and kissed the back of her hand.

"Hello, Maurice," she said, offering him an innocent smile.

I was torn away from them as fans and people familiar with my show came up to say hello, but there was no mistaking the deep voice calling out to me from a few feet away.

"Caroline Isaacs, damn, is that you?"

I turned around to see Tobias, an old flame that'd I'd left behind when I'd moved out to California.

"Tobias Martin, what's happening? I see you're still sexy as hell," I said, having to stand on my toes to give him a peck on the lips. I remembered that Tobias had been a great kisser and great at foreplay, but he had very little swinging between his legs.

"Shit, girl, I can't believe I let your fine ass get away. I ain't been able to get me a woman since you left Philly," he commented while placing his hands on my hips.

"Did you really think you were gonna find someone to

replace Caroline Isaacs?" I asked, flinging my hair back for effect.

"Shut up, girl, and come on out here and let me see if you can still move that sexy ass body."

While I went off to dance with Tobias, I noticed that my brother had pulled Marí out on the floor with him. Good, I thought, she needed to loosen up a little.

I could barely get through dancing one song before a few women were interrupting, dying to fill me in on Philly gossip to put on my blog. The night couldn't have been going better as I learned who was sneaking around Philly doing somebody else's man or woman.

When I looked over to check back on Marí, she'd returned to the bar and was having a drink with Alexis. Finally I excused myself from the crowd that had gathered around me and took a break to have a drink with them—no need in letting my high wear off.

"Who are you two over here plotting on?" I inquired, signaling for the bartender.

"Nobody. I was just telling Marí that I've seen her so much on your show that I'm starting to get jealous," Alexis said, looking Marí up and down.

I didn't know what Alexis was up to, but I didn't like it.

"Please, I don't think anybody could make you jealous, Alexis," I said, sipping on the drink Marí had handed me.

"Yeah, but some of these bitches in here are a little hateful. I've seen them around," Alexis said.

I took a few sips of my drink and said with a wink, "That will happen anywhere you find beautiful women like us as the center of attention. They can't help themselves."

"Now that's the truth," Alexis added.

I was laughing when I felt a cramp across my stomach; it didn't last but a second.

Maurice stepped up between the three of us and said, "Come on, Ms. Marí, show me again how they do it on the West Coast."

"Don't put too much spice in that thing, Marí, you'll never get rid of him," I yelled out to her.

Alexis had already been distracted and was flirting in the face of some thick-necked football player who was trying to get her on the floor. I tried to coax her into dancing but only until another sharp pain hit me in the gut.

"You cool, Linney?" Alexis asked, noticing my discomfort as I grabbed my stomach and grimaced in pain.

"Yeah, I'm going to run to the ladies room. I'll be right back."

As usual the ladies room had a line, but I disregarded it and bogarted my way into the first stall that came open, daring anyone to challenge me. I locked myself in and with my head swirling, I held on to the sides of the wall. Then I felt it. First came a hard hiccup and that's when I tasted the burnt acid from those refried beans. This was the same shit that happened to me the night we opened at Teaz. With my head bent over the toilet, I gagged a few times, dry heaving, and then did something I'd seen countless women do in the bathrooms of Beverly Hills restaurants. I put my middle finger down my throat and threw up everything, splattering the chunky stuff on the toilet seat and the wall behind it. It was atrocious, and instead of feeling better, I felt worse. I was sure that next I'd have diarrhea, and I wasn't about to spend the night on a public toilet.

I emerged sweaty and clammy from the stall; standing

at the sink, I patted my face with the coarse paper towel from the dispenser. My back was perspiring, as was the space between my breasts, yet my body was shivering with cold. What the hell did I have, the bird flu?

I struggled to make my way back out to the bar, and that's when the room started to spin. I could see Marí and Alexis flirting with some guys who looked to be entertaining them, but I didn't feel quite stable enough to walk through all those people. Rather than attempt it and risk passing out in the middle of the floor, I went to the bar and ordered a bottle of water, then headed toward the red exit sign. If I had to, I'd just take a cab. It was then that Tobias walked up, grabbing me around the waist.

"Where you think you're going? The party isn't over yet," he said, holding onto my hips.

"Tobias, stop," I said, practically breathless. "I'm not feeling too good."

He whipped me around so he could see my face. "What's wrong? You want me to get your brother?"

"No, no, don't do that. I just need to get out of here and get some air."

"Come on, I'll take you home."

14
FAMILY AFFAIR

It was the glaring sunlight that woke me up Saturday morning. My body was weak and my mouth tasted like old guacamole. All I wanted to do was fall back into a coma for the day, and I would have, that is until I felt the body of someone next to me. My immediate thought was that maybe Julius had surprised me and come home last night. It didn't take me but a minute to realize that the man lying next to me was not Julius at all, it was Tobias. I was petrified.

I sprung to a sitting position. "Tobias, get up. What are you doing here?"

"Mmm," Tobias moaned, rolling over and dropping his arm across my breasts, pushing me back across the headboard.

I forgot all about being sick and jumped out of bed, snatching his pants and shirt from off Julius's suit rack.

"Tobias, get the fuck up. You gotta get outta here now."

"What's wrong with you?" he groaned, the covers falling off, exposing his small morning hard-on.

"Hurry up, come on," I said, picking up his boxers from the floor and flinging them in his direction.

"Yo, yo, Linney, why you tripping?" he asked, covering his face in anticipation that his shoes would be next.

"Please, Tobias, I don't know how you got here, but you gotta go!"

Noticing the desperation in my face, he sat up and slipped into his boxer shorts. "Damn, girl, it's like that," he said.

I'd managed to get into my robe but couldn't find the belt so I just held it closed with my arm.

"Yes, you have to get out of here. I don't know how this happened or what happened that you . . ."

"Whoa, Linney, hold up. I'm the one who bought your sick-ass home last night, remember?"

Then I remembered how I'd thrown up the night before at the Marbar. I must've had Tobias bring me back to the St. James. How had he known where to take me? Did I somehow tell him before I'd blacked out? What had the doorman thought when I'd come in with another man? I must have passed out from whatever had made me sick, because I would've never brought another man into Julius's bed, no matter how many miles away he was or how drunk I was. I didn't even want to imagine the confrontation I would've had to face had Julius caught me in his bed with Tobias. There would be no explanation good enough.

A perplexed Tobias was now dressed and waiting for me to unlock the door. I would've preferred he used the service elevator so nobody would see him but he had only brought me home. Though I wasn't completely sure that Tobias hadn't taken advantage of me.

"Tobias, look, I'm sorry for being a bitch about all this, and I really do appreciate you bringing me home, but you gotta go."

"Cool, whatever. I'll see you around."

With him gone I remembered Marí. She was staying with me for the weekend. Damn, what would she think, me bringing another man to Julius's apartment? I tiptoed back down the hallway to the guest bedroom to see if Marí was awake. I was relieved to see that she wasn't there, but then I wondered where the hell she was. The way the bed was tightly made, her clothes were neatly hung up in the open closet, and her toiletries and makeup set on the dresser, it didn't appear she'd slept there at all.

Now not only was I confused but also concerned about Marí's whereabouts. She didn't know that much about Philly and certainly wasn't the type to sleep around. Even worse was the thought that someone had slipped something in her drink, but my brother's friends were all stand-up guys. Still, she should've let somebody know where she'd gone.

I dialed Marí's cell phone and it went straight into voice mail. I found the number for the Ritz-Carlton, and when I called, the operator informed me that Marí Colonado had checked out the day before. Marí had never said anything about checking out. Had I mistakenly told her that she could move in with me? She hadn't brought that many clothes with her.

I tried Alexis but her phone was in voice mail. It was Saturday morning, so I should've known she'd be asleep until at least noon. The only other person I thought to call was my brother; maybe he would know who Marí left the party with.

I hurriedly dialed his cell—no answer—then I tried him at home, and after three rings he picked up.

"Maurice, did you see Marí last night before you left?" I asked, the cramps in my stomach making me run to the toilet.

"Sure did."

"I haven't heard from her. Did she leave the party with someone?" I asked.

"Sure did."

I tucked the phone under my ear and washed my hands.

"Maurice, what the hell is wrong with you? Why are you being so damn evasive? I'm worried about her. She never came back to the apartment last night."

"Sis, your little intern is right here, tucked underneath me."

"Marí? Marí's there with you?" I asked, and then sat down on the side of the tub, quite surprised that Marí was actually in the sack with my brother as we spoke.

"Linney, Linney, Linney, there's some things about your hot little intern that aren't for you to know."

"Is she all right?" I asked, sure that she was if she was with my brother.

"Marí, my sister wants to know if you're okay," I heard him ask her.

I couldn't hear her response.

"Marí says she's the best she's ever been."

I sat back on the toilet, praying that whatever was tearing my insides apart would stop.

"Maurice, I can't believe you. You're really low."

"What? What's wrong?" he asked, seemingly getting a kick out of all this.

"I'm telling you, you better not take advantage of her. She's not slick like those trick-ass girls you be bringing home."

Just then my line beeped. Its caller ID read that it was Julius calling from his cell phone.

"Bye, Maurice. I have to go. Tell Marí to call me."

"Sorry to tell you, sis, but that won't be any time soon."

I clicked over to Julius and made my way into the kitchen to start a pot of coffee.

"Jules, baby, what's up? Where are you?"

"I'm at my office in LA. Why, what's wrong? You sound jumpy."

"Nothing. I just wanted to know where you were," I said, feeling better that he was a thousand miles away.

"Caroline, what's up? You don't sound like yourself. Are you okay?"

"Um, not really," I said, then decided against using the curdled cream I found on the door of the refrigerator. "I didn't want to say anything, but I got sick again last night, you know, like before."

"Baby, what's up with that?"

"Nothing. Seriously, I'm fine now. I was going to call you. My mother has invited you to my father's retirement party."

"When is it?"

I took a sip of the strong black coffee and couldn't imagine how people drank the bitter stuff everyday. "It's in two weeks, on a Saturday. Julius, you have to come or I'll be forced to go with some doctor or lawyer she'll try to set me up with," I pleaded.

He started laughing. "I don't know, Linney, it all depends."

"C'mon, Jules, we never spend time together anymore." I was begging because I felt so guilty about Tobias having been in his bed.

"Aww, baby, you sound pretty sweet when you beg."

The second sip went down easy, without any cramps. "Boy, don't play with me. Come on now, Jules."

"Things are pretty tight right now, so I might be able to be back there by Friday."

"Good! I'll let her know. I love you."

I felt like I'd been through a whirlwind in the last twenty-four hours. First I got sick at the club, woke up in Julius's bed with Tobias, and then found out that Marí had spent the night with my brother. The only good thing was that Julius was still in LA. Right now I needed something normal to get back on track.

I took a shower and was sure to feel myself for any signs of penetration, but with Tobias one could never tell. I checked both the bathroom and bedroom trash cans for condom wrappers and didn't find any, which could have been either good or bad. Everything seemed normal, yet I still stripped the bed and changed the linens.

Since Marí was with Maurice and it didn't sound like he was letting her go anytime soon, I had to find something to do. I phoned Alexis to see if she wanted to hang out, and to my surprise she'd already gone ahead and made reservations for us to meet up that evening, around eight-thirty, for dinner.

Still with nothing to do all day, I phoned my mother and we made plans to meet at Bliss for lunch on the Avenue of the Arts.

Now that my day was set, I pulled up a stool to the kitchen counter and turned on my laptop to make a few entries into my blog from what I could remember of last night's gossip.

> Who's creeping with who in Philly? I made my social debut in Philly last night starting at the Marbar and was practically overwhelmed with celebrity sightings. There weren't any upcoming concerts, so why was Sleepy Brown, hiding behind those big ass shades, following R&B artist Shante (girlfriend of Lil Hype) into the Rittenhouse?
>
> Something is up in Philly and believe me, you'll find it all in my blog. Stay tuned . . .

So as not to be late I left the apartment at noon to meet my mother. She was just walking into the restaurant when I arrived. The maître d' seated us at a table near the window.

"Mom, look at you. You look great, all revitalized and glowing! You been to the spa getting another one of those raindrop massages you were telling me about?" I asked, stroking her freshly manicured hands.

"Thank you, dear, but you look a little tired and that makeup isn't hiding those bags under your eyes. Are you staying out late?" she asked, already signaling for the waiter.

"Mom, please, I'm fine," I said, wishing I'd kept my sunglasses on.

"Well, I might as well tell you, your father heard from one of his patients this morning that you were traipsing about the city last night. I told you, Caroline, Philadelphia is a small town."

"Shit, I thought he was retiring. What's he doing still seeing patients? And just so you know, I wasn't traipsing, I was
out with my brother," I stated, not positive that I couldn't
have gone elsewhere with Tobias during my blackout.

"Caroline!"

"Oops, I'm sorry," I said, apologizing for having cursed.
"Mom can we please change the subject?"

The waiter interrupted briefly and we ordered lunch.

"We can change the subject for now, but I'm telling you,
don't go getting yourself a reputation like that Hilton girl."

"You're really funny, Mom, if you think my reputation is
anywhere near that of Paris Hilton."

I watched my mother sip on her drink. She was very
classy, and I hoped that in thirty years I'd be as classy as she
was. Just hopefully not as bothersome.

"If you say so, but if our friends find out you're living
with a man who hasn't even proposed to you, it won't look
nice. He is bringing you to the party, isn't he?" she asked,
then spread her napkin across her lap.

I thought to myself maybe inviting my mother out to
lunch wasn't such a good idea after all. I was getting nause-
ated just from the conversation.

"Mom, if you don't stop badgering me, I'm walking out
of here. Now, how are the plans for the party coming and,
yes, Julius will be escorting me."

"Oh, all right. Stop being so sensitive about everything."

Our lunch arrived and even though the scallop shrimp
rolls were tasty in the chili dipping sauce, I wasn't sure how
much I'd safely be able to eat.

With talk of the party, mother simmered down. I knew
that all one had to do was turn the subject to a social func-

tion and my mother was full of chatter. I couldn't quiet her for at least the next thirty minutes and that's how I liked her, focused on anything other than me.

An hour later as we waited curbside for the valet to bring her car, I noticed celebrity publicist Sasha Borianni sashaying from around the corner of Locust Street. It had to be an omen. How many times had I heard about her and the exposure she'd gotten her clients, which from my understanding was a very short list? It would be awesome if I could talk with her about some career moves for myself. A publicist might have been just what I needed. If anyone could raise my profile for whatever my next career move would be, I was sure Sasha Borianni could.

"Mom, look I'm going to run back inside to talk to Ms. Borianni," I said as I watched the tall, sophisticated woman stroll across the Avenue of the Arts.

"Who?" she asked, looking around to see who I was referring to.

"Sasha, Mom, Sasha Borianni, the publicist chick," I said, pulling on her arm.

"Oh, yes, I've heard of her," she said, then kissed me on the forehead. "Go ahead. I'll talk to you later."

I deftly made my way back into the restaurant, hoping I could catch her before she was seated. The last thing I wanted to do was interrupt her while she was eating. It happened to me all the time and quite often it was annoying. Luckily she was seated at the bar.

"Good afternoon, Ms. Borianni," I said respectfully, extending my hand to her. She was probably about fifty years old and the epitome of class. Sasha had a beautiful set of locks that were sprinkled with gray, and she dressed her ass off—no stylist needed.

Her eyes swiftly took me in, and she replied, "*Top of Da Charts,* Caroline Isaacs." She cocked her head to the side. "Better known to your fans as Linney?"

"Wow, you know me," I said, surprised, my hand across my chest. Boy, did I feel stupid with that move.

"Of course—my grandchildren keep me up with everything hip-hop."

"It's a pleasure to meet you, Ms. Borianni."

"Please, Sasha is fine. Here, sit down," she said, gesturing toward the seat beside her.

"Thank you."

She motioned for the bartender and I ordered a bottle of water—how tacky.

"I've been on your blog a few times. You really keep your audience informed. I've even found some useful gossip on there myself."

"Thanks. Everyone seems to be doing it these days," I said, sounding mushier than I'd ever been. If she was going to be at all interested in working with me, then I needed to come across strong.

"So how do you like being back home?" she asked.

"I like it, but I'm still trying to get my arms around my career as a whole and where I want to take it," I said, holding my glass but not drinking from it, which allowed my sharp eyes to take in her Gucci eighty-fifth anniversary purse. I knew how much that cost.

"I take it you don't have a publicist."

"Not really. Only what the studio provides."

"I see." She reared back on her stool and crossed her long legs. "Your father, he's the retiring plastic surgeon, correct?"

"Yes, ma'am." Long pause while I tried to think of a way to smoothly introduce the subject, then I simply blurted out: "I was hoping I could talk to you about possibly representing me."

"I like your style, Caroline, and you know what I'm going to do?" she said, then paused as if considering what she was going to say.

I didn't say anything because I had no idea what she was going to do.

"How about I give you a little something to put on your blog?"

I leaned forward, glad to see Sasha was taking me in her confidence. "I'm all ears."

Her fingers traced the rim of her glass of Rémy Red. "You know *America's Next Top Model,* the girl who won recently?"

"Of course, she's gorgeous," I exclaimed honestly.

"She won't be for long—at least not her reputation," she declared.

"Why, is she gay or something?"

"That's nothing," she said with a shrug. "However what she is . . ." Sasha took a small sip of her drink. "Well, the girl's a smoker."

"Cigarettes?" I asked, not wanting to assume the worse.

She pursed her lips in response.

"She's smoking crack?" I asked, a little too loud.

"That's right, and she does it right at home with that rock and roll boyfriend of hers."

I was sure my mouth had fallen open. This was a piece of gossip that hadn't even been rumored yet.

"Sasha, can I . . ."

Someone at the door caught her attention, and she waved

over a broad man whom I immediately recognized as T.O. If she could revive his career, then I knew she could assist me with furthering mine.

"Here comes my client."

I stood up to leave, but not before saying, "Are you sure you want me to add that to my blog?"

"What the hell. It'll probably hit the papers, so you might as well get a jump on it."

"You have been way too good to me," I said, and then extended my hand again.

Holding my hand with both of hers, she said, "Hey, we Philly girls have to look out for each other, right?"

"Right, but I wanted—"

"I know. I'll have my assistant call you to set up a time."

That was all I needed to send me on my way. When I returned to the St. James I called Kia and, starting with Marí's whereabouts, I recounted to her all that had taken place in the last few days, concluding with the scoop I'd received from Sasha Borianni.

The only other thing Kia seemed confused about was my having gotten sick again. She insisted I take a home pregnancy test. I told her that was the least of my worries, since I took my birth control pill every morning before I even got out of bed.

The only thing she could think of was that I was working myself too hard. Which all of a sudden reminded me that Marí and I were supposed to go to the Body Klinic for a massage.

I hung up with Kia and dialed Marí to see if she still wanted to meet. Not only did I want the company but I also wanted to know about her night with my brother and how that had gone down.

"Marí, where's your butt at?" I said as I changed into my sweats.

"I'm just leaving your brother's."

"You still want to go to the spa?" I asked as I turned over my watch to check the time.

"Definitely. Do you think we can get an appointment?"

"It won't be a problem. The place is down around Rittenhouse Square. Why don't you meet me there?"

The Body Klinic was set up in an old brownstone at Twentieth and Walnut. I felt relaxed as soon as I entered the reception area. The receptionist said Marí Colonado hadn't arrived yet, and so as not to loose my slot, I followed her to the back to get undressed.

When Marí arrived I was already lounging in my terry cloth robe, sipping on some mint tea. I had to admit she already had a bit of a glow about her. The spa had only been able to fit us in for a couple's massage, which meant we'd be side by side. That was great because then we could talk.

"Linney, I hope I'm not too late," she said as the masseuse showed her where to get undressed.

"No, we're going in together. That cool with you?"

"Sure, sure, just give me a minute to change."

We met back up in the sweetly scented massage room. I slipped out of my robe and under the sheet, as did Marí. The lights went out and the candles flickered, giving the room a golden glow.

"This was such a good idea, Linney. I'm glad I didn't miss out."

"All right, time to dish. So Marí, how'd you get hooked up with my brother last night?" I asked as the masseuses began simultaneously with our necks.

"Your brother is really a nice guy," she said, her head tucked into the table's face rest.

"Yeah, right. Don't let him play you."

"Can you keep your hands right there please?" Marí asked her masseuse, who'd begun kneading her back.

"Trying to get those kinks out from last night, ain't ya, girl," I teased.

"You know, Caroline, I wanted to ask you about some of those people at the party. They were some really big-name players in the club last night, huh? Do you know them all?"

"It was an interesting mix, but it'll become regular once you're around them enough. By the way, did you check out of your hotel?"

"Yeah. I've decided to rent a brownstone over on Twentieth and Mt. Vernon. I wanted something with, you know, a little more space, since I might be staying past the summer if I get the job."

"Really? But I thought the job at Hustler's was only going to be for opening night. And I know it's none of my business, but are you going to be able to afford that?"

"I'll be fine, your brother owns it."

The surprise wasn't that Maurice owned the place; my brother had quite a few properties in and outside the city. The surprise was in just one night she'd gotten him to rent her one in the high rent districts. It must be true that Hispanic women really do have some spice in that thing.

We were quiet for a while as the masseuses worked down our thighs and asked us to turn over. I wanted to fall asleep, but then I wouldn't be able to enjoy the erotic state this always put me in.

"Okay, Marí, now it's time to give up the scoop. I know the party was jumping, but how'd you end up going home with Maurice?"

"Who me? I don't know. Where'd you get to?"

"I got sick again. I didn't know what the hell was wrong with me so I took my ass home."

Marí stopped the masseuse, sat up, and swung her legs over the side of the table.

"Sick? Not like before I hope. Maybe you should see a doctor."

"Come on now, don't change the subject. I'm alright. Lie back down."

Marí lay back down and inquired, "I saw you talking to some guy. Who was that?"

"Tobias, ex-boyfriend, nobody important. Oh, wait a minute. I know what you're doing. . . . No kiss and tell with my big brother, huh?"

"Caroline, you're crazy."

"Seriously though, it's cool. But hey, you want to do dinner tonight? I've made plans to go out with Alexis, but it'll be more fun with the three of us. After all, this is supposed to be our girl's weekend."

The masseuses indicated they were finished. Marí was ready to get changed, but I lay there.

"Thanks, Caroline. But I've already got plans with Maurice," she said, then scooted off the table and into the shower.

I sat there stupefied. Marí had just ditched me for my brother. And had no intention of heeding my warning about his being a playboy. I felt like a used dishrag.

Marí and I left the spa together but went our separate ways. She claimed to have some errands to run before leaving for Atlantic City with my brother. I simply went back to Julius's and took a nap.

Around eight that evening I met up with Alexis at Nectar, a sleek French-Asian themed restaurant in Berwyn for dinner. She was at the bar waiting for me prior to our being seated.

"What's up, Linney? You sure look refreshed," Alexis said after we were seated.

"After last night I was in desperate need of a spa visit, so Marí and I went this afternoon."

"I swear that Marí chick looks familiar to me, but I just can't pinpoint where I've seen her before. You drinking tonight?"

"Now, why you gotta refer to her as that Marí chick, I know that means you don't like her."

"And that you're right about. She just seems to be all up on you."

"Alexis, she's my intern. She traveled with me from LA. Now stop it and give the girl a break."

"Whatever, but I'm telling you, there is something not right about her."

"Why would you think you know her and hell no, I'm not drinking."

"When we were at the Marbar this other Puerto Rican girl came up to her like she knew her, but Marí brushed her off."

The waiter took our order of lobster dumplings, garlic crusted shrimp, and tuna sashimi with soba noodles. Who did Alexis think was eating all this food?

"What are you saying?" I asked.

"Uh-huh, now your ass is curious."

"They always act that way when they see you on TV, like they've known you forever."

"Yeah, I know. But the girl swore she knew Marí was from somewhere in Philly."

"Believe me, Alexis, neither you or anybody else knows the girl. She's from Englewood, California, and this is the first time she's been to Philly—probably her first time on the East Coast."

"Sure, whatever you say, she's your intern. But there's something up with that little Chicana."

"Anyway, since you're searching for dirt on Marí, how about she went home with my brother last night."

"You're bullshitting, right? Oh, so maybe that's who she's been after!"

"She never came home last night and when I called around looking for her, come to find out she'd been lying up with Maurice all night. And to top it off they're on their way down to A.C."

Alexis took a hit of her Tequila. "Haven't these sistahs learned anything yet about Philly's number-one playboy? If she's your friend, you better warn her," she said. I'm sure she remembered that a few years ago she'd almost become one of those girls. Maybe that's why she didn't like Marí.

But Alexis's taste in men varied with her moods. When she was feeling reckless she liked her men hardcore, and when she was being more of the society girl, then she'd chose one of the successful white collar corporate boys. With her looks, she had her choice when it came to men.

After dinner I was too tired to hang out. I think the massage and the day's events had taken their toll on me, so rather than drag myself out to a club, I headed back to the quietness of the St. James. When I got in I put on my robe, turned on the television to an episode of *Girlfriends,* cranked up my laptop, and made myself comfortable on the couch. There was one little thing I needed to add to my blog that would have the wires jumping—the hot gossip Sasha had given me.

Q: Who's strutting the catwalk all the while sucking on the glass dick?
A: America's Next Top Model.

It would've been hot if I could've added that my intern was out creeping with my brother, but I'd never do that without asking Marí first. I'm sure my brother could not have cared less. The more spotlight on him the better.

The more I thought about it that night, the more I hoped that Marí wasn't setting herself up to get her feelings hurt by my brother. I was sure he was spending time with Marí because she was new to the city, and her being young and gorgeous was icing on the cake for him.

I decided to stop worrying about Marí and whatever she was doing with my brother. She was a big girl and I was sure she was quite capable of handling herself.

Later that night when I got in bed, my thoughts turned to Julius. I really missed him and it was no fun being in Philly alone. The partying was great, but when I wasn't out I was here, by myself. I was glad his clientele was growing, only now he was always so damn busy. At least I was able to hold on to the fact that eventually he'd make an honest woman out of me.

15
CLOSE CALL

Monday morning I arrived at the club early so that I'd be able to return the favor by greeting Marí with a cup of her favorite cappuccino. I didn't want her to think it was always about me, plus I was still hoping to bribe her into giving up the tapes on whatever kind of promises my brother might've been filling her head with.

On Sunday it rained so I lay around the apartment watching movies and sleeping. I guess Kia had been right about my body needing some rest and relaxation. I'd even managed to fix myself dinner—it wasn't anything much but cooking was something I hadn't done since leaving California. I would've made the trek out to my parents but my mother insisted it was raining too hard and that she didn't want me to get sick and not be able to attend my father's party. I'd phoned Julius three times over the weekend and had simply been unable to reach him.

Before I could even get to the coffee shop the driver's side tire blew out on my mother's Benz. I managed to steer the car over to the side and was grateful that the cop hadn't given me a ticket as I sat parked in a loading zone on Sansom Street. I had to wait an hour for the Mercedes service people to show up. I made a mental note to talk to my brother about getting a new Benz from his showroom.

When I finally made it to Teaz the parking lot was full, but inside the club as I walked up the ramp it was exceptionally quiet.

"Hello? What's going on, people? Did somebody die up in here? I thought this . . ." I stopped talking as Marí briskly walked up to me and put her arm through mine. Everyone else was seated as if someone were about to make a speech.

"Linney, where've you been? We've been waiting for you," she said.

I turned my face to hers and tried to explain. "For me? Well, my tire—"

"No, no, it's fine. But listen, I have an announcement and I wanted to wait until you got here before I shared it with the crew," she said, positioning herself at the front of the club near the stage.

I didn't know why Marí was beaming and I certainly hoped that she wasn't about to announce to the entire crew that she'd spent the weekend with my brother. Whatever her news, I took heed to brace myself.

"This is it. Remember I shared with you at Caroline's parents that I was up for the job of hosting the opening of Hustler's? Well, it turns out I got more than that—I'm going to be the permanent host of *Hustler's Live,* their new show!" she announced unabashedly.

The crew clapped heartily in response, which made it noticeable that I was the only one standing there with my hands folded across my chest.

"What happens now, Marí? Are you leaving *Top of Da Charts*?" Juan blurted out from behind the deejay booth.

"No. I mean, not unless I have to. Do I, Caroline?" she pleaded, her hands in prayer.

You sneaky bitch, I wanted to call her, but I wouldn't lower myself like that.

"Um, of course you don't, but won't you have to get prepared?" I said, hoping my expression didn't read how I was really feeling.

"I have plenty of time. They're giving me a few weeks and I would never just run out on you guys. . . . I'm so excited. They have all these interviews coming up, *Entertainment Tonight*, BET, and MTV News."

"Well we're all here to support you with whatever you need, right, Linney?" Brad added.

"Caroline, do you think you could put my news on your blog?" Marí asked hopefully. "You know how much your fans love being the first to be in on the latest news. It would mean so much. Please, pretty please?"

All eyes were on me. "Of course, Marí. Whatever you need me to do."

As everyone crowded around Marí to congratulate her and hear more details, I eased away from the crowd and made my way upstairs to the dressing room.

That afternoon, once the show wrapped, I hustled to get my ass the hell out of there, but not before Marí caught up with me and asked if I wanted to celebrate with her and the crew by going out for drinks. I lied and told her I had plans and that we'd find a way to celebrate later. Right then I needed to be as far away from her as possible.

Leaving the parking lot, I phoned Alexis, who told me she had a date for the evening but would be happy to make it a double if I was up for it. At this point I was up for anything. I just needed to get out of my own selfish thoughts, because the green-eyed monster had taken up residence in my body.

It was midnight when I went down to the courtyard of the St. James to meet Alexis, and we headed over to Palmers nightclub at Sixth and Spring Garden.

I wasn't going to bring up the subject of Marí's new job; it was the last thing I wanted to talk about, but I didn't have to because Alexis had already heard. Rather than go into any details, I told Alexis that all I was interested in doing was hanging out and getting loose with my girlfriend.

"No need to say more," she said, then offered me a rolled blunt to light up. I hadn't puffed on one since the last time I'd been to Philly and hung out with her.

"So who are these guys we're meeting?" I asked.

"They're cousins, Simon and Keith Bennett. Keith is mine. I've been doing him for a few months. He's a young Wall Street thug and Simon is, sorry to say, his dope-slinging cousin."

"Are you serious? They're from here?" I took a long toke of the blunt.

"Yeah, parents live in Devon."

"And what's his name, Simon is a hustler?"

"It's not like he's going to admit it, but when a Negro has moved out to Delaware, has two cell phones, is heavy into real estate, drives a rimmed-up Escalade, and has never had a regular job, well, what do you think? Oh yeah, and by the way, I should warn you he's just a tad bit corny."

"Whatever, I don't care. Let's do it."

Once again because of my notoriety we got inside Palmers free. Simon, who'd been waiting inside, proved to be a class act when he tipped the bouncer with a hundred dollar bill. We made our way up two sets of steep and crowded steps and got situated inside the packed club. I could barely see, it was so dark, but once my eyes adjusted I was even more surprised to see that people were actually dancing. At most clubs I went to there was some dancing, or maybe more like swaying, but not like at Palmers. Here people were getting it on, and the later it got, the better it was.

I was standing against the wall bouncing to the music when Simon dragged me onto the dance floor. I finished off my third Rémy Red, sat the glass on the bar, and decided I was no longer Linney from *Top of Da Charts,* I was just a sistah out to get her grove on.

"Baby, I like you," Simon said as I turned around and allowed him to grind up on my ass.

I didn't answer him because I doubted he could hear me. The music was really pumping and I was dying to see this dee-jay Boo I'd heard so much about. If he were really that good, then I surely wanted to invite him on *Top of Da Charts.* Hell, maybe we'd even bring the show to Palmers one night.

I wasn't sure how long I'd been on the hot and sweaty dance floor, but I could see that I was wasted by the way Simon and I seemed to be slow dancing when folks start-ed holding their lighters up to Lil' Kim's song. But still I kept hanging on to Simon, who was rather enjoying all my drunken attention.

"You wanna go outside and cool off?" he screamed in my ear so I could hear him.

I shook my head yes.

I stopped to tell Alexis I was going outside, and before she let me she pulled me aside. "You're going a little heavy tonight, aren't you, Linney?" she asked.

"You think so? I'm doing me tonight, that's all."

"If you say so, but don't go getting sick on me."

"Look, I'll be right back. I'm going outside to cool off."

Rather than stand outside the club with all the other people waiting for the let out, Simon invited me to sit in his tricked-out Escalade. He turned on the air, pumped up the music, and began rolling a blunt.

I offered to lick the cigar paper to seal the weed inside.

"Hell, I'm a lucky ass nigga to be out with Linney from *Top of Da Charts*."

"That's right, baby. It's me and I'm fucked up tonight," I said.

He flicked his lighter and I took a long drag of the strong weed.

"Take your time," he said when I began to choke.

"Whew, I can feel that shit already," I said, pushing my sweaty hair back from my face.

"You always this live, Linney?" he asked after taking a long draw.

I knew I was leading him on, but I didn't care. "I don't know, maybe you got me this way."

I fumbled for the seat controls because it had me sitting straight up.

"Can you adjust this seat for me?"

He reached over to adjust the controls with the added surprise of letting his tongue loose inside my mouth. I tamed him a little by wrapping my arms around his neck as he lowered the seat to a flattened position and attempted to climb on top of me. What the hell was he doing?

Simon was a man about his work, as he wasted no time pushing up my shirt and ravishing my breasts like he was hungry. In the drunken haze I was in I didn't care what he did or how corny he was. So I responded by moving my hands up the back of his shirt, but our legs became entangled and my knees kept hitting the dashboard.

With my eyes closed I felt Simon when he pushed my seat further back, spreading my legs apart with his knees and roughly positioning himself between them. Next thing I knew I heard the unsnapping of my jeans.

That's when it hit me. What the hell was *I* doing?

"Simon, wait, wait. Hold up a minute!"

"What's wrong? Let me just taste this thing. You'll be all right. Ain't nobody gonna see you." His fingers were already trying to get between me and my jeans.

I kneed him just enough that he bumped his head on the visor.

"No, uh-uh. I can't do it," I said.

"Girl, come on, don't do me like that," he said, his hands now clenched to my breasts.

"I'm sorry, Simon, I can't. This ain't me. I'm sorry, I gotta get out of here," I said, and reached for the door handle.

He put his hands up in the air and said, "Yo, you got that. I ain't about to force myself on no woman. It's your loss, I ain't about to sweat you," he said, then flung the door open to let me out.

16

EYES ON THE PRIZE

I'd promised myself that I wasn't going to let Marí's success bring me down, and so far I'd done a pretty good job. Plus Marí was in such a great mood around the set that anything negative I might have said would've made me look like a bitch.

On Friday's show I had the pleasure of interviewing the young boxing phenom, Yusaf Mack, who was about to costar in his first movie, *The Champion Inside.* Teenage girls were wrapped around the block waiting in line to be in the audience. I was the first person to do such an in-depth interview of the celebrity athlete, who had the reputation of declining interviews. The more personal content of the interview reminded me of my goal to one day step away from the world of hip-hop and move onto a more serious side of the industry. Doing what, I wasn't quite sure, because I knew Oprah wasn't about to step aside anytime soon, but I could still see myself sharing the table on the set of *The View*.

To my benefit I now had someone who was going to help me with those decisions. Sasha Borianni had invited me to have drinks with her at three o'clock to discuss my future in the entertainment industry. And then, to top it off, Julius was arriving later that evening.

Sasha had me meet her at Borianni's, an Italian restaurant owned by her family at Twelfth and Spruce. I'd never had such scrumptious calamari with the accompanying spicy marinara sauce. But what really made my toes tingle were the two small glasses of Limoncello they served us.

"How are the plans coming for your father's party? I hear it's going to be quite the event."

"My mother thinks so, and she's about to drive all of us crazy."

"I see. So tell me, how long have you been doing *Top of Da Charts*, Caroline?"

"It's been four years now," I said, dipping the tender fried calamari into the sauce.

"I assume you're ready to make a move."

"I think so, but I'm always being careful because my parents are worried that I'm going to become part of the Hollywood gossip circle."

"So are there any skeletons in your closet I should know about?"

"I don't think so," I said, glad that I'd stopped myself from doing something stupid with Simon.

"You're dating that sports agent, right?"

"Yes, Julius Worthington. He's coming into town tonight."

"That man has made quite a name for himself. What is he, about thirty? Any wedding plans yet?"

"Yes, he's thirty but no official plans yet. He's been wanting to wait until he's financially set. Plus he comes from divorced parents, so sometimes he trips on the whole marriage thing. I mean, anytime it's rumored that Denzel is living in a hotel after twenty-two years with Pauletta, that's pretty bad."

"Some of them last, some of them don't. It all depends on what you're made of. But this is about you, so listen, this is what I've heard. MSNBC is about to start searching for an entertainment correspondent and my thought is that you'd be perfect for that job. They need someone young and vibrant who knows the industry. What do you think? Sound interesting at all?"

"Now, that's some serious exposure. You think I'd really have a shot at it?"

"Damn right, especially if you're my client."

I liked Sasha's confidence. She meant business, and I could see why she'd made such a name for herself in the PR industry.

After lunch I was anxious to get back to the St. James to prepare for Julius's arrival. When I'd spoken with him earlier in the week, he'd told me to be well rested and ready because he was planning a special dinner for the two of us as soon as he arrived. I didn't want to do anything to delay that because my biggest hope was that he might be bringing a big fat engagement ring along with him.

The day before I'd had a bikini wax, with just a touch of hair left on what Julius liked to refer to as my landing strip. I'd had my hair tossed up softly and, of course, the usual manicure and pedicure. I wanted to look exceptionally sexy for Julius, who was supposed to be in Philly by six that evening and to the condo no later than seven. If nothing else, Julius was always prompt. My mother was really going to like that about him.

The first thing I did was set the alarm clock so I could take at least an hour nap, even though I doubted I'd be able to sleep. When after fifteen minutes sleep didn't come I decided instead to make a quick entry into my blog. One would be about Marí, as I'd promised her, and the other about my publicist.

> The first thing I wanna announce tonight is that I have a publicist. Not just any publicist, but Sasha Borianni. Need I say more?
> The other big news is that my intern, Marí Colonado, is an intern no more as she's been offered to host the pop culture show at Hustler's, the brand new nightclub and casino on Columbus Boulevard. Please do check her out!

I turned off the laptop and went in the bathroom, lit a few candles and ran my bath water, sprinkling in some jasmine bath beads. I was soaking in the warm water and listening to Alicia Keys when I found myself beginning to nod off, but it was too late for a nap now. Stepping out of the tub I followed up by moisturizing my skin with my Délices body cream and perfume. I was determined that Julius Worthington would be unable to resist me tonight.

I'd purchased a sheer yellow dress by Stella McCartney that hit me right below my knees, with only four buttons in its low-cut back. There was no need for a bra because the cups held my breasts perfectly in place. The only thing extra was a G-string on my bottom and the dress's matching long scarf tossed around my neck. The bonus for Julius would be the three-inch, two-strap Swarorski crystal studded heels I was wearing. This outfit surely would have Julius going crazy.

I was in the bathroom putting in my earrings when I heard the beep of Julius's door and I knew he was home.

I stepped out into the hallway. "Julius?" I asked, to make sure it wasn't Marí coming back for her things. "Is that you?"

"Baby, damn, look at you," he said.

I'd never displayed myself like this before in such a grown-up way, as Julius would call it. I posed in the hallway, walking its length as if it were a runway. A surprised and approving smile covered his face, as he stood there in a khaki suit, white shirt open at the collar, and a pair of Gucci loafers. That was my man.

"Here, these are for you," he said, offering me an armful of white and yellow roses.

I thought he'd forgotten to close the door behind him, but then I was surprised when three men in tuxedos appeared.

"What's this, Julius?"

"Dinner, baby. Catered just for the two of us."

Part of me was a teensy bit disappointed that we weren't going out, but then I realized all the trouble Julius had probably gone through to set all this up for us. And what I wanted more than anything was to be with him not so much in a crowded restaurant full of strangers but alone all to myself.

He instructed the caterers to do their thing and, lacing his hand through mine, he said, "Let's go out on the balcony while they get ready."

"You sure?" I asked, wondering how he would survive without his eye on ESPN.

"Never been more sure."

The waiter handed him a tray with a bottle of Krug and two champagne flutes. I waited for Julius to slide back the glass doors and then followed him out into the warm air.

"Julius, this is so nice. How'd you know to do all this?" We held our glasses up for a toast.

"'Cause I love you, Linney. You've been working hard—we both have—so we deserve a special night."

The caterer had jazz music playing, Gerald Veasley, Julius said. Julius had been trying to get me interested in jazz and tonight suddenly it sounded so ideal.

"Let's dance," I suggested, and brought his arms around my shoulders. We slow danced across the balcony.

"Are you sure we're not celebrating your getting a new client?" I asked him, just to be sure this was all for us.

"Hell no, baby. I'm celebrating you," he said, then nibbled on my earlobe. "Isn't that good enough?"

Julius and I were halfway through our first bottle of champagne when one of the waiters served us a tray of raw oysters. He sat the tray on the table and we slurped down the tender aphrodisiacs, feeding them to each other. The next thing we were served was fine French caviar, which Julius fed to me. I wasn't sure why but he'd pulled out all the stops.

It all made me giddy with love for him and just plain happy that he'd taken the time out to make me feel so special. Right then the waiter nodded to us that dinner was ready.

"What are we having?" I asked, assuring myself that I wouldn't be getting sick tonight.

"I'm having you," he whispered, his hand reaching under my dress, caressing my thigh.

I patted it away. "First I'm enjoying all of this," I told him, and stepped back inside.

Our meal that night consisted of filet mignon, an arugula salad with what tasted like a honey oil dressing, baby asparagus, and roasted red potatoes. All of this was topped off with a sugary crusted crème brûlée.

"How was your dinner?" Julius asked.

"It's good, you're good, everything's good," I said after filling myself.

"That's the way I like to see you, nice and full, and not off that sushi shit you're always eating."

I smiled at him because he was always so concerned with how I took care of myself.

When we finished eating we retreated to the balcony so the caterers could clean up and let themselves out.

"Wait right here. I'm going back inside to get the champagne."

I stood there against the railing gazing over at the bright lights of the city, which seemed to be competing with the bright lights of the star-filled sky. I could see the Ben Franklin Bridge on one side and the blue lights from the Circa building at Thirtieth Street on the other.

I heard the sliding glass door opening behind me and the warmth of Julius's body pressed against my back. It was going to be awesome spending the entire week with him. I took the champagne glass from his hand and sipped the bubbly stuff.

"Stay still . . . close your eyes . . . I have something I wanna do. Don't turn around, not yet," he said, the tone of his voice already beginning to arouse me.

I closed my eyes, anticipating that this would be the mo-

ment he slipped a ring on my finger, when instead he slipped
the scarf from around my neck and tied it in a blindfold over
my eyes. He gently turned my head around and kissed me,
filling my mouth with his tongue. I moaned with delight
beneath his lips.

"Here," he said, reaching around and helping to bring
the champagne flute to my lips.

"You trying to get me drunk tonight?" I asked, wondering how far Julius would go, and that's when I felt his fingers unbuttoning my dress, turning my skin to fire beneath
his touch.

"Jules, what are you up to?"

He didn't answer.

With my dress hanging loosely at my waist Julius ran his
tongue across my shoulders and down the center of my back.

"I missed this soft skin," he whispered as he tilted my
head forward and kissed all around the base of my neck.

I shivered with delight.

"You like that, baby?" he crooned just like the jazz musi-
cians he loved to listen to.

"Yes, Jules, I like it a lot," I said, not sure if he could even
hear me.

His lips were covering every inch of my back as if it were
the only thing about me that existed. His hands cupped
my breasts and he massaged them gently, then pinched my
nipples—the more excited I became the harder he squeezed—
until I felt my nipples would burst.

"Linney, I missed you, baby," he said softly, and then in a
surprising move he literally ripped off my dress.

"Jules!" I tried to say, but he covered my mouth with his
hand.

Meanwhile, Julius's succulent mouth made its way down my right thigh, and then up the left, saving the cheeks of my ass for last.

This man had never been so freaky with me before, and we were in public. What if someone saw us? Even up here it was possible with all the high-rise condos. Were the waiters even gone? Julius was usually so gentle with me, like he was scared I would break, and now for the first time I was anticipating him showing me a different side. I was ready. I took another swig from my champagne flute, some of its contents dripping from the corner of my mouth I caught it with my tongue and then threw the glass over the balcony and into the street below.

"How about a little more?"

I didn't bother to answer. This was his show.

Then I felt something cold on my skin and that's when I realized Julius had gotten down on his knees and was dripping the cold sparkly champagne down between the spread of my ass. He followed up with his tongue. Had he not held me up I would have collapsed from the sensation alone.

"Oh-h-h-h-h, Jules, don't do that," I murmured, unable to believe this man was actually drinking champagne from out of the crack of my ass. Again he poured.

"Ahhhh, oh, oh, oh."

He did it again and again until I screamed out to those very stars that were lighting up our night.

I was sopping wet from Julius's new style of foreplay. Where the hell had he learned all this? That's when I felt him entering me, not my pussy but my ass. Had he gotten it wrong, did he not know what hole it was? We'd never gone there. But it wasn't his dick, it was the mouth of the Krug bottle. My body tightened but the teasing of his tongue on my clit relaxed me. He repeatedly continued to spit the stream of champagne into my ass and kept at it until I was bent over the railing. Over and over he told me he loved me until it was vibrating in my head.

Our night might have started off romantic but romance had no way of ever touching this. Julius had my body on fire and I could feel yet another orgasm bubbling up from deep inside me. Julius must've felt it too, because he was pushing the bottle harder, in and out. I was scared it would break inside but I didn't want to release the grip my muscles had around it. Slowly, he eased it out and that's when I felt the tears start to fall. How could I ever have thought that Julius could not fully satisfy me? I went limp and he had to hold me. He turned me around and placed my hands on his dick. I couldn't remember it ever being that hard before. It was like forged steel.

Now it was his turn. On the way to my knees I pulled his pants and boxers down at the same time. The first thing I did was open my mouth, letting his balls land on my tongue.

"Git it, girl, git that dick like you like it," my man ordered, signaling me that I was doing everything right.

He pushed the scarf from over my eyes, yanking my head back.

"Open your eyes. Look at me, Linney."

Our eyes locked in the moment, mine full of tears.

"Fuck, Linney, damn it, I love you," he cried out to me, assuring me that he never wanted his dick to leave the warmth of my mouth.

I took him in deeper and when his knees began to buckle. I knew if I didn't stop I'd be swallowing every drop of him. I eased his dick from my mouth and I heard him sighing.

Rather than steady myself on my feet Julius hoisted my legs around his waist and plunged himself inside me so hard and fast that it took my breath away. I closed my eyes and buried my head in his chest for support, except that when I opened them I found myself staring at Marí.

I gasped because I was so weirded out by her presence, but it was too late to stop what was happening and I really didn't want to.

"Fuck! Caroline, fuck!" Julius commanded.

Why was she here? I thought to myself in between Julius's hard thrusts. Why was her face pressed against the patio doors, her knuckles rapping on the glass, smiling at us? I prayed Julius hadn't invited her as part of this sexual feast we were wrapped up in.

I turned my attention back to him. "Come on, Julius. Come on, baby."

"No, no, not yet, I don't wanna come yet," he said, all the while slamming my back up against the wrought iron railing.

I winced from the pain of the railing, my hands gripped his shoulders and he had me by the waist, jamming that dick into me unmercifully. I wanted to tell him to stop, that Marí was watching, but I also had to admit that her presence was somewhat turning me on.

I couldn't think straight, my thoughts were too jumbled. Why was she watching and why was it turning me on, or was she just in shock from catching us like this?

"Julius, stop, no, I don't wanna cum like this, please, please. . . ."

"Come on, baby, you gotta let it out. Cum for me."

To hell with Marí, I had to get my shit off. I concentrated on cumming but kept her in my eyesight.

"You ready, Jules?" I grunted in his ear in a voice that wasn't mine.

"Yeah, come on, baby, let it out."

That was all I needed to hear for my orgasm to burst from inside me, its warmth dripping down my thighs.

By the time we'd finished that night, at least on the balcony, Marí had vanished, almost as if she hadn't been there.

The rest of my weekend with Julius was magical. He had so many things planned for us that I didn't have to do anything but follow his lead. Still feeling uneasy about Marí's appearance, on Saturday morning I had him change the entry code to the apartment, never giving him the real reason why.

We had breakfast that morning at Lacroix at the Rittenhouse Hotel, then we were off to see the Body Worlds exhibit at the Franklin Institute. Afterward we took a helicopter ride, landing atop Trump Taj Mahal in Atlantic City to shop at The Pier at Ceasars and to have lunch at the Palm.

By the time we got back to the St. James I was exhausted. Julius suggested we take a nap, but I wasn't about to let that happen, not before I gave him the best slow neck of his life. Sleep came easy after that. By seven that evening Julius was waking me up so we could have dinner at North by Northwest, and then we drove out to Glenside to hear Dianne Reeves at the Keswick. If I'd never liked jazz before, I was loving it now.

Sunday morning I couldn't have been happier when he suggested his only plan for us that day was to sleep in. I felt like my weekend with Julius had been beyond my wildest fantasies—I never knew I could be that happy, and it was all because of him.

17
ALL THINNED OUT

When Monday morning arrived, I went to work practically skipping, I was so high from my weekend. Julius and I hadn't formally gotten engaged, but I knew it wouldn't be long because all the signs were there. He had never in all the years we'd been dating told me he loved me so many times.

It was undoubtedly the best weekend I'd had since arriving in Philly, and to make it better he'd be there all week, accompanying me to my father's retirement party on the weekend.

When I drove into the parking lot of Teaz I noticed Marí getting out of a C-Class Mercedes, courtesy of my brother, I'm sure. I still had to talk to her about the move she'd pulled at Julius's.

"Marí, yo, hold up," I said as I ran to catch up with her.

"Caroline," she said nonchalantly, and kept walking.

"Wait a minute, I want to talk to you."

She stood still and said, "Go on."

"What was up with you watching me and Julius fucking the other night?"

"Sorry," she mumbled, and walked away.

I couldn't believe her. I didn't know what the hell her problem was. Did she have her ass up on her shoulders because she had her own show or was she really some kind of freak? Maybe she was simply embarrassed that I'd caught her watching us, but if that were the case, shouldn't she have been more apologetic?

It was more than that. During the course of the week Marí was totally uninterested in *Top of Du Charts*. We'd had great guests everyday starting with 50 Cent and his rival Jadakiss. Sasha even stopped by one afternoon to sit in the audience, but Marí had no interest in meeting her. Every time she was asked a question or was asked to do something, it was as if she were being interrupted. Probably because she was either laughing in conversation on her cell phone or using her BlackBerry.

I wasn't about to let her attitude or that of the crew, who clearly noticed the distance between us, take me out of my space. So each day, if Julius was working in the evenings when I got off work, I'd simply drive out to my parents to assist my mother with my father's retirement party.

On Thursday I'd joined my mother for the final taste test with the caterer, which she'd somehow managed to convince my father to sit through with us. As we sat there talking and tasting, I realized that more than the upcoming party, Marí's name had been dominating the conversation.

We were tasting mini desserts when my mother exclaimed, "Maurice and Marí were here for dinner yesterday,"

"That's nice," I commented, having no interest in their developing relationship.

"I left you a message to join us but you never got back to me," she said, passing me her fork filled with strawberries.

"Sorry. I went to a Phillies game with Julius."

"They really seem happy together. Don't you think so, dear?" she asked, turning to my father.

My father was not paying us any attention but seemingly enjoying the food being set before him. "Who?"

"Maurice and Marí," she answered.

He took a sip from one of the three champagne glasses before him. "Oh yeah. This is good—this one," he said, pointing to the glass he'd emptied.

"Marí is a nice girl. I like her and she's been a tremendous help with the party with so many great ideas," my mother added, getting up to make a note.

"She's all right I guess," I answered, becoming agitated and pushing the plate of petits fours away from me. I'd had my fill of desserts and certainly of Marí.

Suddenly interested in my opinion of Marí, my father said, "I don't think your mother means just 'cool,' Caroline."

"Maybe she might be the one. What do you think?" my mother asked, hopefully not of me.

I downed the half glass of one of the sample champagnes in front of me. "The one for what?"

"For your brother to settle down with. Are you even listening?"

I didn't want to dog Marí out to my parents, but I just wasn't feeling that comfortable with her anymore. I wasn't sure how she'd got my brother pussy whipped but that was his problem. It certainly wasn't jealousy on my part. It was just something about the way Marí had changed that had begun to gnaw at me.

"Mom, she's just infatuated with Maurice. I wouldn't expect too much out of it. You know how your son is when it comes to women—he has a short attention span."

As I rode back home that night I passed off thoughts of Marí when I realized I had only two, maybe three nights at best to enjoy with Julius. I didn't even want to imagine how lonely I was going to be when he returned to Malibu.

After we'd played around in bed that night and he'd fallen off to sleep, I got up to take a warm bath. Once out of the tub, I was standing in the mirror combing my hair when I noticed all these strands left in the comb. I tossed them into the trash can and combed through my hair again. This time when I pulled through it there were even more, and when I looked in the trash I realized there were strands in there from earlier in the day when I'd combed my hair that I hadn't even noticed. I picked up my brush and looked at it, where I also found way more strands than normal. What the hell was happening? I picked up my various hair products to see if anything was different. It wasn't. I started to wake Julius up and complain to him, but when I looked over at him he was so deep under the covers I was sure he wouldn't be able to comprehend anything I tried to tell him.

I checked the time on the clock radio; it read 11:30 P.M. I took the phone into the living room and dialed my girl in LA.

"Kia, I need to talk to you before I think I'm tripping."

"What is it, girl? I'm getting my makeup done and I only have about ten minutes before I go on set."

"I think my hair is falling out," I said ruefully, while I studied the ends of my hair.

"What? What are you talking about? Your hair is beautiful."

I fingered through my hair and a few strands fell between my fingers.

"I know, but I'm serious. I mean, it still looks healthy but all these strands keep coming out in my comb and it's been happening for a while, I think. What am I gonna do?" I cried to her.

"That does sound kind of weird. Who's been doing your hair in Philly? You haven't been going to any of those cheesy ghetto places, have you?"

"Hell no. Raphael did it for me a few days ago and I had it tossed yesterday at a place he referred me to. Maybe I should talk to him. He had to have noticed it," I said, lying back on the couch.

"It's probably just stress."

"Stress from what?" I said defensively. "I'm so sick of everyone saying I'm stressed. I'm fine, Kia."

"Calm down. Damn, Linney."

There was no reason for me to lash out at her. "I don't know, you might be right. I think next week after my father's party I'll make an appointment to see a dermatologist."

"Good girl. Now I have to roll. They're calling me to the set. Hey, worse case scenario, you go for a full weave. Gotta go. Love you, Linney."

Hello, Caroline. It's Sasha Borianni."

"Sasha, hi, how are you?" I asked as Raphael did my makeup and I sipped a cup of tea in the dressing room at Teaz.

"I'm good, but listen, I have some pretty interesting leads I'd like to talk to you about. Do you have a minute?"

"Sure, what are they?" I asked, and then informed Raphael I needed a moment.

"Have you ever thought about acting?"

"Not really, why?"

"There may be a role in an upcoming independent film centered on a female deejay, and you've been in front of the camera long enough, so I thought I'd run it by you."

"I don't know. . . . I don't have any experience as an actress."

"Don't take your experience so lightly. You put on an act everyday on the set of your show. I've also spoken to Gayle a few times about some stories she's doing in *O,* and I think if we set this up right, maybe I could pitch you to her for a younger platform that Oprah might be working on. What do you think?"

"You mean Gayle as in Oprah's best friend," I asked, amazed that Sasha had such awesome connections that she could pick up the phone and call such powerful people.

"Yes, the one and only."

"Wow, Sasha, that would be incredible. I'm following your lead from here on out," I said, checking my hair in the mirror. When I'd asked Raphael about my hair he said he'd also noticed the shedding and that it was probably just normal. I didn't think so.

Sasha and I continued to talk as we mapped out the steps for my future, and when I hung up with her I was all charged up for the day. Luckily for me, Marí hadn't come into work that morning.

Maurice and Marí had been spending so much time together that I rarely hung out or talked with her much anymore. We saw each other at work but mostly talked about the opening of Hustler's.

The show that day was off the hook because my guest was Solstice. She was a new artist who was already blowing the top off the billboard charts. Once the show wrapped I was out of there quickly because I had an appointment at the spa, and then that night Julius was escorting me to my father's party.

Julius and I arrived at my parents' around five-thirty so we'd be there to help greet their guests. We both looked so good that I almost didn't want to go. Julius was dressed in a designer tux and I had on a short black dress that my mother had made by her favorite designer. I felt like Julius and I were going to the prom, as the king and queen, of course.

The party planner and my mother had done a spectacular job with the estate. The media was stationed at the front of the house and were taking pictures and rolling film of the guests as they arrived around the circular driveway and passed their cars off to the parking valets.

There were vases filled with calla lilies that lined the walkway through the meticulously manicured grounds to the back of the house. The waiters and waitresses were all in tuxedos. There were hot and cold hors d'oeuvres being served throughout the cordoned off estate.

I'd never seen the grounds look so beautiful. I'd watched my mother and the staff during the week piece things together but the end result was amazing. The landscaping, the tents, the decorations—yes, my mother had gone all out and surely blown whatever budget my father had given her. From now on I was taking lessons from her.

Julius and I were standing inside the entrance to the tent when my parents came up to greet us.

"Julius, I'm so glad you could make it," my mother said, my father on her arm.

"Mrs. Isaacs, you look absolutely beautiful. Now I see where your daughter"—he winked at me—"gets her beauty," he said, smiling at my mother.

Julius was such a charmer, I loved him.

My father gave Julius a hearty handshake. "Good evening, Julius. Caroline tells us you have some pretty talented and well-paying clients on your roster."

I wanted to kick my father for mentioning anything about money. Julius was classy enough to play it off.

"Yes, sir."

"I guess I'll have to start watching more ESPN now that I'll be retired. I'm glad to see you didn't just settle into one sport."

While Julius and my father talked sports and business I walked off with my mother.

"Mom, everything really looks beautiful. You should be proud of yourself, because I am."

"Thank you, dear. Have you spoken with your brother today? I told him to be here no later than six," she said, looking around to see if he'd arrived.

"Nope, sure haven't," I answered, still fascinated by the elegance of the estate. I could've sworn some of the trees and shrubbery hadn't been there the day before.

"What about Marí?" my mother asked.

"No, why? Is she still . . ."

There was no need for me to finish my question. I saw them walking toward us. Maurice had stopped to shake hands with Julius along with Marí, who appeared to be tucked in my brother's hip pocket.

My mother had warned me that they were coming together and that I'd better be nice, but it still surprised me to see her show up on my brother's arm. How could it possibly have gotten so serious between the two of them so fast? Marí never even wanted to talk about him. Hell, I wasn't asking her if he was a good lover; I just wanted to know whatever trash he was using to fill her head so she'd think this could possibly be a serious relationship. Whatever it was, I planned to have a little chat with my brother. He never held back from me, especially when it came to his women.

On the other hand, I'd never seen Marí look so beautiful. No longer looking like the twenty-one-year-old intern who'd showed up at my office in Beverly Hills, Marí now looked like a woman, a gorgeous one at that. Where had she gotten that dress? I knew it was expensive and she certainly didn't make the money to afford it, which only indicated that my brother had taken her shopping.

As they got closer I couldn't help but notice the stunning diamond choker clinging to Marí's neck. He sure was spending a lot of time and money on a girl he was having a fling with.

"Hello, Marí. Don't you look like somebody's million bucks."

"I wouldn't say quite that much, but pretty close. I see you look dazzling as usual," she replied.

"Thank you."

"How are preparations going for your new show?" I asked.

"It's coming together," she said.

I knew I'd be polishing up my small talk technique, especially when there were over two hundred guests arriving that night, so I excused myself from Marí and began making my rounds.

During the cocktail hour so many cameras were flashing it felt like I was on the red carpet of the AMAs. I guess I never realized how big a man my father was. But tonight there was no denying that he was not just an African American plastic surgeon, he was the top surgeon in the world.

Promptly at 7:00 P.M. the velvet rope to the big white tent was removed and people began making their way inside. The interior of the huge tent looked like a white and glass menagerie. There were white roses everywhere and the tables held so many pieces of china and silverware that I wasn't even sure what to use.

At our table along with my parents were Marí, Maurice, my uncle Lee Roy and his wife, and my father's partner, Dr. Carlton Saggs and his wife. At that moment I decided to let my issues with Marí go for the night. It was more important to just enjoy the event, plus this night wasn't about me, it was about my father. Watching Marí and my brother interact, it was easy to see that they actually complimented each other. Maybe, I thought, she wasn't so bad for him after all. My parents surely seemed smitten with her, and they were also enjoying Julius's company. I guess seeing her in a different light, outside of the studio and out of competition, made it easier on the both of us.

After the guests had taken their seats my uncle Lee Roy took to the podium to welcome everyone. He gave an introduction and told some tall tales about my father when they were kids—some serious, some funny. All I'm sure, had been enhanced. Then he read through the program, giving us an overview of how the night would proceed.

During dinner there was too much noise from the silver clanging and conversation among the guests for anyone to speak. The plan was that starting with dessert my brother would be the first to speak, and then Dr. Saggs would be introducing the video highlighting my father's career. All of this would culminate with a short speech from my father.

As the waiters began to serve dessert my brother took to the podium. He used this opportunity to show off all those degrees my parents had paid for. He spoke eloquently as he expressed his love and admiration for our father. It was emotional, though, as he talked about all my father had sacrificed, including time with his family, to be a success. All that missed time with me that I used to complain about seemed not so important after all when I thought about my father's accomplishments.

There were so many aspects of my father's life that I knew nothing about. My father may not have had the son of a sharecropper's story, but money had been scarce for his family as a kid in Newark. And he'd made sure it wasn't scarce for his children or his family members. The next person up was Dr. Saggs, who spoke of their early struggling practice when patients preferred white surgeons rather than black ones. But now my father was the one in demand over any other surgeon in the country. It came as a surprise when he announced that a scholarship was being given in my father's name. The crowd gave a standing ovation, one of many to come during the night.

As Dr. Saggs wrapped up his speech, the video began on the large screen that dropped from the ceiling of the tent. Everything my mother touched had gone without a hitch.

There were photos of the family, footage of my father's speeches, and even some of him performing his great nip and tuck surgeries. I was so proud seeing him accept so many awards and being recognized for sponsoring global philanthropy efforts. It wasn't only that he changed the faces of people who wanted to be beautiful, he worked tirelessly and often without payment on disfigured children and burn victims.

Witnessing so many different aspects of my father's life, I realized that even though we didn't have the normal family life with him gone all the time, he really had done all this for us to be proud of his legacy.

When the film drew to a close the audience was on their feet clapping. I was dabbing my eyes with a handkerchief when all of sudden I heard gasping throughout the tent. Then I heard Outkast singing ". . . Caroline . . . I know you'd like to think your shit don't stank . . . roses really smell like pooh-pooh . . ." and my mother's shrilling scream and Julius's cursing.

I snapped my head up and thought maybe I was imagining things, but the tent had gone quiet and the visual was clear.

There I was on the screen, in that dirty bathroom of Thelma's Diner, my pants down around my ankles, my head banging against the stall door while Vin, the hitchhiker, wrapped a fistful of my hair around his hand and fucked the shit out of me.

"Turn it off! Got damn it, turn it off!" my father belted out as the screen went black.

I couldn't move from my seat. I closed my eyes, praying that what I'd just witnessed and heard wasn't real. My uncle Lee Roy was the first one to jump onto the stage and start talking, but no one was listening. All eyes were on me as my parents came over and escorted me out of the tent.

"Caroline, what the hell kind of stunt was that?" my father bellowed at me as he yanked me over to a cocktail table that was being cleared.

My mother said nothing, just stood next to him crying. Her party had been ruined.

"Do you have any idea what you just did? You not only ruined your own reputation but that of the entire Isaacs family," my father continued.

I didn't know what to say. I'd never do anything to purposely disgrace my family. I couldn't even imagine who'd done this to me. What contact did Vin have with my family to set up something like this?

Then Julius came storming out of the tent followed by Maurice. They were all waiting for me to say something, to make some sense of it all, but I couldn't.

"I'm—I'm so sorry," was all I could say, as tears streaked my face.

The photographers who had come out of the tent gathered around and began flashing pictures of the scene we were making.

"Either get the hell back inside the tent or fuckin' leave," Maurice belted out to them.

Julius let loose on me. I could see the hurt in his face. "Sorry? Fuckin' sorry isn't good enough."

My mother finally spoke up. "You need to go, Caroline, please, so we can try to salvage the rest of this night."

"Julius?"

Instead of answering, Julius yanked me by the arm, practically dragged me past the small crowd that had gathered outside the tent, and took me around to the front of the house.

Yelling at me, he said, "Do you know what the damn media is going to do with that? Have you lost your mind?"

"Julius, I'm so sorry. I can explain," I cried, really not able to. I put my hand on his arm.

Violently he shook it off. "Explain what—getting fucked in a dirty-ass bathroom? How am I gonna show my face around my clients with this shit?"

"Julius, I didn't do this. Please, you gotta help me. You have to understand."

"Ain't shit to understand except you're a dirty bitch, Caroline," he said, spraying spit in my face. He shouted to the valet as he walked away from me, "Bring me my fuckin' car!"

"Julius, wait. Please! Please wait," I said, taking off to run after him as fast as my stilettos would allow me.

"Fuck you, Caroline. I'm done," he said, and took off without me.

As I stood there bewildered and unable to fully grasp what had just happened, I felt someone's hand on my back. I turned around and saw my brother. I fell into his arms, crying.

"Come on, Sis. It's gonna be all right. I'll handle things."

"I'm done, Maurice. I've ruined everything. Julius, Mom, Dad, they'll never forgive me. I've made a fool of myself and the family."

"Here, take these," he said, handing me his keys. "I'll have someone drive you to my place. You stay there until I figure out what to do."

"Are you gonna come home later? Maurice, please, I don't want to be by myself."

"Um, I'll see, but you might need some time alone. Don't worry, you just lay low and whatever you do, don't talk to anyone, you hear me?"

"Where are you going to be, Maurice? What if I need you?"

"I'll be at Mari's. Just call if you need me."

When I got to Maurice's loft at Locust Point I didn't even bother to take off my dress. I just curled up in his bed. I now knew why people always went into the fetal position when they were hurting. You somehow wanted to close out all the pain and wrap yourself tightly so as not to let any more hurt inside.

Sleeping was impossible. I switched on the television and the first thing I heard was my name, so I turned it off. All I kept thinking about was how something so awful could have possibly happened. Who could've been so evil to do such a thing to me? In just one night I'd ruined my entire life, and lost the people that meant the most to me: my parents, my Julius.

An hour later the phone calls began. It was a good thing I was at Maurice's or else the house phone at Julius's would've been ringing as much as my cell. I didn't dare pick it up. Maurice had told me not to talk to anyone. I watched the numbers—some I knew, some I didn't. I wanted to answer when Alexis called but I couldn't. Neither did I answer when I saw Brad's number show up. Even Kia was text messaging me from California. How had she found out so fast? The only call I did reach out to answer was the one from Sasha.

"Hello," I whispered in between sniffles.

"Caroline, it's Sasha, and you already know it's not good."

"Sasha, I swear I don't know how this happened. I swear I'd never do anything like this."

"I'm sure you wouldn't, but it's only been an hour and I've received an abundance of calls. You can imagine how fast and wide this is going to spread. By tonight those photos will be all over the Internet. The media will have a field day with this. I'm not even sure what kind of twist I can put on this one."

"But I don't understand why someone would do this to me."

"I don't know, honey, but I have to tell you that I don't think I'm going to be able to move forward with our plans until we see how this all plays out. You'd better brace yourself because this scandal is going to be huge. I also advise you not to comment on it to anyone, not even your friends. What I will do is call your father's publicist and see if they'd like my assistance."

"Thank you. I'm sorry. I understand."

"And, Caroline, there's one more thing. . . . *People* has cancelled your being on their list."

I held the phone in my hand, squeezing it as the pain of tonight's absurdity traveled throughout my being. Why had this happened? Who hated me so much to want to destroy me?

Chapter 19
UNVEILED

August 2006

It had been a month since the disaster at my father's retirement party and I was basically living in solitude at my brother's apartment. When I went to work that first Monday I'd lost it on the entire crew. They'd been buzzing all day, whispering, trying to treat me as if everything was normal. But how could it be normal when reporters and television crews were not only calling but also hovering outside the building for a chance to interview me.

And of course every time they mentioned me, they had to talk about the fact that my father was the world-renowned plastic surgeon, Dr. Albert Isaacs. Clips from the footage had made their way onto various Web sites and across the covers of the tabloid magazines as well as the papers. My face in addition to that of my family's was splashed over the entertainment shows, and reporters had begun following me back and forth from Maurice's loft at Locust Point to Teaz.

My brother stepped in where he could but basically I was on my own.

One day I was so depressed I'd had to let Marí take the show, and what was sad was that the audience never missed me. *Top of Da Charts* had gone through the roof, making my producers happy, but it was the kind of publicity I could've done without. I refused to be interviewed about it—there was simply nothing I could've said. It wasn't as if I could deny it was my face on the video. There was no doubt about that. So for me, all I could do was count the days until my show returned to L.A.

It was tough to ignore how the entire city was gossiping about me and my sexcapade on the road. Me, who kept track of celebrity lives and their comings and goings, I'd now made a spectacle of my own life and that of my family. My friends in California had been leaving me messages telling me how great they thought it was, even to the point of telling me how sexy they thought Vin was. I guess now I was one of them.

And as for Julius, there was no going back, no forgiving on his part, and I couldn't blame him. So after I'd called him seventy-nine times in two days, leaving him thirty-two messages and receiving no response, I gave up.

Maurice's condo was in dire need of cleaning and my brother's being a minimalist made the dust and trash that had gathered look even worse. He and Marí had come by one day to bring me clothes, but I refused to let her clean up and just ushered them back out the door. But there were memories of my life before that horrid night all around my brother's condo. The one thing he did have a lot of, like my father, was a collection of black and white family photos that he'd enlarged and framed. And he had every magazine I'd ever been in. But now I was sure all of that would be replaced with Marí. She had my brother's love and attention and would soon have that of my family. How could I blame them?

Monday evening I sat alone another night in my brother's loft. I didn't feel like eating any of the leftovers from my take-out meals, so I settled for a bowl of cereal, but since the milk was sour I just sat on the couch and ate it dry. Needless to say I had begun to lose too much weight. When the intercom buzzed I prayed it was my brother with some message from my parents or Julius.

"Who is it?" I said into the speaker on the wall.

"Open the damn door, Caroline. It's Alexis."

I didn't want to open it but I also didn't want to be alone, so I unlocked the door and returned to the chair where I'd been watching reruns of *Will and Grace.*

"What the fuck is up with you?" she asked when she came through the door.

"Nothing, nothing at all," I answered, not even looking at her but still glad she was there.

"How long are you going to hide out in this stank ass apartment?" she asked as she went from room to room turning on the lights.

I shrugged my shoulders, curled my feet under me, and turned up the volume on the television.

"I'm not hiding out. I've been to work."

"Yeah, I've seen you. Wow, great job," she said sarcastically as she cracked opened the vertical blinds to let in the lights from the city.

"And what's up with all this shit?" she asked, referring

to the mess of empty food containers and clothes that were strewn about.

"If you're going to be a bitch, then just leave," I told her.

"Your brother have anything to drink around here?" Alexis asked as she walked toward the kitchen.

"Yeah. Over there in the cabinet," I said pointing to the dining room.

I hadn't had a drink since my parents' party. I'd been so afraid that if I tried to drown that awful night out, I wouldn't have been able to stop.

"Come on, we're having a drink," she said, after searching through the kitchen cabinet for two clean drinking glasses.

Alexis poured us both a half glass of Jack Daniel's.

"I'm not drinking that stuff. What's wrong with you?"

"I think you're going to need it, especially with what I have to tell you.

"The last thing I need is to get sick."

"First of all, where's that Marí at?" she asked.

"Living her life, I guess."

"Well, let me just tell you this—that girl has crossed all lines and broken all the rules."

Trusting Alexis and the stern look on her face, I took a sip of the brown liquid and frowned as it burned my throat.

"What's going on, Alexis? I doubt things can get any worse."

"It's like this—your little intern, Marí . . . remember I told you the bitch looked familiar to me that night at the party?"

"Yeah. What about it?"

"Marí is from Philly."

"No way. She would've told me."

"Obviously she didn't, and that ain't all she didn't tell you. You remember back in our senior year at Branfman when VMT initially came to the school to do that damn reality show you got all hooked up in?"

"Like I could forget," I said, and then took another sip.

"Remember the big scandal with Coach Ramos when our stupid parents accused him of 'molesting' us? Well I should say *you,* since you were his favorite. Anyway, your lil' Ms. Marí is Coach Ramos's daughter."

This had to be a game Alexis was playing on me. Coach Ramos had been our lacrosse coach at Branfman Academy and we all loved him. Some of us even had huge crushes on the handsome Hispanic man.

"Coach Ramos? Get out of here. You're lying. They don't even have the same name," I said, my mind unable to get a grasp on the memory of Coach Ramos and what Alexis was trying to tell me.

Alexis answered me by opening her purse and pulling out a brown envelope, from which spilled out a series of news articles held together with a paper clip. She pounced down in front of me on the floor, dropping the clippings in my lap. "Take a look at these," she said.

I took a big gulp of Jack Daniel's and sat my glass down on the coffee table. The firewater felt good going down.

Skimming through the clippings, I read the headlines along with the photos and their captions. One of the captions was of me and Coach Ramos: "Coach Ramos and his team captain, the young Caroline Isaacs, daughter of the esteemed Dr. Albert Isaacs."

There were also photos of Coach Ramos standing with our entire lacrosse team. The one I stopped to really inspect was a picture of Marí and Coach Ramos, her father, that read "Coach Antonio Ramos and his daughter Marí Colonado-Ramos in happier times."

There was no mistaking it—the young girl was Marí. She looked to be about thirteen.

Everything was fuzzy in my head. What the hell was going on here? In all the months I'd known Marí and through all our conversations, she'd never even mentioned she'd lived in Philly. Or that her father had been Coach Ramos. She had to have known about my relationship with him. I'd even taken her out to Branfman. But then the more I thought about it, Marí had never mentioned much of anything about her family.

I leaned back against the chair and closed my eyes in hopes that through this conversation with Alexis, I'd be able to answer at least one of the questions in my mind.

I had especially taken to Coach Ramos and all the special attention he'd showered on me, always telling me that I wasn't just beautiful, I was smart too. He was constantly telling me how much potential I had and that I shouldn't just rest on my looks or my father's success. The other girls often got jealous at his doting on me. But what Coach Ramos seemed to give me was the attention and time I lacked from my own father. Never had he tried to come on to me or any of the other girls, for that matter.

The problem started when Video Music Television came to our school and based a reality show on wealthy suburban teenagers and our winning lacrosse team. The show highlighted our close relationship with the coach. We thought it was great, all of us being on television, cameras following us around.

All the attention raised concerns from our parents that maybe he was a little too close and had a little too much influence over us girls. Because of this my mother became the one to lead the pack saying that maybe he had been taking advantage of us, especially me. An investigation ensued into possible inappropriate behavior, during which time Coach Ramos was suspended. We students protested but it fell on deaf ears. All of this too was caught on tape by VMT.

Two months later, after a thorough investigation, the coach was found not guilty, but the accusations caused him to lose his job permanently. Branfman wanted no black marks on their institution.

One night about a month after all this went down we were told that Coach Ramos and his wife, Marí's mother, had argued. Supposedly she'd rushed out of the house and gotten into a fatal car accident.

As Alexis and I recalled those vivid details, before I could verbalize what was on my mind, Alexis did it for me.

"You know Marí becoming your intern was no damn coincidence."

"Alexis, I don't know what to say. What does she want with me? I loved Coach Ramos. I even attended his wife's funeral, the whole team did. I had nothing to do with my mother leading that witch hunt."

"More importantly, Caroline, to hell with what happened back then. The real question is who spliced that video at your father's retirement party."

I stood up, poured myself another drink, and began to pace the floor. "Alexis, Marí was the only one who knew about that tape. We thought the hitchhiker stole it."

"Well, now you know he didn't. And that poor guy is probably going through his own hell—or who knows, maybe he's enjoying it. That shit was kinda hot." Alexis raised an eyebrow and smirked at me.

"That's not funny, Alexis." I shook my head. "I can't believe Marí would blame me for her mother's death."

"Why not?"

"I mean, it just wouldn't make sense for someone to go to those lengths."

"Then why didn't she tell you who she really was?"

Alexis had a point there.

"Did any of you check her references when she came to work at *Top of Da Charts*?"

"I guess. I mean she was hired the same day we interviewed her. She really didn't have much to check—she was still in college."

"I'm telling you—you better check her ass out, 'cause she's bad news."

The next morning I woke up with a hangover, but I downed two painkillers with a cup of coffee because I needed my head to be clear. After the discovery Alexis had made, I was determined to find out all I could about Marí Colonado and why she'd come into my life.

My first call that morning before going to work was to Loyola Marymount in California. I asked the operator to put me through to student information. When I reached the receptionist I told her I was calling from VMT and was considering their student Marí Colonado as an intern and was hoping I could get a reference from student affairs.

"What did you say the name was?"

"Marí Colonado." I spelled it out for her as I sat there looking through the news clippings again.

"Okay, hold on."

She came back on the line after a long minute. "We don't have anyone by that name enrolled here."

"Are you sure? Can you check again? It's Marí Colonado."

"Ma'am, I checked."

Holding the picture of Marí and her father, I said, "Wait, can you check another name? How about Marí Ramos?"

"If you want. Hold on," she said, obviously impatient with me.

I waited as I felt my headache ease up.

"I'm sorry, but Marí under Colonado-Ramos, Ramos-Colonado, or any other Marí is not enrolled at Loyola Marymount University. Any other name you wanna check?"

"No, thank you anyway."

This was getting worse by the minute. Marí had totally lied about her background. The bitch wasn't even registered there as a student.

By the time I arrived at Teaz that afternoon to tape my show I was all but ready to kill Marí. How dare she come into my life under the guise of an intern and try to destroy everything I'd built! Because of Marí I hadn't spoken to Julius since that dreadful night. He wouldn't answer my calls nor would he respond to my e-mails. When I'd gone past his condo I found out he'd again changed the code. My parents were barely communicating with me and I didn't dare go out to their house. I was sure any day they'd disown me and write me out of their will, thereby stopping my monthly checks.

It was now time for me to blow Marí's cover.

"What's going on here?" I asked one of the PAs when I walked up the ramp and into a group standing in the middle of the floor.

Nobody answered. They were all engrossed in whatever it was that Marí was saying. I too wanted to hear what she was telling them.

"It's not that I wanted to fool anyone. But I must admit that I embellished my résumé to get the position here at *Top of Da Charts*," Marí stated.

"I was so excited to work with such a great group of people and I'd heard students do it all the time—and now I pray that none of you will hate me."

"Don't you mean you lied, Marí?" I yelled from where I stood behind everyone.

"Hi, Linney. I was just telling the crew—"

"What, Marí? Just telling them how you've manipulated everyone here and my family?"

"Shhhh, Linney, come on. Don't start," Juan said.

"I'll be quiet all right, long enough to listen to more of her bullshit. Go on, Marí, tell us some more."

Marí looked around at the group surrounding her and said, "So that's why I wanted to let everyone know that this will be my last day at *Top of Da Charts*."

"Marí, we hate to see you go, especially right now. We all love you so much, don't we?" Sharon said, looking around at everyone as they nodded in agreement. When the hell did Sharon fall in love with Marí?

I interrupted them again and blurted out, "Yeah, why don't you tell everyone what a fraud you really are? Don't y'all see Marí was the one who set me up?"

Sharon grabbed me by the arm and said, "Caroline, what is wrong with you? Marí has been nothing but a friend to you. Who do you think has been holding this show together ever since you made a fool of yourself?"

It didn't phase Marí; she ignored me and continued.

"I really feel bad for misleading everyone, so I think it's only right that I leave."

"Misleading!" I yelled, and then broke from Sharon's grip. "Why don't you tell the truth, Marí? Tell us how you manipulated everyone just so you could destroy me. What about Coach Ramos and Branfman?"

"Caroline, I'm not sure I know what you're talking about," Marí said.

"I'm talking about my father's party. I know it was you who spliced that tape."

"Linney girl, chill the hell out," Raphael said, clearly disappointed in my behavior.

"No, I won't chill out. I know it was her."

"Caroline, I would never do anything like that. Are you okay? Please don't blame me for that," Marí said, her smarmy tone of voice making me sick.

"Yeah, Linney, it's not right blaming Marí," Brad added.

I couldn't believe that my own crew had turned against me. Why couldn't they see this was all Marí's doing? That she'd planned for everyone to hate me.

I stood there listening as the crew tried to persuade her to stay, telling her that it was okay, that they understood. Yet she kissed and hugged everyone and said her good-byes. I told myself maybe now it was over. She'd used me until she got what she wanted. Maybe now she'd go away.

I left Teaz that afternoon unable to do my show.

The next morning while reading Michael Klein's column in the *Philadelphia Inquirer*, I saw that he wrote about Marí being the first Hispanic woman to head up a nightclub and casino and that she was going to add lots of spice to the nightlife scene in Philly at Hustler's. It also mentioned that her previous mentor, Caroline Isaacs needed to take some advice from her mentee because word from the street was she'd been reduced to covering the opening for VMT and *Top of Da Charts.* Talk about being at the bottom of the charts.

To make things worse Maurice had left me a message that he and Marí were ready to move back into his condo.

The next morning I cleaned myself up and headed into work. I pulled Brad and Sharon together and told them we needed to meet right away.

"Sure, Caroline. What's going on?" Brad asked as we sat in the crammed office space.

"I think we should get back to L.A. This scandal will never die as long as I'm here."

"Well, we can't go yet. You're covering the opening of Hustler's for VMT."

"Is that really true? Nobody asked me."

"The question is are you stable enough to handle it."

"Of course I am. But I can't work with Marí. I'm telling you, she set me up."

Sharon tried to be understanding. "Linney, you can't really believe that. Talk like that doesn't even sound like you. Marí didn't have anything to do with what happened at your parents'."

Brad must've been getting impatient with me when he said, "I'm sorry, Caroline, but this is your responsibility. You're covering Hustler's for us and that's all I have to say on it."

"Yes, Linney. It'll be a good shot in the arm for you at this time. The show hasn't been that exciting lately. You just aren't yourself anymore and the audience knows it. Once this is over we're taking the show back to LA."

"Don't you understand? Covering the opening means covering Marí, and I just can't do it," I cried. But even as I said those words I knew I didn't have a choice. I was under contract and the last thing I needed was to find myself in court.

Kia had flown into Philly for the opening of Hustler's. She'd wanted to come out for something big and this was going to be it. More importantly though, she was in town to offer me emotional support, which was something I was in desperate need of. Poor Alexis had been taking on as much as she could and sometimes I think she was more pissed at Marí than I was. She was certainly disgusted with my brother's behavior. He'd literally fallen head over heels for Marí and I'd simply been pushed out of his life. But for tonight I had my friends Alexis and Kia by my side, and they'd see to it that I got through this night.

Alexis was meeting us at Hustler's since Kia went there early with me. Even though Kia had heard the Marí story before, my anxieties had me rambling on about how violated

I'd felt when I found out that Marí had lied about her past and aired my sex tape. Having heard the story a month ago when it all happened, Kia nodded along, listening patiently, but that's what friends were for. I guess I repeated the story so much because somehow I still couldn't believe it.

I took my time getting ready that night and drove Raphael crazy with what I should wear and how my hair should be styled. I wasn't usually nervous before I went in front of the camera, but this was different. This time I'd be interviewing Marí. The day before she'd requested a prepared set of questions before she'd agree to allow the interview, which was good for me because that way I was sure to stay on track.

I told myself in the mirror that I was Linney from *Top of Da Charts,* but even as gorgeous as I looked, I still felt depressed.

Since the show was live I had two cameramen following me, including Juan for my audio. We hit the red carpet interviewing arriving celebrities as they entered Hustler's then moved inside to the casino floor. I was beginning to relax. This was my thing. Next we went inside first the club and then the casino, so viewers could get a firsthand view of Hustler's.

The casino floor was jammed with gamblers at every table, and people were waiting in line for a chance at the slot machines. The press was huddled throughout, interviewing any celebrity who crossed their path.

I interviewed the club's owner and some of his partners. The mayor was present along with some bigwigs from Harrisburg. Everyone had a hand in the success of this venue.

I met up with Marí at the top of the stairs leading to the restaurant and hotel, where she was holding her interviews.

Before we rolled the camera I politely asked her if she was ready.

"Not yet, Caroline. Give me a few minutes," she said, and then turned her back to me.

I didn't take offense as she was presently being swarmed by a host of Hispanic publications all wanting to know how it felt to get so far so fast and what her plans were for *Hustler's Live*. I hung around for another fifteen minutes until she was free.

I stepped over to where she sat propped up in a chair. Alexis and Kia were right there with me, like bookends in case I fell.

"Marí, I need to get this started. I have to interview Mimi out front in about twenty minutes."

She snapped her head around. "Shit, can't you see I'm talking!"

"What did she say?" quipped Alexis.

Kia wasted no time repeating it. "She said, 'Shit, can't you see I'm talking.' "

Marí gave the three of us a look as if she were repulsed we were there, and then flung her hair, dissing me, because in her mind I guess I no longer mattered.

"Don't feed into it, Kia," I said, seeing that the trailer trash was about to come out of her.

Kia and Alexis could see I was getting antsy. I had to get this interview or Brad and Sharon would kill me. I kept telling myself, "This is business, not personal. Don't get it confused," but it was hard not to because my personal life was in a shambles and it had been Marí's fault.

Calmly, without warning, Alexis bypassed Kia, walked over to Marí, and tapped her on the shoulder.

"Are you gonna let her ask you some questions or what?"

"When I'm ready to be interviewed I'll let her know," Marí said, then turned her head to speak with someone else.

I held Alexis back and said, "Forget it, let's go."

"Oh no. Fuck that. I'ma handle her 'cause I been rehearsing for days how I was gonna cuss this bitch out."

"Alexis, just chill out. You don't have to do that. She's not worth it."

She got up in my face like she was going to fight me. "No, but you are and ain't nobody going to play you—especially her. Here, hold my shit," she said, then dropped her earrings in her purse and passed it to Kia.

In her stilettos Alexis strutted over to where Marí stood talking with Jenice Armstrong of the *Daily News* and commenced kicking Marí's ass.

Before I could reach out to grab Alexis, she caught Marí by the hair, held her head down and punched her in the face and the back of the head until she fell to the floor. Marí never saw it coming.

"Hell yes, this shit is about to get crazy up in here!" Kia said, doing nothing to de-escalate a situation that had already turned into mayhem.

What the hell had happened to Alexis? I'd never seen her act as if she'd come straight out of the ghetto. She was always talking about beating somebody's ass but I didn't know she could actually fight.

Marí tried to fight back with the microphone that was still in her hand but she couldn't control Alexis, who was swinging like a prizefighter. I was afraid that if somebody didn't stop them, Alexis would kill the girl.

"Whup that bitch's ass, Alexis!" Kia screamed out, standing up on a chair to get an aerial view.

"Kia, shut up. You're making this worse! Stop, Alexis, please!" I screamed at my friend. Then I saw the light of the camera rolling and I realized my microphone was on. Damn it, everyone was seeing this right as it unfolded.

A crowd had grown around us and was cheering them on. Did they even know who to root for? My eyes swept the crowd for my brother but he wasn't in sight. Hopefully he hadn't arrived yet. And I hated to think of my parents' reaction when they found out about this fiasco.

Casino security seemed to appear from out of the walls. There were about ten of them pulling Marí and Alexis apart until both of them were being picked up off the floor by the muscular men, simply dangling in the air with their stilettos hanging beneath them.

When the Philadelphia police arrived I felt bad seeing Alexis and Marí being carted away in handcuffs. I knew it was my fault, just like everything else had been. But Alexis wasn't the least bit embarrassed as she strutted past the television cameras, holding her head up high. Plus she knew she wouldn't spend more than a minute in jail; her father was the mayor.

Juan and Raphael managed to get Kia and I out a back exit before the media swarmed on us. Kia was way too excited about all of it as we rode in a taxi back to her hotel.

"Linney, if I knew it was like this in Philly, I would've been here a long time ago!"

"Kia, it's not funny. I could lose my job. My family's already disowned me."

"But, Linney, you gotta admit it, Alexis was kicking her ass and I mean the girl never lost her stilettos. You gotta give it to her."

I had to laugh at that one because I'd never seen anybody fight the way Alexis had and still come out of it looking good. If nothing else she was more than a friend. As the brothers said it, Alexis was my dawg.

I dropped Kia off at the Four Seasons, and when I finally got back to my brothers' it was 1:00 A.M. I almost expected the locks to be changed. This shit with Marí was getting worse by the minute.

Maybe I was just desperate, but after I'd gotten into bed I put in another call to Julius. I'd planned that when his answering machine picked up that I'd not only apologize again but I'd tell him what I'd discovered about Marí, since my brother hadn't wanted to listen. Instead of getting his service I got him.

"Caroline, what do you want?" he asked, sounding too weary to argue with me.

"I need to talk to you."

"Go ahead, talk. You got two minutes."

I sat up in bed so I could get out all I needed to say. "I wanna explain, Julius. Let me do that much."

"What can you possibly say? The video was pretty self-explanatory."

"All I can say"—I stopped to choke back the tears—"is I'm sorry."

"Sorry what, that you got caught?"

"Sorry that I got caught, yes. But, Julius, I'm more sorry that I hurt you and our relationship."

"We don't have a relationship anymore."

I couldn't hold back the tears any longer. "Julius, don't do this to me. I mean, can you honestly say that you've never made a mistake?"

He didn't say anything for a while and I thought that maybe he'd hung up.

"Julius?"

"Linney . . ." he paused. "I've made some mistakes. There were times when I wasn't faithful but—"

"Julius, I don't care what you've done. I don't wanna hear it. It's me that needs to be forgiven. Please give me another chance. Please forgive me," I begged, squeezing the pillow to my chest.

"I've been trying my best to hate you, Caroline, but it ain't hard to see that somebody was out to get you."

"It was Marí, Julius, I can prove it."

"It doesn't matter, you're coming home. I'll be there to get you tomorrow."

"Julius, what about my parents?"

"Don't worry. When I get there we'll go out to see them."

"I love you, Julius. Please hurry, please."

Maybe this is what light looked like at the end of the tunnel. Within the hour he'd called back with his flight information and I began to pack. He told me he'd have the doorman let me in at the St. James. To hell with VMT and *Top of Da Charts*—Julius was coming to get me.

Now Marí could have everything she had ever wanted and lied so hard to get, including moving in with my brother. I phoned Maurice.

"Caroline? What's going on? What was that stunt you and that stupid ass Alexis pulled tonight? You ought to be glad we're not pressing charges."

"Maurice, stop. Just listen. I'm going back to LA."

"When?"

"Julius is flying in tomorrow to get me. His flight gets in at three, so he'll be here around four to pick me up and move my stuff to his place until we leave."

"Yeah, all right. Just leave me a message when you're gone."

"Good-bye, Maurice," I said solemnly, wondering if this would be the last time I'd speak to my brother. But with Julius coming I was now optimistic that he'd fix everything with both my parents and Maurice. If he could forgive me, then so could they.

With everything slowly piecing itself together, I phoned Kia and told her she was free to return to the West Coast because Julius was coming. In the morning I'd talk to Brad and Sharon about my plans, but they'd already promised me that once I covered the opening of Hustler's we'd be able to return to Los Angeles.

For the first time in months I was able to sleep. I knew Julius's arrival would be a far cry from the fanfare of the last time he'd visited me in Philly, but it didn't matter. I was just grateful that he was returning at all.

The next morning I woke early to drive Kia to the airport and was headed into Teaz when I received a call from Brad.

"Hello, Caroline, it's Brad Cohen."

"Brad, I'm on my way in. I'm sorry about last night. I swear I had no idea Alexis was going to go after Marí."

"I'm sure, but that's not what I'm calling about."

"So why are you calling and why are you being so formal? I'm not late for the show. Please tell me we're still going back to California."

"That's just it. *Top of Da Charts* has been cancelled."

"What? You have to be kidding me! Because of last night? Please tell me this is a joke!" I cried as I screeched to a halt in the middle of the George Platt Memorial Bridge in an effort not to hit the car stopped in front of me.

"No, it's not. Believe me, Caroline, it's out of my hands. Your ratings have been weak and not to pour salt into the wound, but you've been overshadowed by your intern. And the other thing, Caroline, is that you've become too much of a risk."

I ignored the beeping of horns behind me and the passing motorists giving me their middle finger.

"What is it, Brad? Marí's convinced you that I can't do my job anymore, is that what it is?"

"Caroline, you're good at your job, but you just might need a break. You know, get some rest, take a vacation. Things have been tough for you lately."

"But I do my job, Brad."

"I know that, but our format is no longer exciting. Kids just aren't tuning in like they used to."

"How can that be true? Things are—" I stopped, refusing to beg Brad not to fire me, not to take away the only thing I had to hold on to. But then I remembered Julius. I had him. Plus I had to hold on to some dignity because in spite of it all, I was still an Isaacs.

"Can you at least have someone send over my things?"

"Of course, Caroline. And I do wish you a lot of luck. You're still young and . . ."

I hung up on him.

Since I no longer had a job, I went back to Maurice's to wait for Julius. I hated having to add the bad news of losing my job to the already fragile state of our relationship, but he was all I had. Just seeing him and having him hold me would make me feel better. Since I was already packed, I took my bags and put them in the car and headed over to the St. James.

I pulled out of Maurice's garage around 3:45 P.M. His place was at Twenty-ninth and Locust and Julius's place was at Eighth and Walnut. It would only take me a few minutes. When I got to the corner of Twenty-ninth and South streets, I found myself stuck in bumper-to-bumper traffic. I looked around to see if I could back out or take a side street, but there wasn't any room to move. I looked over at the clock on the dashboard. It was nearing 4:15 and I was sure Julius was wondering where I was. I dialed his cell phone but it went to voice mail. I tried not to panic and think that he'd changed his mind. Maybe his flight had been delayed. . . . If so, then why hadn't he called me? I prayed he hadn't had second thoughts, but how could he not? Would I have taken him back if the situation were reversed?

Finally, traffic was diverted around what had been an accident on the Schuylkill. I began to crawl behind the traffic on Chestnut Street, where I saw there were several emergency vehicles, a news helicopter flying overhead, and people standing on the bridge trying to see the accident.

But my focus was on Julius. I needed to make sure he was still coming for me. I pulled into the courtyard of the St. James and, breathless, I ran into the lobby, only to be disappointed that the doorman had not seen or heard from Mr. Worthington.

Once again I was distraught, with nobody to turn to. Kia was gone, my job had fired me, and Julius hadn't showed. I drove back to Maurice's apartment and drank until I passed out.

Chapter 21
PANDORA'S BOX

I was awakened in the morning by the blaring sound of the television and its morning videos, which reminded me about the one-woman pity party I'd conducted the night before. On the floor beside the bed was the phone book, where I'd searched for an airline to get a flight back to California. At least there I'd be able to blend in like any other celebrity who'd been exposed by a sex tape. I knew that in Hollywood, sex tapes were just part of the culture.

I patted the covers in search of the remote so I could change the channel. The last thing I wanted to see was a reminder that I'd lost my job at Teaz. I was about to get out of bed when I landed on Fox news. I thought I'd glimpsed a photo of Julius up in the corner of the screen. It couldn't be. I turned up the volume so I could hear what the newscaster was saying.

"Noted sports agent Julius Worthington was killed yesterday afternoon in a bizarre car accident. He was attempting to exit the Schuylkill Expressway at Thirtieth Street when his car was hit from the rear and pushed over the embankment into the river. Authorities are searching for leads on the hit-and-run driver. Witnesses report it was an SUV with no license plate."

This couldn't be right. I turned to channel 6 and eventually watched the same story. Channel 10, there again his picture and photos of the car being pulled out of the river by a tow truck. Before I could change the channel there was the body bag being carried by two policeman into a police van. Then I remembered the accident yesterday on my way to the airport. My God, I was there.

I grabbed the phone and dialed Julius's parents—no answer. I couldn't stop crying to dial another number. I threw the phone against the wall, but by now it was ringing, as well as Maurice's house phone. I knew everyone was trying to call me to tell me that Julius was dead. I turned the ringer off both.

I went out onto the balcony and screamed out to whoever could hear me. My life was over. My heart had been ripped from my chest. I went to the bathroom and looked through the medicine cabinet. Motrin, Tylenol, Mylanta, nothing that would help ease me into a peaceful death to end my miserable life.

Inside my brother's liquor cabinet there was rum, vodka, and scotch. I lined the bottles up and sat down at the kitchen table. I poured my first glass and added some apple juice to sweeten the lethal mix. Finally, I had to end all the misery I'd been dealing with. I'd drink myself into oblivion, then maybe I'd have the courage to kill myself.

Around ten that night I knew I didn't have the guts to commit suicide and all the drinking I was doing was just making me sick. I had a better idea. I'd go out and pick up a lover; maybe he could erase the pain. That's what started this trouble anyway: Marí, the road trip, and Vin, the hitchhiker.

I turned on my cell phone to ask the doorman to arrange a car service to pick me up, but before I could dial, Alexis's number came up.

"Alexis, come get me. I wanna go out."

"Caroline, why the hell haven't you been answering the phones? I was on my way over there."

"For what?"

"Listen, I know about Julius, and I am really so sorry."

"He was coming back for me, you know. We talked yesterday. He still loved me, Alexis. It's all my fault. If he hadn't been coming . . ."

"Please, Linney, stop it. None of this is your fault. But right now you need to turn on the television."

"For what? You want me to suffer through seeing that body bag with my Jules in it?"

"Caroline, shut your drunk ass the fuck up and listen to me."

I stopped talking. Alexis never talked to me like that, and after the ass whipping she'd given Marí I wasn't taking any chances.

"I'm sorry," I mumbled, and clicked the television back on.

"Okay put on channel seventeen."

I knew this was the local station that carried Marí's show but I followed Alexis's instructions and turned to it anyway.

There he was, my brother, on *Hustler's Live*—down on one knee proposing to her on national television. I couldn't even cry anymore. This joke was way too cruel. Here I'd lost everything and Marí had gained it all.

"Linney, you see that shit?"

"Yeah. I see it. You know what? I don't even care anymore. Hey, maybe they'll be happy."

"Happy my ass—and you're gonna care about this shit I got to tell you."

"What now, Alexis? I can't stand another Marí story."

"Listen, before you go crazy on me and do something stupid, you should know I took it upon myself to dig a little deeper into Marí's background."

"So what."

"That bitch is beyond crazy. I'm talking psycho, and you need to watch out for her."

"Marí's through with me—she's got everything she wanted. She has my job, my brother, my—"

"Shut the fuck up, Linney, and listen. Damn. The private dick I hired went to her apartment in LA, and the shit he found was so damn bizarre that he took pictures and e-mailed them back to me."

I didn't say anything.

"Are you listening? Now those pictures, Linney, were all of you. All kinds of pictures she had plastered all over her walls. The bitch had a fuckin' Caroline Isaacs shrine. Do you understand what I'm saying? This shit she's been doing is some real thought-out bullshit."

"What are you saying, Alexis?"

"She's obsessed with you, girl, and people like her are dangerous."

It wasn't getting through. "What are you saying, Alexis? Marí's crazy for real?"

"That's right. And she was seeing some doctor who had her taking lithium. The bitch is obviously psychotic. There were bottles of pills lying all around her dirty ass apartment. She's crazy, Linney, and you gotta warn your brother."

It was hard to sleep thinking about Marí's sick obsession with me, so I just lay there staring up at the ceiling, letting my mind race. I didn't think Alexis would lie to me, and right now she was the only person Marí hadn't corrupted against me. Alexis had wanted me to call Maurice and tell him what she'd discovered, but I couldn't do that without real evidence, especially since he'd hung up on me when I'd attempted to tell him about Coach Ramos. Or maybe I was scared that he'd think I was the one who was crazy. Still though, I was puzzled as to why Marí had gone through all of this. How could she possibly blame me for what happened to her family? Granted, my mother and her friends had been responsible for her father losing his job, but I'd had nothing to do with that.

Her intentions all along, it seemed, had been to pick my life apart piece by piece. She'd planned it all, starting with her interview when she'd been knowledgeable of my background. And she'd already admitted she'd lied on her résumé. And then that great idea of hers about taking *Top of Da Charts* on the road, which I'd given her all the credit for—I always did, and she always seemed so naive. When all along I'd been the one who'd been naive.

I turned on my laptop and logged onto the Internet. It was the first time I'd done so since the party. There were 312 messages. I went through and deleted all of them without even reading them. Checking my blog was out of the question, as I was certain the studio had cancelled my account. The only e-mail I saved was the one from Alexis; the subject, Marí.

The investigator had put together a slide show of Marí's apartment. I stared at the screen in amazement; it was like something out of a Stephen King story.

It was apparent that Marí was a slob, far from the neat freak she pretended to be. I clicked on the slide show and it was just as Alexis said. There were pictures of me working with my one-time trainer, shots of me getting tea from some dinky coffee shop, me shopping at Country Mart in Malibu, me pumping gas with Kia waiting in the car, and so many news articles and magazine clippings, as well as the three *People* magazine covers. There were even pictures of me from Branfman. But what really scared me was something I saw—pinned to Marí's wall. About two years ago when I'd cohosted a Save the Children concert I'd thrown out my monogrammed towel to the audience. There it was, hanging on Marí's wall. Alexis was right. Marí had truly created a shrine of Caroline Isaacs.

All along she'd played me, just waiting for the right moment. And the finale had been my father's retirement party. Her plan had worked perfectly. I'd lost everything and everyone. And then, just when I thought Julius and I still had a chance, his car was hit and he was gone from my life too.

As crazy as it all seemed that someone could be so cruel, Alexis was right. Marí's fingerprints were all over this—all over the plan to destroy my life. Now it was my turn to try to put those pieces of my life back together, at least what was salvageable. I knew my brother would never marry Marí once I exposed this sick side of her. And my parents would feel the same way too when I made them realize that it was Marí who'd cast a dark shadow over our family.

Without even planning it I slipped on a pair of jeans, a T-shirt, and sneakers. I went to the garage, got in my mother's car, and drove to the brownstone at Twentieth and Mt. Vernon where Maurice and Marí were living. I'd never been there but I'd gotten her address from a card she'd sent me—more of her bullshit.

I parked on Twentieth Street where I could get a clear view of her comings and goings. It was early so I knew at least my brother had to be leaving for work by 8:00 A.M. I got lucky in just twenty minutes. Hand in hand they walked out the door together. It pierced my heart to see them so happy and carefree, all at the cost of my being miserable. But could I really blame my brother?

I sat in the car for about a half hour trying to convince myself that I really wasn't crazy to be sneaking around Marí's house. But I had nothing to lose, so there was no reason for me to be afraid. I told myself that this was the only way I could reclaim what was left of my life, which wasn't very much. I stepped out of the car and swiftly made my way toward her house. I didn't doubt that the front door would be locked I certainly had no idea how to pick a lock and I wasn't strong enough to break the door down. I jiggled the doorknob anyway but froze in place when the next door neighbor came out.

"Good morning. I think they already left for work," the man said.

"Good morning. Thanks, I have a key," I lied.

I stood still until he pulled off in his car. While keeping my eye on the street, I pushed at the front window, but what the hell was I going to do if it opened? I couldn't very well climb through the front window of Marí's house. I decided to go through the alley and around to the back of the house.

I immediately noticed that the kitchen window had been left open a crack. I pushed the window up as far as it would go, then hoisted myself inside. If somebody saw me, they'd waste no time phoning the police, especially in this neighborhood. Well, I'd just have to take that chance; once again nothing to lose.

I doubted if Marí would keep anything around her to indicate her obsession with me, but I searched through the house anyway. I was scared to touch anything because I didn't want any evidence that I'd been there.

I tiptoed around the house for what reason I don't know, since nobody was there. The house was pretty basic, furnished mostly with what looked to be rented items.

There were only two bedrooms and one was completely empty. I rifled through her closet and was not surprised to find my Gaultier bustier, another thing supposedly stolen by Vin. I went back downstairs and was walking out the kitchen to leave when I looked over at the garbage can. Either I'd been watching too much television or my life had truly hit rock bottom. I dug in Marí's garbage can to see what I could find. I was about to pull my hand out from her leftover breakfast when I noticed a crumbled piece of notepaper in the trash. I would have ignored it except for the fact that I saw Julius's name. I straightened it out and read: Flight 207 arriving 3 P.M.

"That was Julius's travel info!"

I was so dazed about what the note implied that in an effort to sit down I knocked over one of her kitchen stools. Ruining my life, my job, even my family was one thing, but the thoughts that were going through my head were beginning to scare me. Could Marí have been crazy enough to have killed Julius?

I folded the note and put it in my pocket. She might not be guilty of killing Julius, but I had enough evidence to make it clear to everyone that Marí had destroyed my life.

22
DEATH BECOMES HER

barely made it back to my car before I broke down in tears. I couldn't even attempt to put the last three months of my life together. I pounded on the steering wheel until people on the street began to stare from the blaring of the horn. I mashed my foot on the gas pedal and screeched off down the street. If Alexis could fight for me, then I had to find a way to fight for myself. There was nothing else to do but to confront the enemy. I called Marí.

When her phone rang for the fourth time I prepared myself for the message I'd leave on her voice mail. Maybe if I threatened to expose her, she'd leave me and my family alone. Her line beeped and I told her everything I knew, from her taking the internship, the footage of Vin and I, the undermining of me at work, and those photos plastered in her Englewood apartment. I told her if she didn't drop everything and get out of the lives of both my family and me, that I would go to the police.

By the time I finished I was shaking. I lay back on the bed and waited for Marí to call back.

An hour later as I sat on my bed pondering how I would approach my parents, who I still hadn't heard from, the house phone rang.

"Marí?"

"No, it's me, your brother. What the hell is wrong with you, Caroline? Why are you fucking with Marí?"

"Maurice, what are you talking about?" I asked, pacing from one room to the other.

"I'm talking about the fuckin' message you left her. Do you know how upset you got her with that bullshit? She had to leave work early today because of your accusations."

"Maurice, you don't understand. Come over. Let me talk to you, please."

"I've heard enough. She forwarded me your message. You're sick, Linney. I just didn't think you'd stoop so low as to accuse Marí of fucking up your life. I'm sorry, sis, but you need to get some help." He hung up abruptly.

Now I was spent. Marí had once again flipped things as if I were the crazy one. This was no time for tears. She was so confident of her relationship with my brother and my parents that she'd forwarded my message to Maurice, certain he'd never believe a word of what I'd said. He now thought I was the one who was psychotic. And at the rate I was going, I was beginning to feel just that. Maybe it was time for me to give up and surrender.

But it was still shocking to me that my brother had hung up on me. What's more, that he was even mad at me. Any situation I'd ever gotten myself into Maurice was always there to help out. How could he have been so weak to fall for Marí? Now I knew that a mere threat to call the police hadn't been enough. Maurice as well as my parents would need to see the real Marí. I'd have to prove what I knew was true.

If Marí were truly responsible for killing Julius, then I at least had to keep fighting for him. I called Alexis to tell her how things had gone and that she need not dig any deeper into Marí's past, that I'd found out all I needed to know.

"Where are you? Have you talked to your brother and told him about his crazy ass fiancée?"

"Alexis, it's too late. She's got him thinking I'm crazy. I know he'll convince my mother and father of the same thing and they'll probably put me away somewhere."

"You want me to talk to him?"

"Hold on, my line is beeping," I said, and then glanced at the caller ID. It read Private Number.

"Alexis, I'll call you back. Let me see who this is."

"Hello?" I asked cautiously.

"Caroline, I see you've been busy, but you do know it's too late."

"Too late for what, Marí? What else can you do to ruin my life? Haven't you gotten what you wanted yet?"

"Not yet. You see, Linney my friend, in just a few hours my plan will be complete."

"What the hell are you talking about, Marí? What plan?"

A sickening laugh escaped her, the kind that only emotionally unstable people can emit.

"I'm stealing them all away from you, Caroline, all the people you love, just like you did mine."

"Marí, I don't know what you're talking about. I had nothing to do with your mother dying in that accident."

"What about my father—my father who could never praise you enough. That's all I heard at home. Linney Isaacs this, Linney Isaacs that. Anyway, there's no time for that."

"Marí, I'm so sorry about your family, but you know it wasn't my fault."

"Nothing's your fault, is it, Caroline? Well, it's too late to be sorry anyway, because in a few hours you'll lose everyone you love too."

I was desperately scared for the first time in my life. I'd never encountered anyone as sick and demented as Marí, and I had no one to turn to. What could Marí possibly be planning to do in a few hours?

I hit redial and got Alexis.

"Alexis, you have to help me," I said. "She called. She wants to kill someone, I know it. She wants them all, she said."

"Caroline, please slow down just a little bit. Tell me what she said."

"You were right. She wants me to pay for her family with mine. I don't know what to do."

"You gotta warn your parents about Marí. If your dumb ass brother doesn't want to listen, then you need to get your ass out to Villanova."

"But—"

"But my ass, Caroline. If I have to, girl, I'll kill that bitch myself."

"Alexis, what are you going to do? I don't want anybody else to get hurt."

"Just do what the fuck I told you. Now go."

I went into the hallway and pushed the button for the elevator, then I dialed my parents.

"Gladys, it's Caroline. Listen, please don't think I'm crazy. Are my parents there?"

"No, just Ms. Marí. We're getting ready for the engagement dinner with your parents."

"Where is she?"

"Ms. Marí?"

"Yes, Gladys, where the fuck is Marí?"

"I don't know . . . in the house . . . outside, I'm not sure right now."

"Listen to me, Gladys, you can't let her near my parents or my brother, you hear me?"

"Ms. Caroline, I don't understand. She's your brother's fiancée."

"Gladys, have I ever acted irrational or crazy? Have I, Gladys, have I?"

"You're scaring me, Ms. Caroline. What's wrong?"

"I'm sorry, Gladys, but I'm scared too. All I'm asking is that you please don't let anything happen to my family before I get there."

I could hear in her voice that she'd thought I'd lost it, and I almost had, but who wouldn't be crazed with all that I had before me?

Rather than wait for the elevator, I took the stairs and ran to my car. Thank God there wasn't any traffic because I made it to Villanova in forty-five minutes flat. I hadn't had a decent conversation with my parents since the party, and certainly hadn't been to their house, but I needed to reach them. This was serious and Marí was dangerous.

When I opened the front door I half expected to be shot

by Marí, but the house was quiet except for Gladys, who was busy supervising the kitchen staff.

"Gladys, where is she?"

"Ms. Marí?"

"Gladys, please, this is very serious."

She pointed toward the pool and I ran the distance. When I got on the other side of the doors I was face to face with her.

"Caroline, you got here rather fast. Here, please have a seat," she said casually, as she pulled out a chair for me.

My eyes took in the patio, the pool, the poolhouse. We were alone.

"Where's my brother?" I asked, wondering how she was able to remain so calm knowing I was about to expose her.

"You mean my very rich and handsome fiancé? I bet you can't believe he fell for me, can you?" she asked, then sat down as if this were a casual conversation. I remained standing.

"Of course he did. You fooled him, Marí, like you did me and everyone else," I yelled ar her.

"Oh calm down. He was no fool. Actually he's a very smart man—you know that. But the way I see it, if you're patient and develop the right plan, you get what you want. You wouldn't know that because you've never had to plan for anything. Everything came to you easily, remember?"

"Fuck you, Marí. Where's my brother?" I asked again, hoping she hadn't already gotten rid of him.

She rapped her knuckles on the glass table. "Your brother is no fool, Caroline. He loves me. Those other women couldn't hold on to him because they were all used up. But I had something that every man desires. I was a virgin, never been touched. Your hear that? Virgin."

"But you told me . . ."

She covered her mouth. "Oops, I lied."

Then she stood up and circled around me as she went on. "Now imagine, your brother the playboy got to enjoy the taste and feel of a Latina virgin, something as new for him to experience as he was for me. You can't imagine all the things we've planned. He'll do whatever it takes to keep me, so you see, that's why he hasn't believed any of the lies you've told him about sweet Marí. I wasn't a used up whore like you, who screws hitchhikers in roadside bathrooms, but then you rich girls are nasty anyway, 'cause you're better than us, right?"

"I never said that nor did I ever treat you that way," I said turning around.

"You didn't have to. It was always there, right in the air between us."

"Is that why you set all this up? To destroy my life?"

"If you wanna know, I'll tell you how you lost everything."

Motionless and speechless, I waited.

"Let's see, first it was the job, easy; the road trip, even easier; and if you could've seen your face all desperate searching for that camera, my God, I almost peed myself." When she finished, she leaned over the back of the chair watching me.

"I just can't believe you set all this up. You're sick, Marí," I said, pacing back and forth wondering what to do next.

"I know. I'm good, though, aren't I? Do you want to know how good? Did you ever wonder why you kept throwing up at all the right times? Simple again—contact lense solution—just a few drops in your drink, your food, and you were fucked. It was so funny seeing you like that, having you under my control."

I hated to ask. "And Julius?"

Again that sickening laugh. "Do you think he would really marry you after that video? Awww, but you loved him, didn't you?"

I felt myself beginning to tear up and sat down so I wouldn't fall. She stood over top of me.

"Don't cry, because you surely weren't thinking of Julius when Vin was fucking you in that bathroom. Tell me, Linney, was he better than Julius?"

My hands were trembling. I didn't want her to see how scared I was, so I held onto them and began wringing them.

"Why Julius? He didn't have anything to do with this."

"He made you happy, so he had to go," she said, flicking her hand as if Julius's life meant nothing.

"You bitch."

"Call me what you want, but I took care of him, didn't I? With just a little push over the Schuylkill."

She'd done it. She'd admitted that she killed Julius. Where was everyone to hear this?

"You're sick, Marí. I swear I'll never let you hurt another person in my family."

"They're not your family anymore. They're mine now, and as far as who to hurt, you're the last person who's gonna suffer, and your family will be here to see it all go down," she said menancingly, like I was her prey.

"But why? Whatever you do isn't going to bring back your mother."

"My father either, you little cunt." I could see she was getting more angry. "But you didn't know about that, did you? No, you didn't. Because of you, Caroline, he's a crackhead bum. He's probably somewhere on the streets of the Badlands still mumbling your name."

My voice cracked "And my hair," I gasped.

Again she laughed. "Just a thimble full of Nair mixed in with all your fancy hair products and you never knew—not even that white faggot who called himself your stylist knew. See what I'm saying, Caroline? In the end I really am better than you," she said with her face so close to mine I could smell the wine she'd been drinking.

I don't know where the courage came from—I wasn't a fighter like Alexis—but I lunged for Marí, grabbing her by the face and pushing her back, holding onto her hair. She managed to throw me off and I stumbled backward, giving her a chance to grab hold of my hands, but I used that opportunity and as hard as I could, I kneed her in the pussy. She let loose my hands and winced in pain.

"I'm not going down like this, Marí," I said. Just in that moment she grabbed me around the neck in a chokehold, cutting off my breath.

Holding me by the neck, she dragged me over to the pool and dunked my head in the water. I went under, once, twice, but the third time I held my breath and flipped her into the water with me.

I could hear Gladys screaming and see my mother running from the house, flailing her arms and crying hysterically while Marí and I tussled in the water. I managed to break from her and get up the steps to climb out of the pool, but she was right there behind me.

Her hands reached out and I felt her fingernails rip the skin across my cheek. I touched my face and felt the wet blood on my fingers. My anger was at the boiling point. This girl had killed Julius and wanted to kill me. I had to save my life. I punched at her and she grabbed my hair, pulling so hard I could feel it coming out at the roots, but I didn't stop until I got my hands around her neck.

I heard people screaming, felt my brother pulling at my waist trying to free my grip, but I just squeezed harder, with all my might. She began to fall backward onto the flagstone, with me landing on top of her. Desperate, she reached out and grabbed my blouse, tearing it from my body. But still I wouldn't let go until finally her wiggling stopped and her body went limp.

I must've blacked out because when I came to I lay shivering on the chaise lounge. Over top of me stood my parents, Gladys, and more Montgomery County police officers then I could count.

I turned my head to look around me, afraid that Marí would come after me again, and that's when I saw my brother kneeling over his precious Marí as she was being zipped up into a body bag.

My father, meanwhile, stood haggling with the police that I'd been defending myself and that I needed help. I was too distraught to explain or to even care what happened to me because my life was done, regardless of who believed me.

Then things got really clear when the female cop stood me up in my wet clothes and handcuffed me.

"I'm placing you under arrest for the murder of Marí Colonado," she said.

But then like a miracle, I heard Alexis's voice cursing and making her way through the police tape. Her father, the mayor, was in close pursuit.

"Get the fuck out of my way," she boldly told the officers. "You're not taking her anywhere. Dad, come on," Alexis ordered her father.

"Officers, uncuff Ms. Isaacs."

"Sir?" the detective asked.

"I think you'll want to hear what my daughter has to say."

I'd saved my family but it was Alexis who saved me. She told my family and the police everything that had happened and even had some of the evidence with her to prove it. She'd truly come through as a friend.

TWO MONTHS LATER

October 2006

I'd finally made it back to California. My parents didn't want me to go, but once I was cleared of all charges I got the hell out of Philadelphia as fast as USAir would take me. I'd lingered in my apartment for two months, suffering from a depression I didn't think I'd ever be free from.

This day though the sun couldn't have been shining any brighter, making me not notice the smog that usually draped itself over Beverly Hills. It was all clear and I was ready to start living again.

My brother had a hard time dealing with the fact that he'd been played and, unlike me, he refused to go into therapy. Not only did he just open up another dealership but he was also in talks with some Hollywood types about a movie deal based on what happened. I guess that was his way of dealing with it.

My parents on the other hand were going through their own emotional turmoil. They couldn't apologize enough for having abandoned me and not seen through to who Marí really was. My mother had come up with all kinds of things— she wanted to take me to the islands, take me to Paris, anything so I wouldn't have to keep reliving that night. But I'd just wanted to come home.

I wasn't sure where my career was headed, but once I'd come out of my cocoon I'd discovered I was in high demand. When your life had unraveled in the public eye the way mine had, you have to hire someone to be a liaison for you, and for me that was Sasha Borianni.

But before I did anything or made any moves, there was one person I needed to call.

"Kia, hey, it's me. I'm home."

"Girl, I haven't heard from you in months. What the hell happened in Philly? I been trying to call you but all your numbers have been changed."

"She was crazy, Kia."

"Shit, I know that. I wanna know about the fight. You actually killed her?"

"I was fighting for my life, Kia, and I don't know . . . I just started choking her and couldn't stop."

"Ouch. Shit. Are you going to be okay?"

"I have to."

"What are your plans now that you're back?"

"You're going to love this. How about I'm in therapy just like the rest of Hollywood?"

"That's pretty fly. I mean, hey, everybody we know is doing it. Hell, I might even get me one."

"You want to pick me up and go over to the Ivy for some lunch so I can fill you in on the details?"

"Sure, Linney, but you should know that I had a fender bender and your Benz is missing its bumper."

Hysterical laughter escaped me.